CW01160620

THE TEMPLAR LEGACY

PART 2 OF THE RICHARD CALVELEY TRILOGY

PETER TALLON

authorHOUSE

AuthorHouse™ UK
1663 Liberty Drive
Bloomington, IN 47403 USA
www.authorhouse.co.uk
Phone: 0800.197.4150

© 2017 Peter Tallon. All rights reserved.

No part of this book may be reproduced, stored in a retrieval system, or transmitted by any means without the written permission of the author.

Published by AuthorHouse 10/13/2017

ISBN: 978-1-5462-8238-9 (sc)
ISBN: 978-1-5462-8239-6 (hc)
ISBN: 978-1-5462-8237-2 (e)

Print information available on the last page.

Any people depicted in stock imagery provided by Thinkstock are models, and such images are being used for illustrative purposes only. Certain stock imagery © Thinkstock.

This book is printed on acid-free paper.

Because of the dynamic nature of the Internet, any web addresses or links contained in this book may have changed since publication and may no longer be valid. The views expressed in this work are solely those of the author and do not necessarily reflect the views of the publisher, and the publisher hereby disclaims any responsibility for them.

With thanks to Richard Maylam for thirty years of
encouragement, ideas and constructive criticism

Norfolk and Suffolk 1424

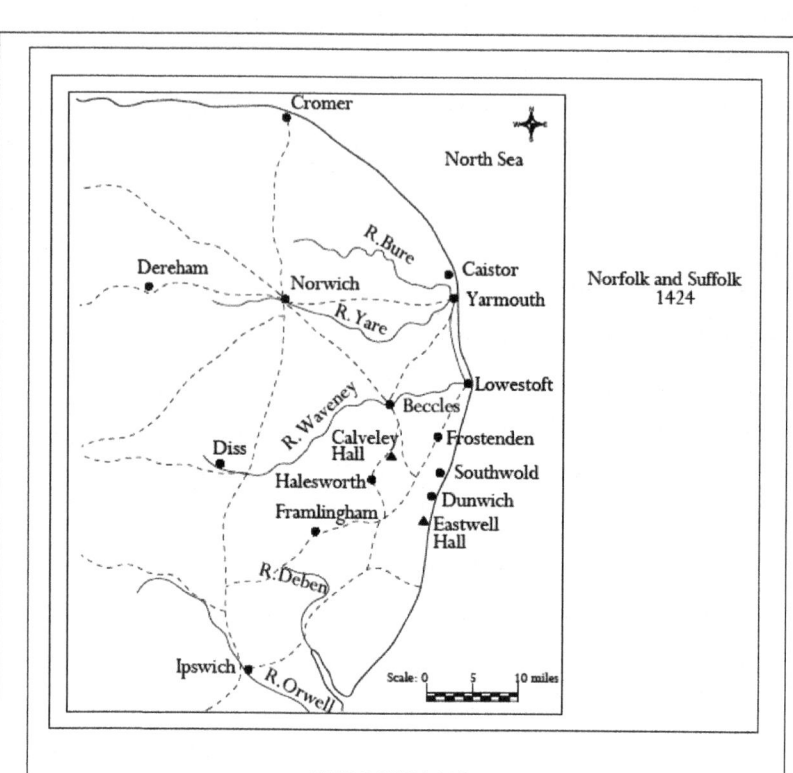

EUROPE IN 1424
Richard's Journey from Venice to Pilgrim's Castle

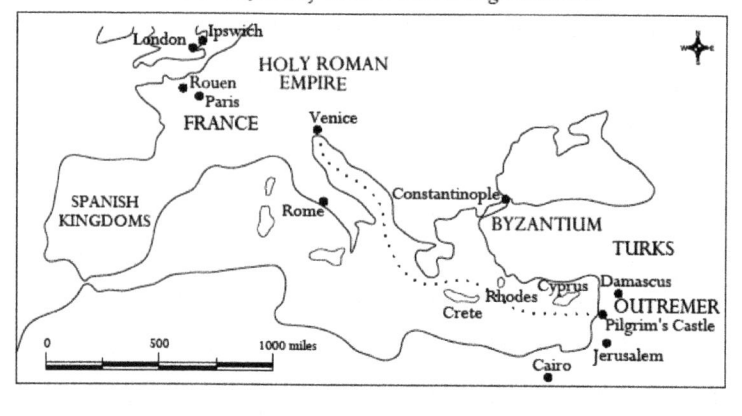

CHAPTER ONE

The evening was warm and sticky like so many that had gone before during that hot, humid summer. In some of the towns plague had broken out again and now the priests were warning of God's retribution returning once more to smite his unworthy flock. In the forest of Vincennes just outside Paris, a small group of Burgundian soldiers was lighting sentinel lamps and preparing to retire for the night. The commander had decided it would be healthier to remain outside the city as long as possible; tomorrow would be quite soon enough to enter the cramped, smelly French capital.

The sound of a horse approaching at speed disrupted the quiet of the forest. The Burgundians quickly stood to arms for although Paris had been occupied by their English allies more than two years ago, French raiding parties from south of the Loire frequently penetrated as far north as the capital ambushing convoys and carrying off prisoners worthy of ransom.

The road through the forest was broad and straight so the Burgundians were able to see the horseman a good bowshot away despite the gathering gloom. He was coming from the direction of the city mounted on a fine, tall destrier which galloped along the dusty road with long, ground devouring strides. Within a few seconds the horseman was near enough for the Burgundian commander to see that he was a high ranking knight dressed in armour of the latest, uncomplicated English fashion who would fetch a fair price if he was handed over to the French for ransom. Like most of his countrymen, the Burgundian had little sympathy for his arrogant English allies, feeling a far greater natural affinity towards the Valois king of France who was for the moment, so it seemed, making war on his own people. The unnatural alliance with England could not last, and here was an opportunity to gain favour with the French and at the same time make an easy profit.

But such mercenary plans had to be abandoned as a knot of horsemen appeared from the direction of Paris struggling in the wake of the lone knight. At first the Burgundian wondered if they were in pursuit but, as they drew nearer, the red cross of Saint George emblazoned on their white surcoats confirmed that they too were English. Must be the escort, thought the Burgundian as he ordered his men to stand down and let the horsemen pass.

The knight galloped on for another mile until he reached the castle of Vincennes which guarded the eastern approach to Paris. The gate was already open for he was expected and, as his mount's iron shod hooves thundered across the wooden drawbridge, an equerry came out to meet him. The knight dismounted in the courtyard, patted his horse's sweating neck and asked breathlessly,

"What news of my brother? Am I too late?'

"Not good My Lord," answered the equerry nervously. "The physicians say he is dying."

The knight ran across the courtyard to the tall keep remembering, despite his distraction, to acknowledge the two burly archers who stood guard outside, and pushed open the heavy, oak door just as a shout from the drawbridge announced the arrival of his exhausted escort. Taking the broad, stone steps three at a time, tears already moistening his large, brown eyes, he burst into the bedchamber where his elder brother lay dying.

Such tragic little scenes were common enough in the great conflict between England and France, which had been fought more or less continuously for almost a hundred years, but this time there was a difference; the lone knight was John, Duke of Bedford and his dying brother was Henry V, the Plantagenet King of England.

* * *

II

The sight that met Duke John confirmed the equerry's gloomy prediction. King Henry, looking like a living skeleton, sat in bed propped up by cushions and surrounded by physicians and clerics. To John they seemed like buzzards hovering around a dying lion but that, he knew, was hardly just for all that could be done for the king would be done because he was adored by his English subjects. With great effort Henry raised a skeletal hand of acknowledgement to his younger brother and, in a voice which seemed incongruously strong for such a wasted body, ordered everyone to leave the chamber so that he might speak in private to his noble brother. The duke pushed away a pomander offered to him by a departing cleric, the stench of dysentery was nothing new to a warrior of his experience, and sat down at the king's bedside. As soon as Henry and John were alone they abandoned the formality of their public status and spoke as two brothers might, for they had always been especially close.

Holding back his tears with difficulty John said, "Harry I am grieved to find you thus but I understand there is still hope?"

Henry looked at his brother with unnaturally bright eyes. He was burning up inside. "Then you understand wrong," he sighed. "There is little time left and much to discuss. I give thanks to our merciful Lord that you arrived in time."

"What would you have me do?"

"You will be the executor of my will and take personal control of the war. The French are cowed but not yet beaten, nor will they be while the rebellious dauphin continues to defy his father."

John distractedly wiped a bead of sweat from his brow. "Surely the French will respect the wishes of their own king. He has promised the throne of France to you after his death, in solemn treaty at Troyes. The war is won apart from some minor trouble-making in the south."

The king smiled and placed a bony hand on his brother's. "Not everyone is as honest and trustworthy as you John. The dauphin has more support than we might wish because many French claim their king was unsound in mind at Troyes."

John reflected for a moment on the senile French king, Charles VI and admitted, "They may have a point but a treaty is a treaty. The crown is yours after Charles and will remain a Plantagenet possession for ever."

"Not without more fighting. Now listen carefully. Maintain Philippe of Burgundy as your ally but do not trust him. He will support you while there is profit in it for him but not a moment longer. He is a noble duke of France forced into war against his sovereign by the treacherous murder of his father at Montereau, but even now my agents say he is in covert contact with the dauphin."

"Then he shall pay for it," muttered John ominously.

"But not yet. You will have need of him until the dauphin is captured and his army put to the sword. If things should take a turn for the worse and Burgundy rejoins France, hold on to Normandy whatever the cost. Normandy is becoming home to more and more Englishmen who will fight to keep their newly won lands without payment."

"Aye," agreed John, "money is always a problem. Parliament is becoming resentful of the cost of the war. It feels the war was won at Troyes and sees no reason to continue pouring money into France, especially now that the profits from booty and ransom are remaining with the new English landowners in Normandy instead of swelling the coffers at home."

"Exactly so," said Henry. "If the dauphin continues with his hit and run tactics instead of facing us again in battle, all our good work may yet be undone by money, or rather the lack of it."

"Money, money, always money. Nowadays it seems that wars are won and lost through bankers and parliaments instead of guts on the battlefield. Small wonder they say that money is the root of all evil." The king smiled at his uncomplicated brother, but in truth he was concerned lest the subtleties of statecraft should prove too much for him. Henry could feel his strength ebbing fast yet the purpose of his summons to the duke was still unfulfilled. He said,

"John, it is upon the matter of money I wish to speak to you. The English warrior, brave and patriotic though he is, expects to be paid unlike his downtrodden French counterpart. An archer will move mountains for six pence a day but if he does not receive his just reward he will quickly resort to plunder. We have won the battles but we have yet to win French hearts. Plundering Englishmen will not assist our cause."

John scratched his head and asked, "Then what can we do without handing over our royal authority to parliament and the Lombard bankers?"

A stabbing pain gripped Henry's stomach. He winced, closed his eyes willing the agony to dissipate for a few more minutes. When he recovered he could barely whisper.

"Inside the chest below the window you will find a casket. Bring it to me." John did as he was bid and returned to the king's bedside carrying a heavy, locked, iron box about the size of a knight's tournament helm. "Beneath my pillow is the key," said the king. "Unlock the casket."

John's eyes widened as he saw the contents. "These are Venetian gold ducats," he gasped. "There are hundreds of them."

"Enough to keep an army in the field awhile at least," agreed Henry, "and there are plenty more where they came from."

There was so much John wanted to ask he hardly knew where to begin but the king, now desperate for time, spoke without waiting for his brother's questions. "After Agincourt I received a strange embassy in London. It was the day before Christmas and you may remember that you and I were staying at the Savoy Palace. I was preparing for morning mass when the commander of the guard came to my chambers with a message from a certain Charles d'Evreux who claimed he could finance the war for us in return for some unspecified arrangements. Normally I would have dismissed such an approach and at the time the war seemed all but won, but it was Christmas. I was light of heart and curious to meet a man who believed he could pay for a war. Not even the Lombard bankers ever claimed that."

A little hurt, John said, "You did not tell me."

"It seemed of no consequence then but times have changed since those heady days after Agincourt."

"That is true enough," acknowledged the duke wearily.

"Charles d'Evreux had sent the commander of the guard to me with the casket you see before you now, so you will understand my curiosity. When he arrived I dismissed the commander because d'Evreux would not speak to me unless we were alone."

"That was foolhardy Harry. He might have been an assassin."

"True, but I judged I could withstand an attack from a man who was at least twenty years older than me should it prove necessary."

"So what did he want?"

"In exchange for the finance to bring the war to a conclusion, he wanted me to re-instate the great military Order of the Temple when I became King of France."

John's mouth opened but no words would come. Henry's stomach pains had eased for the moment and he was able to smile at his speechless brother. "John you look like a stranded fish. I confess I too was surprised at the time."

"But the Templars were suppressed by King Philippe of France more than a hundred years ago."

"Suppressed but not destroyed apparently. Enough of the warrior monks escaped to maintain the integrity of the Order in secret. More importantly for us, most of the immense Templar wealth, the real reason for Philippe's attack on the Order, slipped through his grasp. The portion which he did manage to secure was only a small fraction of the fortune amassed by the Order from two centuries of plunder, banking and bequests. That fortune is at our disposal if we agree to d'Evreux's terms."

"But Harry, the Templars were convicted of terrible things; heresy, sodomy and idolatry to name but three."

"The Templar confessions were only extracted after torture and many later recanted. Few people believed the charges then and no-one does now. The root cause of the suppression was Philippe's imminent bankruptcy. The wealth of the Templars was an obvious target. Remember, the last strongholds in the Holy Land had but recently fallen to the infidel so the Templars, whose arrogance had made them unpopular almost everywhere, were seen as expensive failures."

"Was d'Evreux a Templar then?" asked John.

"Not just a Templar. Charles d'Evreux is the Grand Master."

"He still lives?"

"Yes. He has maintained contact with me regularly since our first meeting."

"Where is he now?"

"I do not know but messages can always be sent through an intermediary who lives in Rouen. Now listen to me carefully John. After I am gone make contact with d'Evreux and agree his terms. We need the Templar fortune and re-instating his Order is but a small price to pay for it. Who knows, the Templars may yet form the spearhead of another crusade, but be cautious. I sense danger, especially from those whose families still live on the profits reaped from the Templars' suppression You will need the services of a brave, resourceful and utterly trustworthy warrior, preferably a garter knight."

"Sir John Talbot?"

"I think not John. Talbot is undoubtedly brave and trustworthy, but he is young. We need someone more canny, someone who can decide when caution should take priority over boldness but who will act with bravery when the time is right."

"There is only one man I know who fits all those requirements; Sir John Fastolf."

"My thoughts exactly," agreed Henry.

Suddenly the king's wasted body twitched. He cried out in pain. When he recovered himself his voice was barely audible and John had to lean forward to hear his laboured whisper.

"Take the casket John. In the lining you will find the name and residence of the man who is d'Evreux's intermediary. As my regent you will have full royal authority to deal with d'Evreux though I doubt not that you will have more pressing matters to attend to for a while after my soul departs this wretched body. The French king's health is also failing and when he dies you must proclaim my son Henry VI, rightful King of England and France. Only then will you discover who among the French accept the Treaty of Troyes. Guide my son in the ways of honourable kingship until he is old enough to rule in his own right, and watch that hothead brother of ours. Humphrey's temper and appetite for women could be the undoing of us all."

"You know I will do my best Harry," said John whose tears now flowed freely.

"Aye, I thank God I have you John. When you feel the time is right, contact d'Evreux but remember secrecy is everything. No news must get out of what you are doing until the Templars' treasure is safely under lock and key in England."

The king closed his eyes and sighed, "My time is almost nigh. Bring back the priests; I am ready for the last rites. Do not grieve for me John. I will soon be with Alexander, Julius Caesar and Hannibal; what fascinating discussions we shall have!"

Henry Plantagenet, King of England, died during the night on the thirty first day of August in the year of Our Lord 1422. His forecast concerning the French king was accurate, for only two months later Charles VI of France, who had spent much of his later reign in his own private mad house, followed him to the grave. As soon as Charles's tomb was closed, Duke John of Bedford proclaimed the nine month old Henry as 'Henry by the grace of God, King of England and France'. He need not have bothered. Amongst the dignitaries who attended the funeral of the old king, there was not a single peer of France. They all acknowledged the dauphin, his son, as the next true King of France.

Duke John now truly understood the magnitude of the task that confronted him.

* * *

III

The clear waters of the River Yonne in Burgundy ran red. Bathed in warm twilight, knots of English archers and men at arms moved around the battlefield laboriously gathering the dead in preparation for a quick mass burial. To avoid disease in the heat of the summer it was vital to get the corpses underground as soon as possible and, scattered in and around the small town of Cravant, there were nearly six and a half thousand of them. Most were Scots, some were French; hardly any were English.

The fighting had been particularly fierce at the only bridge across the river, where the Scots had desperately tried to hold back the English advance only to be cut down to the last man. Yet again a small, highly disciplined English force had won an unlikely victory in France against overwhelming numbers, but this time there was a difference for within the English ranks there had been a contingent of Burgundians.

Sir John Fastolf, the Norfolk knight, was not impressed with his allies. "Their heart is not in it. They might as well have stayed at home for all the use they were," he said as he downed a goblet of red wine in a deserted tavern near the bridge which had survived the fighting unscathed.

"Aye sir," agreed Henry Hawkswood, his senior sergeant. "Those there Burgundians speak French, look French and even smell French. To me that makes them French whatever their duke says." Both men had been slightly wounded but eight years of non-stop campaigning had taught them to steer well clear of the army medics whose cure for all ills was the leech. Fastolf's left shoulder had been bruised by a Scottish pike which dented, but failed to pierce his expensive armour. Hawkswood's injury might have been more serious, for although the cut on his cheek was only superficial, it was dangerously close to his one surviving eye. His left one had been poked out by a pitchfork during haymaking on the Wiltshire farm he had lived on as a lad. He took a pull at his mug and grimaced as the insipid French ale trickled apologetically down his throat.

"Think you Sir John that there may be good ransom from this fight?"

"Not this time Henry. The French ran off as soon as we forced the bridge and the Scots fought to the death as usual. Mind you these Scots are so poor they wouldn't have been able to afford much ransom anyway."

"But they fight well Sir John."

"That they do. They fight like the French used to fight before they lost their confidence against us."

"But they hate us more."

"True, and that sustains them no matter how often we beat them. They only need an occasional success like Bauge to keep them going. As for ransom, we shall know more when Captain Richard returns."

Fastolf and his company had done well out of the war. Drawn from his estates in Wiltshire, Yorkshire and especially Norfolk, many of his men had been campaigning since the resumption of hostilities in 1415. Originally a small band of just thirty archers and ten men at arms, Fastolf's personal command had grown to a company of over one hundred experienced warriors, three quarters of whom were archers. But since his knighthood in 1417, Sir John had been called upon to carry out more and more administrative duties, and although his wealth and status had increased as a result, he had been obliged to relinquish direct control of his company for long periods of time to his deputy, Richard Calveley. The two men had met nine years previously in 1414 when Richard's family had been cruelly murdered by agents of his avaricious cousin, Geoffrey Calveley. In return for Richard's personal allegiance, Fastolf gave him the lieutenancy of his Norfolk family home, Caistor Manor, and provided him with the means to vengeance upon Geoffrey. Richard in turn saved Fastolf's life at Agincourt and now, after many years of shared dangers, an unbreakable bond had developed between them. That did not mean they always agreed, far from it. Henry Hawkswood had witnessed more than one blazing row between Sir John and his company captain, usually caused by money. Sir John had a particular fondness for it which sometimes clouded his judgement, but Richard only saw it as a means to an end rather than an end in itself.

Henry wondered aloud, "What will happen now?"

Fastolf stood up, looked inside the taproom which had been well stocked in anticipation of a French victory, and returned to his settle with another pipkin of good Burgundy wine. "This battle will clear the French from the country south of Paris," he said. "We will soon drive all the dauphin's forces beyond the Loire."

"Some of the men are saying they would like to see their families again. What can I tell them Sir John?"

Fastolf paused for thought. Men like Hawkswood had not been home since the war began; the request was not unreasonable. "This winter all men who have served more than four unbroken years may go home if they wish to. I shall pay for their journey but I shall want the sergeants back by the beginning of March. Those men who wish to remain at home beyond that date may do so on condition they send back able bodied replacements approved by their sergeants in advance."

Henry smiled, "That will do well Sir John."

"Will you be going too Henry?"

"No, I have no family. My home is with the company. When the war ends I shall probably buy land in Normandy and live like a gentleman."

The tavern door swung open and a tall, raven haired man at arms entered carrying a sealed scroll of parchment. His armour was old fashioned, containing too much chainmail and not enough plate, but Richard Calveley wore it out of loyalty to his father who had used it to campaign in France a generation ago.

"Good news Sir John," he said. "Our victory was more complete than we thought. Both the French and Scottish commanders have been captured and, considering the scale of the battle, our losses are trifling."

"Then find a goblet and enjoy some of this fine Burgundy wine," smiled Fastolf, "for tonight we celebrate."

Richard sat down with his comrades, goblet in hand, and gave the parchment scroll to his commander saying, "This message arrived at headquarters shortly after the battle began. I could not help but notice that it bears the royal seal."

Fastolf broke the seal and quickly scanned the message. It did not take long and when he had finished the furrows on his brow revealed his disquiet. "I am commanded to attend upon the Duke of Bedford without delay."

"Return to England in the middle of a campaign?" asked Sergeant Hawkswood incredulously.

"Bedford is in Rouen," replied Fastolf. "I will not be away for more than a week or two but my senses tell me to be wary. Why should Duke John want to remove one of his most experienced commanders at so critical a time?"

"Perhaps it no longer matters," volunteered Henry. "We have beaten the French yet again and their Scots allies. They will not trouble us again this year."

Richard shook his head, "But Duke John could not have known that when he wrote this letter."

"Quite," agreed Fastolf. "Under the circumstances I think I would like you to accompany me Richard. Henry, you are my senior sergeant so you will be in command during my absence. I know you will look after the company as I would."

Henry's one brown eye blinked in surprise. His father had been a lowly farm labourer without an acre to his name, but now his son was to lead a hundred English warriors, albeit briefly, and report directly to the Earl of Salisbury, the commander in chief of the English army in France. He felt he should say something profound but the words would not come. All he could manage was a simple, "Thank you Sir John." He wished his father could have witnessed this moment but a return of the plague had taken him many years ago. Now there was nothing left to tie Henry to England.

Sir John Fastolf, now in his mid forties and nearly six feet tall, typified the professional English officer around whom the army was built. His brown hair and short beard were streaked with grey, and his was one of those companies that never lacked replacements, for Fastolf's reputation as a soldier was amongst the best. Men followed him confident of victory and the spoils that went with it. Richard Calveley on the other hand was a different sort of soldier. Taller even than Sir John and ten years younger, he was a little more gentle than a captain should be. Each time the French killed or wounded one of the company, Captain Richard seemed to think he had somehow failed his men. He knew them all by name and placed their welfare above all other considerations even, so some said, victory. The men loved him for it. One glance from those jade green eyes and the company would cheerfully follow him to the ends of the earth. He had no need to exhort them; their greatest fear was not his anger but his disappointment. There was no need for explanations; everyone knew that Richard would look out for them.

Henry had often noticed how women looked at Richard. The captain's open, clean shaven face somehow reflected his generous spirit, especially when he smiled, but Richard discouraged womanly favours because he was devoted to his wife Mary and daughter Joan who lived near the cathedral at Rouen. Henry knew he was fortunate to follow Sir John and Richard and, if they considered him capable of leading the company in their absence, he should have nothing to fear.

Fastolf raised his goblet and announced, "A toast! Here's to Sir John Stewart and his wild Scots. May today's battle make them think twice before crossing the sea again to meddle in our affairs in France!"

"I'll drink to that," said Richard, "but knowing the Scots they will want revenge rather than peace."

"Aye," agreed Fastolf, "they'll be back, you can count on it. We will need to give them at least one more thorough beating before they see the error of their ways."

The three Englishmen drained their goblets and left the tavern. Henry went to the company's rallying point near the church while Richard returned with Fastolf to the Earl of Salisbury's headquarters to ask for leave to go to Rouen. The earl was not at all pleased to lose Fastolf but Duke John was the infant king's regent so his orders had to be obeyed. Salisbury's last words to Fastolf were, "I need you here John so return as quickly as you can. I shall now march west to Anjou and Maine where there should be rich pickings to be had." The fifth King Henry had always forbidden plundering because he regarded the French as his own rightful, if misguided subjects, but now financial stringencies imposed by an increasingly obdurate parliament had consigned such noble sentiments to the midden heap. Organised plundering was fast becoming a substitute for regular pay, and with it any faint hopes of winning French hearts were fading fast. The more far sighted English commanders were just beginning to realise that France could never be conquered, but at least there was still time to make some money out of the war. Richard already understood that the English would ultimately fail but from the way Fastolf's eyes glazed over at the thought of plundering Anjou and Maine, he was fairly certain that his commander secretly shared his view. Whatever it was that the Duke of Bedford wanted, it was unlikely to prevent Fastolf from hurriedly rejoining the army. Only a foolhardy man would stand between Sir John and booty.

Richard's forecast about Fastolf turned out to be accurate but as for Richard himself, the Fates had very different plans.

* * *

IV

At last, thought Geoffrey Calveley, after all this time I've found my man. A happy co-incidence had resulted in Geoffrey being called to stand in for the sick Ipswich magistrate on the very day that Henk de Groot was brought before the assizes for brawling in a dockside tavern. De Groot had singlehandedly beaten up two tough archers and dealt more than one bloody nose to the sheriff's men before he was finally subdued. Now, on this bright Thursday morning, he stood manacled to two large turnkeys awaiting his sentence.

But de Groot was up before no ordinary magistrate, for Geoffrey Calveley had been painstakingly searching for someone to replace his erstwhile steward, Titus Scrope, whom he had lost eight years ago. Titus had been much more than a mere steward to Geoffrey. Unburdened by a conscience or morals, Titus was the instrument through which Geoffrey achieved his ruthless ambition for wealth and status in Suffolk society. Nothing seemed to be beyond the reach of Titus' evil tentacles; all obstacles to his master's avarice were swept aside by fair means or foul, in return for which Geoffrey ensured that his steward was paid well enough to allow him to indulge his personal lusts and cruelties.

Everything had been going so well until the day Geoffrey was thwarted by his cousin Richard over a land auction in Beccles market square, after which a series of uncontrollable events took place. Titus exceeded his master's instructions by murdering Richard's family and burning down his house before Richard had returned from Beccles. But Richard quickly found out who was responsible and although his retribution was slow in coming, it was effective for he was able to prove Geoffrey had been born a bastard and his inheritance was therefore illegal. Consequently Richard, being the closest legitimate male relative to Geoffrey's father, ejected his cousin from Calveley Hall, at Holton near Halesworth, and acquired title to the property himself. Even now Father Hugh, the Franciscan friar and personal friend of Richard, managed the hall and the land attached to it while Richard was away fighting the French.

Finally everything was ruined when Titus Scrope discovered love at the ridiculous age of forty three and tried to put his evil ways aside. But the object of his affection was a Lollard preacher, Mary Hoccleve, who had already committed herself to Richard. When Titus realised his love was spurned, he provided the evidence which convicted Mary of heresy and caused her to be condemned to the terrible death of burning at the stake, ironically in Beccles market square where all Geoffrey's troubles had begun. But Titus must have loved her still, for on the day set for Mary's execution he drowned himself in the River Waveney though his body was never found.

A last minute rescue by an unknown knight saved Mary from the flames but Geoffrey had never been in doubt that the man inside the unmarked armour was his cousin. If proof were needed, Richard and Mary had reappeared together a few weeks later in Normandy where they were beyond the reach of English heresy laws.

Geoffrey had no intention of allowing Calveley Hall to slip from his grasp permanently, and now the means to this end stood in the dock before him. His instincts could smell out pure evil but first he must ensure that the law was seen to be applied. He put down his quill on the ornate wooden desk in front of him and affected the pained expression he always used before sentencing. His unweathered, middle aged chins wobbled as he spoke.

"Henk de Groot, I find you guilty as charged. Do you understand?"

De Groot, like most of his Flemish countrymen, spoke English well. He was barely five feet tall and incredibly ugly. His huge barrel chest and long, hairy arms suggested immense physical strength; two normal sized men could have fitted comfortably inside his black, brigandine jacket. He reminded Geoffrey of one of the trolls he had heard about in Norwegian folklore.

"Yah, I understand," said the troll.

"Have you anything to say before I pass sentence?"

"No."

"Very well," said Geoffrey. "In view of the fact you are a subject of the Duke of Burgundy, our ally against the detested French, I shall be lenient, but the extreme violence you showed towards the sheriff's men cannot go unpunished. You will pay a fine of ten marks or go to prison for six months."

For the first time the bland expression on de Groot's large, red face altered. The heavy brows knitted and the dark eyes flashed. "I do not have de money."

Geoffrey of course knew this and smiled inwardly. "In that case you will spend the next six months in Ipswich gaol unless you can find someone to pay your fine."

"But my ship sails for Antwerp dis evening."

"I cannot help that de Groot. You broke English law so you must accept English punishment. Sheriff Fletcher, take him away." Geoffrey closed the charge book, which lay on the desk beside his quill without filling in the sentence, and said to the recorder, "That concludes the business for today, the fifth day of August 1423. The remaining cases will be held over until tomorrow."

The battle of Cravant had been fought the week before.

"Make yourself scarce while I speak to the Flemish man." Geoffrey placed a silver shilling in the grubby hand of the turnkey of Ipswich gaol.

"Thank you sir," croaked the turnkey, "but is it wise to enter his cell on your own? He's very violent."

"Just take me to him," replied Geoffrey impatiently.

"Very well sir." The turnkey led him down some well-worn, stone steps into the heart of the stinking gaol. Green slime clung to the grey walls and from somewhere ahead the noise of dripping water echoed through the darkness. Worst of all was the stench of stale humanity, for as far as Geoffrey could see, there were no windows to bring air into the place. The only light came from burning torches fixed into brackets on the unforgiving walls. Small, circular rainbows created by the damp air enclosed the torch flames and within seconds Geoffrey's clothes became soaking wet and his thinning grey hair clung to his head as if he had just stepped out of a cold bath. God's teeth, he thought, no-one could survive long in this.

The turnkey unlocked the heavy, oak door to a cell barely two paces square; the smell was dreadful. A single candle hanging from the ceiling gave just enough light for Geoffrey to make out a dark, animal-like shadow crouching in the far corner as if ready to spring at any moment. Geoffrey took a second or two to gather his courage then said, "Turnkey, lock me in here but stay within hailing distance." He knew he must show no fear in front of de Groot, but as he looked down at the gnome-like troll crouching just a pace away from him, ice cold fingers seemed to claw at his stomach. De Groot could snap his spine like a dried twig if he chose to. The door slammed behind him; they were alone together.

Trying to keep his voice steady, Geoffrey said, "Do you remember me de Groot?"

The massive, ugly head slowly turned towards him and, in the flickering half-light, the dark eyes looked balefully at Geoffrey with the same cold menace as a hawk before it strikes. "Yah, I remember."

"I bring you good tidings. You may embark on your ship this evening. Your fine has been paid."

"Who by?"

Geoffrey listened at the locked cell door to make sure the turnkey was out of earshot. "Me."

If Geoffrey had hoped for thanks he would have been disappointed as de Groot simply asked, "I can go now?"

"Not quite. First I wish to speak with you."

De Groot sighed impatiently and shrugged, "Well?"

"I want you to work for me."

"Why?"

Geoffrey did not answer immediately. He tossed a Venetian gold ducat onto the floor in front of the Fleming and enquired mildly, "Do you like gold?"

"What man does not."

"Take it, I have much gold."

De Groot's hairy hand slowly gathered in the gleaming coin like a huge, voracious spider. A hint of respect entered his voice. "What must I do?"

Geoffrey had won his man. "I will make you rich de Groot so that you can live like a lord if you wish, but in return I demand your complete loyalty and total discretion."

"What is meaning of word 'discretion'?"

"You will work for me in secret."

"What work you want me to do?"

Geoffrey smiled wickedly, certain in the knowledge that this man would have no scruples. "Anything I ask. Gold must be earned. You will be my agent based in Rouen, Normandy. I shall send money to you each month and, when necessary, orders too. There may be long periods when I have no work for you but you will still be paid. Apart from that my only rule is that you must be at your dwelling in Rouen on the first day of each month so I can contact you when I need to. Do you read?"

"Yah and I can write a little."

"Good. What age are you?"

"About thirty five I think."

"You agree my terms then de Groot?"

The Fleming drew breath to speak but checked himself. He pulled out a small phial from his brigandine jacket, removed the stopper and poured a few drops onto his right forefinger. Then he rubbed the liquid over his gums and said, "I agree."

Geoffrey wrinkled his nose and asked, "What is that? I could smell it in the courthouse today."

"Oil of cloves. My teeth hurt and give me much trouble. Dis oil bring relief from pain. It come from somewhere beyond de land of Turks, which is why I have to use it not often. It cost much money. I only use it when de pain is great."

"Well now you can afford to use it whenever you like de Groot." Geoffrey reached inside his cloak and drew out a small pouch containing nine more gold ducats, the universal currency of Christendom. He handed the pouch to the Fleming, "Use this to find suitable lodgings in Rouen. When you have done that, write to me at my home at Eastwell Manor, which is about five miles south of Dunwich on the Suffolk coast. Inside the pouch you will find a seal as well as more gold. Use the seal when you write to me so I can be sure no-one else has seen the message, but once you have told me where you are dwelling in Rouen contact me sparingly, only when you have important information."

"How much will you pay me sir?"

Geoffrey noted the 'sir' with satisfaction. "One gold ducat each month. On occasion I may pay you more if you have carried out my instructions particularly well. Your first task, which will be a continuous duty, is to observe my cousin Richard Calveley who lives in Rouen with his wife and daughter. He is my sworn enemy."

"Why not let me get rid of him for you? It would be easy for de Groot."

"Because suspicion would immediately fall on me and he has proven difficult to kill in the past. Anyway, I need to disgrace him before dispatching him so that I can inherit what is rightfully mine. Any other way is likely to fail because Richard has powerful friends."

"I understand," acknowledged de Groot, who still preferred the simple solution.

"On your way to Rouen," continued Geoffrey, "there is another matter I wish you to deal with which will require careful planning."

The warm, afternoon, summer air was a delightful contrast to the putrid, clammy Ipswich gaol and, as Geoffrey walked slowly back to his lodgings, he looked across the harbour to the southwest quay where de Groot's ship was making ready to catch the tide. What an excellent day it had been! For the last eight years, ever since Richard had thrown him out of Calveley Hall, Geoffrey's life had seemed to drift aimlessly. He had soon plotted his revenge but his plans could not progress because he had lost his faithful steward, Titus Scrope, the evil and reliable agent who carried out his dark desires. Geoffrey had neither the skill nor nerve to do these things himself and, in any event, he would never break the law in person; he left that to others.

But now, as he watched the Flemish sailors start to cast off from the quay, Geoffrey felt his life had regained purpose again. Titus was always going to be difficult to replace and even de Groot was not going to be a complete substitute because Titus had been the nearest thing to a friend Geoffrey had ever had. There was no question of confiding in the Flemish troll or sharing fears and triumphs with him the way he had done with Titus, but on the other hand there were some advantages too. De Groot possessed the low, fox-like cunning of the wild but he was no intellectual. This would make him easily biddable because his only desire was gold; the purpose of Geoffrey's grand design was of no interest to de Groot. Titus, especially towards the end, had frequently questioned Geoffrey's orders, not their morality but their efficiency, and had usually been proven irritatingly correct.

Geoffrey knew that all he needed to do to ensure de Groot's obedience was to maintain a regular supply of Venetian ducats. Fortunately money was easily accessible to him because his wife, Beatrice, had been endowed with a large acreage of good farmland in East Suffolk. She was no beauty but Geoffrey could hardly expect to secure an eligible bride after losing his own estate to his cousin. He had not intended to marry but the sudden need to find somewhere decent to live had forced his hand; part of Beatrice's endowment was Eastwell Hall. She had also produced an heir. God's holy balls! What an effort that had been, reflected Geoffrey. Still, all women look the same in the dark and at least there was someone who would ultimately benefit from his life of knavery, for young Thomas had survived the perils of infancy and was now a healthy six year old.

Geoffrey reached the entrance to his lodgings and took a last look at de Groot's ship as it glided down the Orwell estuary. A great day indeed but, he cautioned himself, at the rate he was now spending Beatrice's endowment he must not take too long to achieve his aims.

"A year at most," he murmured to himself. "That should be time enough."

CHAPTER TWO

Richard and Fastolf drew rein on the heights of Saint Catherine to enjoy the view below them. Rouen, the capital of English occupied Normandy, hugged the east bank of the winding River Seine, and in the fields outside the city golden corn swayed in the gentle summer breeze. The English had captured Rouen in 1419 following a bitter six month siege, after which there was an orgy of rape and plunder which did nothing to endear the English to French hearts. Dominating the view was the Cathedral of Notre Dame, which was quite the most magnificent building Richard had ever seen. He imagined he could see his own house, which lay half way between the cathedral and the market place, where Mary and Joan would be carrying out their daily duties unaware that he would be with them within the hour.

Sea going vessels lay moored at the city quay. The Seine was navigable as far upstream as Rouen, a fact which had not passed unnoticed to the Viking raiders of yore, who had carved out the original Duchy of Normandy at the expense of the Kingdom of France. The landward side of the city was protected by four miles of formidable walls and lofty towers, which had delayed the conquest of the victor of Agincourt for an entire winter, until famine weakened the inhabitants so much that they could not resist the final assault. That was four years ago. Since then there had been an influx of English folk like Richard and Mary, who hoped to make their homes in a part of France which looked destined to remain an English possession for ever.

"There'll be an early harvest this year," said Fastolf inconsequentially, then letting an uncharacteristic touch of wistfulness enter his voice he added, "I wonder how things are at home." For him, home was Caistor Manor, two miles north of the busy Norfolk port of Yarmouth, where he had been born and bred.

Richard smiled, "Your Lady Millicent will have everything under tight control Sir John, you can be sure of that."

"Aye," agreed Fastolf, "but I have not seen my dear wife for two years and I miss her. Some of the men will be returning home this winter. I may request leave from the Earl of Salisbury to spend Christmas at Caistor this year. You are fortunate Richard; you will be with your Mary this very day."

"True, but not by choice. We cannot go home because of the unjust heresy laws in England, and I would give much to see Suffolk again, if only for a month or two, as would Mary. My real home is Calveley Hall though I have yet to spend a single night there."

"At least you have a good steward to care for Calveley Hall until times change for the better."

"There is no-one I trust more than Father Hugh," acknowledged Richard, "and managing my estate at least keeps him beyond the confines of Dunwich priory."

"How he became a Franciscan I'll never know," said Fastolf.

"Hugh and the priesthood was never a comfortable match," agreed Richard, "but I daresay many of us might find Holy Orders a preferable alternative to poverty. Still, I look forward to the day when I can return to Calveley Hall and manage the estate myself."

Fastolf chuckled, "Then I shan't live to see it. You will never be a farmer again Richard, not while you have the strength left to fight the French."

Richard stroked his horse's ears and said thoughtfully, "I suppose you are right, but going home is a pleasing dream. I would like to think that Mary could manage as well in my absence as Millicent does in yours."

"We are both fortunate husbands but if you cannot return to England with Mary, you will have to accept Normandy as your home."

Richard looked down at his old fashioned armour and then glanced at Fastolf's superb Greenwich plate, which bore the Norfolk knight's azure and gold coat of arms containing the motto 'Me faut faire', roughly meaning 'I must keep busy'. He said wistfully,

"While we English are obliged to travel in full armour for fear of being murdered on the road, we can never regard Normandy or any other part of France as our home."

Fastolf shrugged, "People are attacked on English roads too."

"Yes, but that is straightforward highway robbery. Here we are murdered for being English."

The conversation was getting too deep for the urbane Fastolf, who brought them both back to day to day reality. "Well at least we can try to make as much money as we can while the good times last. I will go straight to Duke John at the Hotel de Ville and then visit you this evening. Hopefully we will be able to return to the army tomorrow."

"You will dine and stay the night with us?"

Fastolf dug his heels into his horse's flanks and called back as he cantered towards the city, "Indeed yes. I shall look forward to sampling Mary's cooking again."

Richard walked his huge black warhorse, which he had captured from the French at Agincourt, slowly through the city's crowded streets. He did not hurry; a homecoming should be savoured, especially an unannounced one, but even so, his heartbeat quickened as he entered the street that led to the small square between the cathedral and the market place. At the entrance to the square he stopped to purchase some beef pies from the butcher Mary always used, then remaining dismounted, he led his horse towards the neat, whitewashed house at the far end of the square.

Joan, his nine year old daughter by his first wife Ann, and the only survivor of the slaughter instigated by his cousin, saw him as she played with two other children outside the house. "Maman! Maman! Papa is here!" Richard smiled wryly. Joan knew no other home but Rouen; her first language was French. She ran to him and threw her arms round his armoured waist. He lifted her up onto his horse where she sat in the high backed saddle like a pimple on a lion.

"Have you been looking after your mother well my young lady?"

"I think so Papa. Have you brought me anything?"

"Of course." He patted a small leather bag which hung from his saddle. It contained a skilfully carved set of painted wooden farm animals plundered at Cravant. He knew Joan would love them but, if asked, he would have to tell Mary he bought them; she did not like his profession and disapproved of plunder. He led his horse with its tiny rider to the back of the house, unsaddled it in the small manger, checked there was plenty of water in the trough and spread some summer hay which the noble creature began to devour immediately. Then, gathering up Joan in one arm and the meat pies in the other, he walked into the house.

Mary was in the kitchen preparing some food. She had her back to the door and assumed the new arrival was Joan. "Would you like to help with this pastry dear?" she said as she washed down a chopping board. She was wearing a tight, embroidered bodice and a dark blue skirt. Her fair hair was gathered up into a working bonnet exposing her long, elegant neck.

Richard paused briefly to admire her and answered, "I'm not much good at pastry making my darling but I'll give it a try if you wish."

Mary span round, her brown eyes wide with surprise and delight. "Richard! It's you!"

"Nothing wrong with your eyesight my dear."

Her brow furrowed as she touched her hair with her flour covered hands. "I must look dreadful."

Richard put down Joan and the meat pies, "Never more beautiful. Come here." Mary flew into his arms. They kissed and held each other for a few minutes saying nothing, just relishing the moment of the unexpected reunion until Joan, who had been the essence of patience for a nine year old, could wait no longer. "Can I see what you've brought Papa?" Richard released Mary and handed Joan the leather bag. The wooden animals were received with gasps of pleasure. "Papa, they are beautiful. May I show them to my friends?"

Mary answered, "Of course dear and I will arrange for you to visit Genevieve and have supper with her too."

"I would rather have supper with you and Papa."

"Very well then. It is now nearly four o'clock. You can stay with Genevieve until six."

"That's all right Maman, I only need half an hour."

"But I have things to do. I will collect you at six."

"But…."

"No buts. Six o'clock."

"Yes Maman."

Richard was still in the kitchen munching one of the pies when Mary returned from delivering Joan. She said, "I hope you don't think me harsh with Joan but I have not seen you for months. I want to love you properly my handsome hero. Thank God you are still in one piece; I am always so fearful." She began to unbuckle his armour.

The clock near the market place chimed half past five. Richard looked contentedly at Mary's naked body as she lay snuggled up against his. The afternoon sun shone through the shuttered windows casting stripes of golden light across her back. She really is a lovely woman mused Richard to himself. Her long, fair hair lay spread haphazardly across his chest and her breathing was heavy as she slept after their lovemaking. Her skin was not the milky white colour the bards admired so much, but Richard preferred a slightly darker hue. What a pity they had been unable to have children of their own. He suddenly found himself comparing Mary with Ann, his first wife. This was something he tried to avoid, for as much as he loved Mary, she would never be able to replace his beloved Ann. Tall, elegant Ann Calveley, the mother of his children and his ardent supporter when times were hard; it would be at her side his body would lie when the Lord called him.

Mary stirred and murmured, "What time is it?"

"Half past five."

"I'll just lie here a little longer then. It's so warm."

Richard swallowed and said, "Did I tell you Sir John Fastolf is coming to dine with us tonight?"

Mary sat up, horror writ large across her face. "What! Why did you not tell me sooner?"

"And miss this? There is time enough yet. I will help."

Mary leaped off the bed and reached for her clothes. She was thirty five, the same age as Richard, but her body would have graced a woman ten years younger. "When will Sir John arrive?" she asked.

"We did not fix a time, that depends on the Duke of Bedford, but I doubt he'll be here before eight." Richard leaned over, grabbed Mary by her narrow waist and dragged her back onto the bed. He kissed her neck and shoulders and whispered, "We can spare another twenty minutes."

Mary did not object.

* * *

II

"God's teeth! Mary, your dinners are worth travelling a hundred miles for!" exclaimed Fastolf as he pushed his empty platter to one side.

"Thank you Sir John," she replied coquettishly. "Have you had enough?"

"More than enough, too much in fact. I'll be needing a new suit of armour at this rate." They sat round a rectangular, oak table in a small, low beamed room at the front of the house reserved specifically for dining with important guests. Even quite humble dwellings in France boasted separate dining rooms which reflected the importance of food in French society. Another French custom adopted by the Calveleys was to encourage Joan to join the adults at dinner instead of hustling her off to bed early. Somehow the French seemed to enjoy their children more than the English.

"Did you kill as many Frenchies as Papa in the battle Uncle John?" asked Joan in her heavily accented English.

Mary scolded her, "Joan! You must not ask questions like that!"

Fastolf laughed, "I don't manage to kill many these days. I prefer to capture them for ransom."

"What is ransom Uncle John?"

Fastolf beamed as he warmed to his favourite subject. "The idea is that I capture a French knight, then he pays me money called ransom to release him. After that I do my best to capture another one at the next battle and he pays me also and so it goes on."

Joan frowned, "It all seems rather silly Uncle John."

"I daresay it is but it beats working for a living!"

Richard glanced sidelong at Mary. As a Lollard she had preached against the evil of war but he knew she would say nothing to embarrass him; Fastolf meant no harm.

To ease the strain, Richard quickly changed the subject of the conversation, "Sir John, you have said nothing yet about your visit to the Duke of Bedford."

Fastolf suddenly seemed ill at ease. "A strange matter Richard. I know I can speak freely here so I will tell you it concerned money, an immense amount of it. The war is draining England of gold, but if we can get our hands on the treasure the duke spoke of, we may yet conquer France."

Mary became more attentive. Anything that might bring the war to an end interested her. "But if we fail to secure this hoard Sir John, what then?"

Fastolf shook his head sadly, "Then the war will drag on and ultimately we shall be driven back to England. That, at least, is Bedford's opinion."

Mary looked at Richard who read the concern in her eyes. "Don't worry my dear. Sir John speaks of many years hence. If the Lollard persecutions have not ended by then we can make our home elsewhere, Burgundy or Switzerland perhaps."

Fastolf cautioned, "Even if the Lollards have been forgotten you must remain wary because Mary's conviction for heresy still remains on record. The church courts in particular have long memories and if they forget, your cousin will not hesitate to remind them. While Geoffrey Calveley lives, England will be unsafe for Mary."

"So what will happen now Sir John?" asked Richard.

"Tomorrow you and I will pay a visit to the custodians of Bedford's treasure. They are not far away and we should be back in Rouen by sunset. I shall report to the duke then we can rejoin the Earl of Salisbury while there is still some plunder left in Maine."

Richard cringed but Mary seemed not to notice Fastolf's cheery reference to plunder; she was lost in thoughts of her own.

Early next morning Fastolf and Richard left Rouen by the south gate and followed the road to Louviers. The cooling breeze of the previous day had died away and the cloudless sky heralded a return to full summer heat. It was going to be unpleasant for men in full armour.

"How far are we going Sir John?" asked Richard as he brushed away a cluster of black flies which had settled on his horse's sweating neck.

"We are heading for a small manor near Igoville which, according to Bedford, is about six miles south of Rouen."

"You have not yet said exactly who it is we are visiting."

"The Knights Templar."

Richard gasped, "Did I hear you correctly? The Knights Templar?"

"Yes."

"But how can that be? The Templars were destroyed a hundred years ago."

Fastolf shrugged, "My response was the same as yours Richard when I first heard, but Bedford assures me that some Templars escaped the great suppression. The Order has been maintained in secret ever since."

"But even if that is so, what use can they be to us?" asked Richard. "There cannot be many in number else we'd have heard of them."

"It's not their fighting qualities we need but their money. Only a fraction of their wealth fell into French hands at the time of the suppression. The Templars claim they can finance our war to its conclusion."

"And what do they get in return?"

"Assuming we win, we will re-establish their Order with or without the Pope's consent and return to the Templars the property and estates stolen by the French crown."

"So that is why they cannot support the French," observed Richard. "Too many influential French families live off land once owned by the Templars."

"Exactly. If the French win, the Templars will gain nothing."

The two Englishmen cantered their mounts along the rutted, dusty road which ran close to the Seine. Neither spoke for a while, each unsure of what danger lay ahead. Although it was not yet ten o'clock, Richard could feel sweat dripping from his body. His gambeson was already soaked inside his armour and he wondered if this was how the Templars of yore must have felt each time they rode out to battle with the infidel under the blazing Holy Land sun. They had been a special breed of knights, predominantly French, spurred on by the cold fire of religious fanaticism and dedicated to a cause they knew was right. Such fervour combined with rigid discipline and well-honed fighting skills had made the Templars and their kindred order, the Knights Hospitaller, the terror of the Muslims. If their successors were anything like them, the lives of two English warriors would be of little consequence in the grand plan to re-establish the Templar Order and its estates. This was an alarming thought, and as Igoville came into sight nestling inside the next bend of the Seine, Richard broke the silence.

"The Templars were known for their ruthlessness Sir John. Do you not think we are taking a risk by meeting them without a company of bold English archers behind us?"

"Possibly. They are men who live outside the protection of the law. At present their interests and ours appear to coincide, but if ever that ceases to be the case, who knows what will happen. Anyway, we will soon find out. Yonder a small track breaks away from the road. We follow the track for two miles into the hills where we will be met and blindfolded for the last part of our journey."

"Blindfolded! But we'll be helpless."

"Bedford agreed the terms Richard so we must adhere to them. Best be on our guard though."

When he saw the four men who were waiting for them at the edge of a large oak forest, Richard felt a little more reassured. None wore armour and, apart from short, all-purpose daggers hanging from their belts, they seemed to be unarmed. Subconsciously Richard had been expecting to encounter large, mailed knights wearing the feared white surcoat emblazoned with the blood red, eight pointed Templar cross, but these four could have been simple woodsmen such as you might see on any Suffolk estate. He smiled inwardly at his rustic simplicity as one of the four came forward to meet them.

The Templar said, "Mes Seignieurs, welcome." Seeing the coat of arms on Fastolf's shield he addressed the Norfolk knight. "We will escort you from here. I believe the blindfold and disarming arrangements have already been explained?"

Fastolf, never at ease with the French language, turned to Richard. "You speak to him; he's talking too quickly for me." Poor though he was, Richard's father had appreciated the value of education and sent him to be instructed by the Franciscan friars at Dunwich Priory on the Suffolk coast where, among other things, he had learned French and geometry. Now, after dwelling eight years in Normandy, Richard was almost as comfortable speaking French as his native tongue.

"We accept the blindfold," he said, "but we will retain our arms."

"But this is not what was agreed," said the Templar.

"We were told nothing about disarming. You are French, we are English and we are at war. We will not give up our arms to you."

"Our orders are that you must give up your arms."

Richard unsheathed his huge sword and said menacingly, "Then come and get them if you dare."

"God's holy balls!" rasped Fastolf. "What in Hell is happening?"

Richard whispered, "They want us to disarm."

"And you told them 'no'?"

"Was that wrong Sir John?"

"Certainly not. It will do no harm for these Templars to learn we are not to be trifled with."

The spokesman for the Templars backed away and consulted with his comrades for a few moments. Then, with an air of bored resignation he said, "Put away your sword Englishman, you may keep your arms."

After such an unpromising start, Fastolf and Richard felt even more vulnerable as they were led away blindfolded by their escort. Both kept their hands tightly wrapped around their sword pommels, but such a precaution would have availed them little if the Templars decided to turn nasty. Richard tried to maintain some sense of direction by using the position of the sun which penetrated his crude blindfold, but such basic measures were rendered useless once they entered the shade of the oak forest.

The forest shade came as a welcome relief from the full heat of the day but soon, in Richard's mind, the shade turned to gloom and the peaceful quiet of the forest became oppressive silence. How would the Templars react to his little show of defiance? Such rigid disciplinarians might choose to make an example of him to show they also were not to be trifled with.

* * *

III

The journey through the forest lasted about an hour and as soon as they re-emerged into the sunlight, the escort halted and removed the blindfolds. As Richard's eyes slowly adjusted to the light again, he could see that they had not actually left the forest but had halted in a clearing in which about a dozen large, white tents were pitched. Moving quietly between the tents were grim faced men wearing ankle length, white cloaks emblazoned with Templar crosses on the front, back and left shoulder.

Fastolf spoke softly, "Somehow I could not really believe it until now. It's as if we have travelled back in time more than a hundred years. You don't suppose this forest is bewitched?" This last remark was made more than half seriously.

The escort leader entered the largest tent, which was pitched in the centre of the clearing, while the two Englishmen looked nervously about them. Richard noticed that the Templars were mostly middle aged or older and began to wonder if the Order was withering away. Perhaps the secrecy and the lack of a cause to crusade for were making the recruitment of younger men difficult. After all, there was a perfectly good war raging in France which should easily satisfy the young bloods. It would take a special sort of man to give that up in favour of a covert, celibate monasticism without the protection and benefits of the Church. The prime purpose of the Templars had always been to fight the Muslims, yet for more than a hundred years this had been denied them. Richard sensed that the alliance with the English was the last throw of the dice for them which, if it failed, would see the ultimate demise of the greatest of all the military orders.

The escort leader emerged from the tent and addressed the Englishmen. "The Grand Master will see you now. He respectfully requests you to leave your arms outside his tent." This time Fastolf and Richard acquiesced and planted their swords in the soft, forest earth before entering the presence of Charles, Sieur d'Evreux, the Grand Master of the Templars. Inside the square tent were four men, two standing at the far corners and two sitting at a simple wooden table facing the entrance. Light penetrated through ventilation apertures cut into the tent walls at eye level to keep the air cool. Neither of the two seated men stood up when Fastolf and Richard entered, which would have been customary in normal society for Fastolf was a garter knight, nor were the Englishmen offered a seat; there were no other chairs in the tent. Richard felt the pores in his skin open as his eyes met those of the older of the two seated men; there could be no doubt that he was the Grand Master.

The Sieur d'Evreux was over fifty but age had not dimmed the fire that burned in his soul. His cold, grey eyes seemed to reveal a restless, implacable spirit which, though disciplined by iron self control, could never be subdued. The gaunt, bony face and thin, aquiline nose warned of a predatory, intolerant nature which would brook no opposition. A natural aura of authority surrounded him creating a powerful, threatening presence which no ordinary man could fail to sense. Even Fastolf, who feared no-one, swallowed nervously.

"Welcome gentlemen," said the Grand Master in almost perfect English. His voice was thin and nasal and his greeting as warm as a midwinter frost. "I assume you understand the purpose of this meeting?"

Fastolf answered, "Certainly Grand Master. My Lord Bedford explained all to me in Rouen. You require English help to re-establish your Order."

D'Evreux raised his eyebrows in mock surprise, "And you require our finance to complete your conquest of France. We need each other do we not?"

"My Lord Bedford said as much," agreed Fastolf.

"You speak on his behalf?"

"And with his authority, Grand Master. We need evidence that your wealth really exists before we can proceed further."

The Grand Master smiled, but no humour accompanied the minimal movement in his thin lips. "First you will tell me who you are."

"I am Sir John Fastolf, a garter knight, and with me is the captain of my company Richard Calveley."

"Calveley," mused the Grand Master. "I have heard that name before."

Richard said, "A distant kinsman of mine, Sir Hugh Calveley, fought with distinction under the Black Prince's banner in Gascony. My father also fought in France."

The Templar did not trouble to acknowledge Richard's reply. Instead he addressed Fastolf again. "While I understand that garter knights are well respected, I thought Lord Bedford would have sent someone from the upper nobility."

"We were chosen for our skills, not our blood line," answered Fastolf starkly.

"Then I shall require you to swear an oath to the effect that all matters passing between us shall remain secret."

Irritation began to displace the Norfolk knight's initial anxiety. "We shall do no such thing. You have our word; that should be enough. An Englishman's word is his bond. Oath taking is not our way." An ominous silence followed during which Richard feared they had overstepped the mark. He looked sidelong at Fastolf, who now seemed quite at ease; if he was nervous he was not showing it. When at last the Grand Master spoke again, his words chilled Richard to the marrow.

"The reason for the delay in my replying to you is simple. If anyone speaks to me with disrespect, in the manner you have just done, the normal penalty is immediate execution. My authority here is absolute. Even though you might claim ignorance of our ways, I would still have you punished for defying me. Fortunately, none of the brothers here present speaks English otherwise you would most certainly suffer, but I warn you, there will be no second chance." Neither Englishman doubted the Templar meant exactly what he said and they were well beyond the protection of English law here, but d'Evreux did not insist on proceeding with the oath taking. Too much was at stake to allow the unholy alliance to fall at the first obstacle.

"Very well," continued d'Evreux, "you say you require proof of our wealth?"

"We do," answered Fastolf more respectfully, "but it is a mere formality." The Grand Master turned to the man sitting beside him and spoke in a strange guttural language Richard could not identify. Until then Richard had hardly noticed the second man because d'Evreux's huge presence overshadowed him, but now there was time to observe him in more detail. His provenance was clearly beyond the bounds of Christendom because the olive brown colour of his skin was too dark to be explained solely by exposure to the sun. Deep brown, almost black eyes set close to a thin, arched nose, and a natural sharpness of movement gave the impression of a small falcon, though unlike d'Evreux, this man understood humour for his narrow face broadened generously when he smiled at something his master said.

When they finished conversing, the Grand Master introduced his companion. "This is Mamoun al Rashid, a brother from the east. He agrees that you should have your proof so you shall see our fortune for yourselves."

"Thank you," said a relieved Fastolf. "Is it here?"

"No, but it needs to be moved here. Perhaps you will help us because it will take many men to transport it."

"Of course Grand Master. Where is it now?"

"Castrum Peregrinorum." Fastolf looked blank so the Grand Master translated the Latin into English for him. "Pilgrim's Castle."

The Englishman was none the wiser. "I have not heard of it."

Richard's heart sank for he was better versed in history than his liege. "I have Sir John," he whispered. "There is only one Pilgrim's Castle; it was the last stronghold of the Templars in the Holy Land."

Fastolf's mouth fell open, "Outremer! The treasure is in Outremer!"

D'Evreux seemed unconcerned. "Does that surprise you Sir John?"

"Well, yes. How do you know it is still there? Surely the Muslims stole it when they took the castle."

"The Muslims did not take the castle. The Templars abandoned it when Acre fell though there was insufficient time to make arrangements to move our treasury. It was no simple matter to move hundreds of thousands of gold ducats, we could only carry away a small fraction of it, so the Grand Master at the time, Guillaume de Beaujeu, ordered the treasury to be hidden in the hills near Pilgrim's Castle. Although he drew a map, the precise description of the location of the treasury is passed down by word of mouth through each successive Grand Master. As well as telling his successor, he tells one other brother to ensure the secret is not lost in the event of an accident."

It took Fastolf a few moments to recover his numbed wits. He had not bargained on a trip to the Holy Land. A song thrush began to warble from a leafy bough at the edge of the forest clearing. Its merry song seemed to accentuate the stunned silence that hung heavy inside d'Evreux's tent. At last the Templar asked, "Is something the matter Sir John?"

Fastolf rubbed his chin and frowned, "The Turks are still in Outremer. Surely they will not permit us to enter their territory and remove a fortune from it? They already persecute and murder simple Christian pilgrims. Heaven knows what they would do to their old Templar enemies."

"It is as you say," replied d'Evreux, "therefore our mission must be carried out with care. Until now there has been no point in taking such a risk, but the alliance with you English means our time has come at last."

"But even if we succeed, you cannot store your treasure in tents like this. Or are you intending to give it to us all at once?"

"Hardly Sir John. Do not concern yourself about security here in France. We do not permanently dwell in tents but live ordinary lives like everyone else for most of the time. Normally you would not recognise a Templar if you saw one, for we do not parade our identity. But once a year we meet to renew our pledge to the Order and swear in new brothers. Lord Bedford sent for you now so that you could see us in our true aspect as warriors of Christ. When we recover our treasury it will be scattered throughout France in secure locations under the supervision of individual brothers."

Fastolf raised a sceptical eyebrow, "Will that not be a temptation to some of them?"

"No brother breaks his vows. The retribution is too terrible to contemplate." The Grand Master turned to Mamoun al Rashid and they briefly spoke again in their guttural language, then he concluded the audience with the Englishmen saying, "The appointed meeting place for the start of our little crusade is the Basilica of San Marco in Venice. The date is the feast of The Immaculate Conception, which you will remember, is the eighth day of December. There will be forty two of us and we shall travel as pilgrims not warriors. Therefore you will not need your armour. I shall provide you with weapons and chainmail hauberks, which can easily be rolled up and packed away and only used if the need arises."

Fastolf looked guiltily at Richard and said quietly, "I'm sorry about this but I have no choice." Then he said to the Grand Master, "It is with regret that I must decline this venture. I have more than a hundred men in France who look to me for leadership, pay and welfare. While I may leave them for a week or two, the journey you propose will take many months. Captain Calveley will go in my place and, with your permission, will bring one other Englishman with him."

"That will be in order," agreed d'Evreux, "though unnecessary because there is already an Englishman amongst our brotherhood. I will have him brought here." He signalled to one of the sentinels standing at the back of the tent and ordered him to fetch the English brother. Meanwhile Richard glared at Fastolf who, he knew, could easily have gone with the Templars to Pilgrim's Castle and delegated the command of his company in France to his captain. Fastolf's real motive for staying behind was, of course, not to miss out on the plunder to be had in Anjou and Maine. While they waited for the English Templar, Fastolf, who studiously avoided Richard's baleful eyes, said quietly,

"Richard, I know exactly what you're thinking but it's not true. I must be with my men in time of war. Rest assured, I will reserve a captain's share of any plunder we secure for you while you are away. You will not lose out."

"Will that be enough to assuage your conscience?"

"And I will give you paid leave until it is time for you to depart for Venice so you can organise your affairs in Suffolk and then be with Mary and Joan for the next few months." That was an attractive proposition but Richard was not yet mollified. "And you will give me the sergeant of my choice to accompany me to Outremer?"

"Depends on who you choose."

"Not good enough because I have not yet decided. You know very well that Bedford would prefer you to go with the Templars."

Fastolf shrugged, "All right then, you may have the sergeant of your choice." Before Richard could respond Fastolf ended the awkward conversation by addressing d'Evreux again. "Grand Master, how will you travel from Venice? By sea I suppose, but how can you expect to land unopposed in any port under Turkish control?"

D'Evreux nodded, "Arrangements have already been made with the Doge of Venice for the hire of a fast galley. We shall avoid the Outremer ports but the galley's draught will be too deep to allow us to disembark directly onto the beach below Pilgrim's Castle. Therefore we shall carry rowing boats with us to ferry us ashore."

The tent flap opened and the sentinel returned accompanied by a tall, gaunt, white haired Templar who would not see fifty again. A slight stoop and a short, grey beard made him seem older than he really was, but this particular warrior of Christ would hardly have struck fear into the heart of the infidel.

He bowed to the Grand Master and said, "You wish to see me Grand Mast-" The last syllable remained unspoken. The Templar's dark eyes widened. He backed away in abject terror. A movement at Fastolf's elbow gave him no warning of what was to come as he was suddenly brushed aside. In an instant Richard had forced his way past his liege and grabbed the English Templar by the throat.

"In God's name!" bellowed Fastolf but Richard seemed not to hear. He wrestled the English Templar to the ground and tightened his grip until his victim's eyes bulged out of their sockets like quail's eggs on a salver. At a signal from d'Evreux, the two sentinels and Mamoun rushed to their comrade's aid and tried to drag Richard away, but his grip did not slacken. The English Templar's face turned red, then purple and it was not until Fastolf himself prised Richard's fingers away from the scrawny throat that air at last re-entered the bursting lungs.

"You bastard!" snarled Richard, "Bastard! Bastard!"

The Grand Master, white with anger, demanded, "What is the meaning of this!"

Richard, his voice shrill with emotion, appealed to Fastolf, "Let me kill him. This vile animal is Titus Scrope!"

Fastolf had not met Titus before but he knew of the part he had played in the destruction of Richard's family. "Richard, are you sure?" he asked incredulously.

"Sir John, how could I be wrong! To be sure he is grey haired now and wears a beard, but I could never forget that voice and those evil snake eyes. I always felt he cheated death but now his time has come." He lurched towards Titus again but the three Templars managed to hold him back with difficulty.

"Enough of this disgrace!" shouted d'Evreux. "Sir John you have some explaining to do."

Before Fastolf could reply, a gasping Titus Scrope answered from the tent floor, "Grand Master, may I speak?" D'Evreux nodded and Titus clambered unsteadily to his feet. "Grand Master, you know I came to you as a sinner many years ago. Since then I have repented and done my best to serve God by dedicating what is left of my unworthy life to your Order." He looked at Richard and continued, "It is true I wronged this man not once but twice in a most terrible way. I deserve to die at his hand and if Master Calveley chooses to dispatch me now I shall not resist. I would, however, ask him to stay his hand awhile so that I may have an opportunity to serve him in some way and try to compensate, if only a little, for the evil I have done him."

"A pretty speech Scrope," said Richard coldly, "but it will not save your neck."

The Grand Master took little interest in the lives of his brothers before they joined the Order. Provided they served him well as Templars, he was prepared to overlook the past. Titus was no exception; it was time to put these insolent English emissaries in their place, but first he must reprimand Scrope.

"Brother Titus, you have no right to offer your life to anyone but me. You are pledged to the Order, no-one else."

"Yes Grand Master," acknowledged Titus humbly.

"As for you Sir John, you will instruct your brawling compatriot in the basics of self control and good manners before he joins me in Venice."

Fastolf replied, "The circumstances are extreme. Your English Templar is a murderer, a thief and a liar. He destroyed Captain Calveley's family and I do not doubt that my response would have been at least as violent as his had it been my family your Templar murdered."

"Has Brother Titus been convicted of these crimes in one of your English courts?"

"Well, no," admitted Fastolf.

"Has a warrant been issued for his arrest."

"No."

"Then he is not a convicted criminal so he shall continue to enjoy my protection. His conduct has been exemplary since he joined the Order seven years ago and I shall tolerate no more assaults on his person by your captain. Our mission will be dangerous enough without breaches of discipline within our own ranks. I must have assurances from both of you about this."

Fastolf recalled Bedford's remarks about the importance of co-operating with the Templars in England's quest for final victory. He disliked forcing his loyal captain to accept a situation which he himself would find impossible, but England's cause must come first.

"Richard," he said, "are you in control of yourself now?"

The initial pulse of blind rage that swept through Richard when he first saw Titus had passed, and although he was still determined to send Titus on the road to Hell, he realised that this was not the time. The change in the old English Templar was remarkable. Far from the evil assassin Richard had once known, he now beheld an old, almost pious looking man who, to the uninformed, might pass as a priest. But Richard knew the true Titus Scrope better than most; the plausible, repenting sinner could not fool him. He thought back to that terrible autumn morning, nine years before, when he had ridden home from Beccles to find his house burned to the ground and his two young sons beaten to death. Above all he recalled the violated, mutilated body of his beloved Ann, who had fought Titus and his henchmen until her dying breath. A few days later Richard had seen a Halesworth doxy wearing Ann's brooch and found out she was given it by one of Titus' men. Although no court would convict on such evidence alone, it was enough to reveal the truth to Richard. Even if Titus truly repented, God might forgive but he never could. He felt the anger welling up in him again fuelled by guilt that he had not been with his family when they needed him most.

"Yes Sir John," he replied, "Scrope is safe, at least for now."

The Grand Master signalled to his men to release Richard, and Fastolf said, "Richard, from the moment you reach Venice you must give the Grand Master your loyalty as if he were me. Your retribution must be suspended until you return from Outremer, after which I shall not only release you from that bond, but will also do all in my power to help you to bring Scrope to justice. You have my word on that; do I have yours?"

Richard looked once more at his sworn enemy. Titus saw the cold, green fire blazing in Richard's eyes and instinctively took a step back.

"Aye Sir John," said Richard in an expressionless monotone, "you have it."

CHAPTER THREE

While Richard was discovering that Titus Scrope had not drowned after all, two hundred miles away Father John Chadwick was walking slowly back to his church from Calais market. He had been the parish priest for less than a year, but that was long enough for him to realise he had made a mistake. When the living became vacant, the prospect of a large parish in English occupied France seemed exciting to the quiet Hampshire curate, so he had grasped the opportunity with both hands. But the great venture had proved a disappointment.

Calais was a strange town. Despite repeated attempts by a succession of English kings during the last eighty years to anglicise the place, Calais remained stubbornly French. Certainly the governors, mayors and most of the merchants were English, and many shops bore English names, but in the taverns, the markets and the streets the language was still predominantly French. This in itself need not have concerned Father Chadwick, who spoke French fluently enough and, after all, any soul English or French is of equal value to God, but the practical effect for his parish was devastating. The French refused to attend the church of the invader, which was not altogether surprising, but the English merchant class was notoriously irreligious, presuming that a few good donations would purchase enough indulgences to make the chore of attending mass unnecessary. Consequently Father Chadwick found himself giving sermons to an almost deserted church every Sunday. The feeling of not being needed accentuated his lonely life; he regarded himself as a failure but in truth his task was impossible.

He stopped in front of his church and looked at the sandstone plaque outside. Painted on it in white were the words 'Church of our Lady,' but beneath the faded, flaking paint the words 'L'Eglise de Notre Dame' could be seen carved deep into the stone.

"That neatly sums up the superficial nature of our conquest," said Father Chadwick quietly. Since his arrival in Calais, he had developed the habit of talking to himself otherwise he would have gone mad. There was no-one else to talk to; or was he mad already?

He entered the quiet, gloomy church observing wryly that it was empty as usual, and headed for the presbytery which adjoined the south transept. He was only half way along the nave when he noticed some large splinters of wood on the stone floor. Hurrying between the pews like a silent, black cloaked phantom, he turned the corner into the transept and beheld the remains of the presbytery door. The heavy, iron hinges had been smashed by a mace or similar weapon, but the intruder had not cared about limiting the damage because most of the thick oak which supported the hinges to the door had been split apart and lay scattered across the transept floor.

The priest stood still and listened; he had no wish to confront the perpetrator of this violence who must have used considerable physical strength to gain entry. No noise came from the presbytery and so, satisfied he was alone, he stepped through the dismantled doorway and entered his violated home. His first reaction was surprise. Apart from the door there appeared to be no damage. He went to the chest where the church finery was stowed but the great lock was unbroken. Then he checked his personal effects and church items of lesser value but nothing had been touched. Now, more confused than afraid, he went into the records room which led off from the presbytery. Here were kept the church diaries and ledgers of births, deaths and marriages. Father Chadwick hardly ever needed to come in to this room but the intruder had because there were large footprints in the thick dust which covered the wooden floor.

After spending nearly an hour checking all the ledgers were in place, Father Chadwick satisfied himself that nothing was missing. Whatever the intruder had come for, he appeared to have left empty handed. Perhaps he had been disturbed, or more likely he had chosen the wrong church. That would be true to form thought the priest bitterly; even a thief's visit to my church was a mistake. The other odd thing about this strange affair was the smell that permeated the records room, but John Chadwick's experience of spices was limited, so he was unable to recognise the distinctive aroma of clove oil.

* * *

II

The ride down the coast road was a poignant journey for Richard, for the twenty five mile stretch of highway between Yarmouth and Dunwich had been the link between most of the dramatic events that had changed his once peaceful farming life. His ship had come in with the tide at Yarmouth shortly after dawn, so he should be able to reach Calveley Hall by nightfall comfortably enough. Although once his cousin's property, Richard felt that Calveley Hall at Holton near Halesworth was where his true roots lay. The hall was only three miles from the smallholding at Westhall where he had lived with Ann and the boys until their murder, but although that had been rented to Fastolf long ago, he was pleased that his final dwelling place would not be far from memories of his first family.

The yellow gorse, clustered in clumps across the heathland south of Lowestoft, was enjoying a second blooming and a myriad of butterflies hovered over the meadow flowers in the pastures which always bordered the roadside villages. How very English it all was! No war here for centuries. Somehow the relationship between nature and village life seemed most at ease here and Richard quietly rejoiced at being a son of Suffolk, that most English of English shires.

The hot summer had brought the crops forward, and the part of Richard that was still a farmer was satisfied to see the harvest well advanced, though as yet it was still only the last day of August. He wondered how far his own harvest had progressed and looked forward to enjoying farm talk with his steward, Father Hugh. The other great pleasure about travelling in England was the security. Apart from the heavy sword he always wore to mark his rank, Richard had dispensed with the accoutrements of war. His armour was stowed in a warehouse in Yarmouth and instead he wore light hose and a dark green, short sleeved tunic which was far more suited to the summer weather.

It was a little past noon when Richard rode through Frostenden. Just outside the village he dismounted to allow his bay palfrey to rest for a few minutes and looked wistfully at the overgrown track that led into the forest on the western edge of the village. This was the path that had once led to the thriving Lollard community where he had first met Mary in the aftermath of his family's destruction. The Lollard heresy held a certain appeal for Richard. These followers of John Wyclif believed in mankind's direct communication with God through the reading of the Bible in English. They had no time for the church hierarchy which, in their view, stood between God and his people. The bishops, cardinals and pope lived off the toil of the poor like parasites. There was no mention of these prelates in the Bible, and even some of the poorer clergy sympathised with this particular Lollard view until a law against heresy was passed by parliament which threatened heretics with death by burning.

A uniquely novel aspect of Lollardy was the belief in complete equality between men and women. Mary had been the leader of the Frostenden Lollards and was, to all intents and purposes, a priestess. The concept of women priests was something the Catholic clergy abhorred but the idea found support amongst many ordinary people. Richard held no strong views either way but Catholicism had been ingrained too deeply in him at a tender age by the Dunwich friars for him to abandon the faith of his childhood without an overpowering reason. Ironically the friars, who were Franciscans, partly shared the Lollard view of the church hierarchy in that they also believed the wealth accrued by the prelates should be distributed more evenly amongst the faithful. But thanks to Titus Scrope, the Frostenden Lollard community had been scattered to the four winds; now they were just history. Richard remounted his horse, flicked the reins and rode on.

He stopped just once more to buy some smoked herrings from the waterfront at Blythburgh, then turned inland for home following the winding course of the River Blyth. The bell in the round tower of St Peter's church at Holton chimed a quarter past three as Richard reached Holton village, less than a mile from Halesworth, where the northern boundary of his land began. A surge of anticipation swept through him; he had not been home for so long. He kicked on his horse and cantered through a small copse, but when he emerged into the open again his excitement quickly dissipated as he looked around.

Wide swathes of ripe wheat flanked the gentle, south facing slopes either side of him like carpets of gold but, pleasant though the spectacle was, Richard had expected to see only stubble because this was where the harvest on his land traditionally started. Instead the crop was still untouched. Not wanting his homecoming to be blighted, he told himself that Hugh must have had reason to begin the harvest elsewhere this year, after all, Hugh was now an experienced steward. But by the time Richard arrived at the brick built hall, his disappointment was turning to irritation for he had passed blocked ditches, broken fences, overgrown hedges and a host of other little indicators that hinted to the tutored eye the beginning of neglect. The sward of grass, which flanked the cobbled pathway leading to the great oak front door of Calveley Hall, had not been cut for many weeks and, leaning idly against one of the massive door frames, a farm worker was munching a large pie.

Richard rode up to the pie-muncher and waited for his reins to be held while he dismounted, but the farm worker made no attempt to help. Instead he looked Richard directly in the eye and took another large bite out of his pie. Sliding off his mount with practised ease, Richard tied the reins to one of the stone lions which sat either side of the front door, walked up to the arrogant yokel, and asked quietly,

"Who are you?"

Although at least a head shorter than Richard, the ruddy faced, pock marked farm worker was not overawed. He finished chewing his mouthful of pie, swallowed, wiped his greasy lips on the back of his hand and replied,

"More like who be you my dandy peacock strutting round here like you own the place." Richard's patience was already stretched and, though normally considerate to those below his rank, he decided to make an exception in this case. Bracing his feet slightly apart, he swept the back of his gloved hand across the labourer's face, felling the unfortunate man as if he had been poleaxed. Richard watched the half eaten pie fly through the air until it landed somewhere in the overgrown grass then, standing over his crumpled adversary, he calmly repeated his question.

This time the reply was more respectful, but only a little more. "Luke Cotter. It's not right you striking those below you. I shall tell the owner."

"You just have."

"That cannot be," smirked Cotter. "He be away in France, but his steward's here so be warned."

"And where do you think I have just come from. Take me to Father Hugh at once. Allez vite!"

Luke Cotter knew only English but those last two words sounded sufficiently foreign to convince him he had made a terrible mistake. He quickly got to his feet and simpered, "You must be Master Calveley -"

"Captain Calveley."

"I didn't realise. Very sorry sir, hope you won't hold it against me."

"Is that how you treat all visitors?"

"Lord no sir! I'll fetch Father Hugh directly, please follow me."

Richard waited in the great hall and looked round while Cotter climbed the broad oak stairs to search for Hugh. At least the interior of Calveley Hall seemed well cared for. The embroidered tapestries which Richard had sent back after the capture of Melun three years ago had been hung on the red brick walls with care and good taste. The floor and furniture were spotlessly clean and fresh, summer flowers graced the long dining table and window recesses. He smiled a little mollified, and thought, almost a woman's touch; perhaps there is a reasonable explanation for the state of my land. I shall try to be patient.

His renewed determination to be sympathetic began to falter as the minutes passed with no sign of Cotter or Hugh, but at last his steward appeared at the top of the stairs closely followed by Cotter.

"Richard! What a surprise!" exclaimed the Franciscan as he bounded down the stairs to meet him. "If I had known I would have arranged a proper reception for you." Richard could hardly believe his eyes. Hugh had changed almost beyond recognition. Gone was the long, grey Franciscan robe and simple open sandals. Instead a confident man of thirty one wearing a smart, black tunic and hose embraced him at the foot of the stairs. No grey yet tinged Hugh's almost shoulder length, brown hair, and the only evidence of his priestly state was the long rosary and heavy, silver crucifix he wore round his neck. The pleasure of seeing his friend again momentarily displaced Richard's worries about his land, but only until Hugh turned to Cotter and said,

"Attend to Captain Calveley's horse." Cotter did not reply, but the look of defiance that showed on his face as he departed to carry out Hugh's order convinced Richard all was not well at Calveley Hall. He decided not to mention his concern just yet and said,

"God's teeth Hugh, I hardly recognised you! You look more like a knight of the shire than a Franciscan friar. You are still a priest I hope?" Then glancing down he added, "Your crucifix is the wrong way round."

Hugh quickly turned his crucifix so that the dying Christ was facing outwards. "Of course I'm still a priest but a friar's garb is not well suited to stewardship so I obtained a dispensation from the prior at Dunwich to wear ordinary clothes during the day."

Richard asked, "How is Father Anselm?" Anslem had become a substitute parent when a return of the plague carried off Richard's mother and father. An only child, the young Richard had been taken in by the Dunwich friars where Anselm was given the thankless task of tutoring the unruly boy. He quickly abandoned any hopes he may have harboured of training his charge for the priesthood, but he did give him an education worthy of an earl.

"Father Anselm is well enough considering his age," answered Hugh, "but he has given up his duties as prior and lives in quiet retirement in the priory."

"What about the new prior? Does he mind you stewarding for me? I know Anselm found it difficult to let you go."

"On the contrary, Father Simon would be disappointed if I returned. He values the salary you pay the priory for my services too highly to want me back."

Richard frowned, "That hardly seems in line with Franciscan values."

"True," agreed Hugh. "Father Simon is more a career priest than a caring one. Anselm's prime concern was the moral wellbeing of his flock whereas Simon's is Simon. I don't like him; I think he sees his role at Dunwich as just a stepping stone to greater things."

"The ambitious priest is a common enough article these days and I daresay the Franciscans are just as prone to them as any other Order. I should be interested to meet this Simon. We can call on him on our return journey."

Hugh took a step back and winced as if he had just been struck. "We?"

Richard laughed, "It's all right, I'm not sending you back to your cloistered brethren, far from it. I have come to take you on a journey most men can only dream about. We're going to Outremer!"

"But Outremer is Turkish land now."

Richard quickly scanned the stairs and asked, "Are we alone in this house?"

"Probably."

Peter Tallon

"Well just to be sure, let us walk outside where no-one can overhear us. What I have to say is for your ears alone."

They took the path that led to a water meadow, which flanked the winding River Blyth, and Richard recounted the strange events that had occurred since the Battle of Cravant. By the time they reached the small, wooden footbridge which crossed the river linking the two halves of his land, the story had been told and Richard concluded by saying,

"So you see Hugh, quite apart from your companionship, which I value highly as you well know, you will also be a powerful counterweight to the religious zeal of the Grand Master. He will have to listen to you. As a fully fledged priest your voice will have greater impact than mine, especially since I tried to throttle Titus Scrope right under the Grand Master's nose."

Richard stepped onto the footbridge and began to cross but stopped when he sensed that Hugh was not following. "What's the matter Hugh? Are you not excited by our venture to the Holy Land?"

The Franciscan looked pale and uncomfortable. He lowered his large, brown eyes and said quietly, "I cannot come." Richard was momentarily lost for words. Remembering how his friend had thrived on the Agincourt campaign, he thought Hugh would have been delighted at the prospect of a new adventure. The refusal came as a bolt out of the blue. Richard looked at the clear water eddying beneath his feet where a shoal of small silver, fish with bright red fins swam idly amongst the weeds which festooned the gravelly river bed. He spoke in a voice devoid of expression, "Why not?"

Hugh picked distractedly at a small splinter in his forefinger and mumbled, "I am not the man you once knew. Years of quiet stewardship in peaceful Suffolk have taken away my thirst for adventure."

"I can easily get someone else to look after Calveley Hall while you are away."

Hugh shook his head, "I would be a liability to you if I came. The thought of foreign travel, especially to a land occupied by ferocious Turks, fills me with dread."

Richard thought back to the Agincourt campaign when Hugh had accidentally got caught up in a cavalry charge against the French. Then he had shouted 'Saint George!' and wielded a mace with the best of them. It was difficult to believe a man could change so much.

"Are you telling me everything Hugh?"

The priest's pale face blushed. He nervously rubbed the back of his neck. "Of course."

"Then I will not order you to accompany me, but if you are hiding something tell me now as a friend. Do not wait until I find out or my attitude might change."

An uncharacteristic touch of aggression entered Hugh's voice. "I told you the reason. That's all there is to it."

Richard knew he would get nowhere by pressing Hugh further, but seeing his oldest friend undergoing such obvious turmoil worried him deeply. He tried to remove the tension between them. "Very well, I accept what you say. If you need help while I'm away, call on Millicent Fastolf at Caistor Manor. Sir John himself intends to winter there this year so you will not be alone if Cousin Geoffrey decides to cause trouble."

"That is good to know. How long will you be staying here Richard?" Richard now had no desire to remain at Calveley Hall any longer than necessary because he knew he would be unable to stop himself questioning Hugh again. It was better to part as friends even though all was not well.

"I shall leave as soon as we get back to the house and stay the night at Dunwich Priory. I have much to do if I am to reach Venice by the eighth of December."

Instead of expressing disappointment, Hugh sounded almost relieved. "I shall arrange for some food to be packed for your journey. We roasted a suckling pig only yesterday and the bread was fresh baked this morning."

Talk of bread served to remind Richard of the poor state of his land. The wheat harvest had not even started. As they slowly walked back to the house he said, "As you are going to stay here, there is a matter we need to discuss that disturbs me. I am referring to the condition of my land. Compared to the last time I was here it has deteriorated. You know how I hate to see neglect, yet there are blocked ditches, broken fences, weeds amongst the crops, not to mention the fact that this must be the only farm in Suffolk yet to start its harvest."

Hugh stared at his feet and answered almost in a whisper, "I'm sorry Richard, I have been unwell for much of this year, a malady of the humours, but I am better now and will attend to the harvest and all the necessary improvements immediately."

"I am sorry you have been ill, but your farm foreman should have kept up the maintenance and supervision when you could not. Where is Jacob? I shall speak to him before I go. He was always so thorough."

The awkwardness that had punctured Hugh's voice a little earlier returned, "Jacob suddenly seemed to become old. The job was too much for him. I had, er, to let him go."

"Then who is foreman now?"

"Luke Cotter."

"That insolent wretch! That explains it. Get rid of him, he's no good." Richard sensed Hugh wanted to object but the desire to see him go quickly was even greater.

"All right, I shall deal with him," agreed the Franciscan limply.

"Shall I dismiss him for you?"

"No, no. I took him on so it should be me who dismisses him."

"Very well and do not trouble to arrange food for me. I shall leave immediately. If I have done something to offend you Hugh then it was unintentional, but never have I felt unwelcome in your presence until now."

"It is not you Richard. You have shamed me and rightly so, for failing in my duties as your steward. Believe me, when you return all will be well; that I promise."

Richard smiled, "Then we part as friends. That's all that really matters."

* * *

III

Hugh watched Richard until he disappeared round a bend in the Blythburgh road. The late afternoon sun cast long shadows and a warm, red glow across the fields, but the Franciscan could take no pleasure in any of it. He felt utterly wretched. He turned, opened the great front door to the hall, and slowly walked up the stairs where his nemesis awaited him. He paused briefly outside the door to his private chamber, took a deep breath and entered.

"Can I come out now or must I stay hidden like a harlot from a vengeful wife!" Annie Mullen was wearing only a thin, linen shift through which Hugh could easily distinguish the outline of her delightful body as the sunlight flooded through the window behind her. Their afternoon lovemaking had been interrupted by Richard's unexpected arrival but Hugh still felt the hunger of frustrated desire despite the scolding he knew she would give him.

"Come now my dear," he said soothingly, "you know we must take no chances."

"But it's all so humiliating. It makes me wonder if it's all worthwhile." Annie knew exactly how to deal with the inexperienced Hugh. Four years older, and vastly wiser in the ways of the world, she had held the upper hand in their unequal relationship from the start. In the beginning she was sure she loved him, it was not just the excitement of sleeping with a priest, but now his vulnerability was no longer novel and the enforced secrecy had become irritating. At times like this she wanted to hurt him simply because he was such a soft target, but usually these feelings left her when she saw the pain she inflicted; she was basically a good hearted woman. This time however, she needed to strike harder for he had deserted her in the middle of their love-making to scurry to his master like a beaten cur. She straightened her long, golden hair and sneered,"

"I might as well return to my husband; at least he is master in his own house."

She stood up and picked up her gown which lay crumpled on the floor, but Hugh had been humiliated enough for one day and at last the fire that had lain dormant in his heart for so long roared into life. "No you don't," he snarled, and gripping her by the shoulders he flung her back onto the bed. Annie's shift rode up and the sight of her slender legs dissolved the last vestiges of his self control. He bent over her and tore off the shift, ripping it to shreds as he did so.

"Hugh, what are you doing! You wouldn't take me against my will would you!" But Annie's words were more forceful than her resistance for this was an aspect of Hugh she had not seen before. Perhaps her priest lover had backbone after all, maybe even a dark side which could be interesting. She would not do too much to discourage it.

He made love to her more forcefully than ever before, but she was still damp from the previous interrupted attempt so no pain was involved. Instead Annie enjoyed herself; she knew she could easily stop him if she really wanted to but instead she gave in wantonly, uninhibitedly and her cries of fulfilment drove him on to even greater passion. Blood rushed through her veins like torrents of fire; this was true lovemaking! She was vaguely aware of fierce growling noises in her ear as Hugh finally reached satisfaction moments after her, and as the passion began to subside she was convinced once more that she still loved him.

Mistaking her replete silence for anger, Hugh whispered, "I'm sorry about that, I don't know what came over me."

"Shut-up or you'll spoil it."

The confused priest said no more and within seconds fell asleep in her arms.

The meeting next morning with Luke Cotter proved to be every bit as difficult as Hugh expected. The interview took place in the small upstairs study where Hugh worked out the business accounts and where, many years before, Geoffrey Calveley and Titus Scrope used to plot their ruthless plans for the enrichment of Calveley Hall and each other. Cotter walked in without knocking and planted himself on the chair opposite Hugh's desk.

"You want to see me young Hugh?" The Franciscan hated Cotter's familiarity but at least he would not have to put up with that much longer.

"Yes Luke, I have bad news for you. When Captain Calveley came here yesterday, he was angered by the neglect of his land and by the fact that the harvest had not yet started, while every other estate is well advanced. Regrettably he ordered me to dispense with your services."

The smug look on the foreman's face suddenly disappeared. "Why did he not dispense with your services then? You are steward here not me; or did you blame everything on me?"

"Of course not Luke but you must admit that the farm yield has deteriorated since you took over from Jacob. Anyway, this is a direct order from the owner; I have no discretion in the matter."

Cotter leaned forward menacingly and said, "I think you have, my randy young priest. Your master will be away for months, years even. You can stay your hand for a while."

"How do you know that?"

"My sister told me." Hugh was angry with himself for careless pillow talk. At least that's all Annie does know, he thought, though I wish I'd sworn her to silence.

"And where is it our strutting peacock landlord be taking himself I wonder," continued Cotter, "plundering and murdering hard working folk like me in France I'll warrant."

"That is neither your business nor mine," said Hugh, finally abandoning his conciliatory tone. He placed a leather pouch in front of Cotter and added, "Here are ten silver shillings to help you on your way. Now pack your things and leave by tonight."

The foreman stood up and towered threateningly over Hugh. "So that be the way of it eh? Well it won't be that easy. Annie won't like it."

"I cannot help that. I only removed Jacob and took you on because you're her brother."

Cotter smiled an evil grin as he made the threat that Hugh feared most. "And what if I tell big Will Mullen about his wife's visits to your chamber? He's not known for his sweet temper. He'll come looking for you I shouldn't wonder."

"Then let him."

"And if I be correct, a priest that gets up to the sort of games you've been playing with my sister cannot be in a state of grace."

"So?"

"Well consider all those sacraments you've carried out during the past year. If you be in mortal sin they count for nothing. What of all those good folk who think they're married but aren't, and all their bastard children who aren't truly baptised. It gets worse. How think you will the relatives feel of all those that have died unshriven? Their loved ones might spend eternity in Hell thanks to your bogus confessions. They will be wanting retribution for sure if I open my mouth."

Hugh had already thought about this. "God would never send their loved ones to Hell because of my sin. All my sacraments have been received in good faith. Anyway, there have been mercifully few because I am not a parish priest. I only perform a sacrament when I cannot avoid it."

"Oh, so it makes no difference to you if I stay silent or not?"

"Of course it does. It will be the end of me if you speak out."

"Then change your mind," urged Cotter.

"No Luke, you must go and before you decide to destroy me speak to Annie. She will not want it."

"I'm not obliged to do my sister's bidding," he glanced at the money pouch on the desk and grinned, "though we might be able to come to an arrangement."

"How so?"

"If that there bag was to be filled with gold instead of silver, I may have a loss of memory."

Hugh was under no illusion. He well knew that if he paid up, Cotter would be back for more but the prospect of a reprieve, if only temporary, from humiliation and disgrace was worth ten gold sovereigns. He could easily arrange the accounts to cover for this amount of money and meanwhile Annie might persuade her brother to stay silent, or better still, he might drink himself to death after coming into such a large windfall. Even if Cotter did demand more, the estate could pay provided the sum was reasonable.

Hugh went to the strongbox in the corner of the study and said, "Very well, I agree."

Until that moment Hugh had done no personal wrong to Richard beyond keeping his problems to himself, but the payment to Cotter marked a turning point, the crossing of a threshold from which there was no going back. He had betrayed his master and closest friend.

CHAPTER FOUR

A chill northeasterly brought with it a penetrating drizzle as the blunt nosed cog *Morning Star,* hove to outside the lagoon of Venice to await a pilot. Richard wrapped his black pilgrim's cloak tightly around himself and looked at the fabulous city which stood amongst the still, lagoon waters on man-made dykes and islands. Venice, the Pearl of the Adriatic, was probably the richest city in the world and certainly the most powerful. Despite her limited manpower, she controlled a maritime empire which covered most of the islands in the Eastern Mediterranean and much of the seaboard of Dalmatia and Greece. Now she had taken over the leading role from the defunct Byzantine Empire in holding back the western advance of the Turks.

"I thought these Mediterranean places were always warm," grumbled Henry Hawkswood who stood at Richard's side, "but this cold drizzle would be just as much at home in Southampton." Richard had been forced to use all his powers of persuasion to get Fastolf to release his most experienced sergeant for this venture. Apart from Hugh, there was no-one Richard would rather have to accompany him and, if it came to a fight, Hawkswood's skills would prove invaluable.

"It's surprisingly cold," agreed Richard, "but whatever the elements throw at us I shall be glad to get off this leaking pile of planks. There were times I thought we'd never get here."

"Two days late is not bad going considering the storms we went through Captain. It's just as well the master refused your demands to be put ashore or we would have been later still." Henry's face was mask-like but his eyes were laughing. Richard, never a good sailor at the best of times, had suffered agonising sea sickness during the rough weather and, to make matters worse, Henry's stomach remained untroubled through it all. But the solid Wiltshireman was almost as relieved as Richard to see the end of the journey because the pounding of the waves had forced open some of the cog's timber seams; one more storm would have finished them.

A six oared rowing boat pushed off from the lagoon's Lido entrance and rowed across the choppy, grey water like a drunken water beetle. Seated in the stern was the pilot who wore a bright red cloak and a fine ostrich feathered hat which, Richard presumed, were his badge of office, but by the time the reeling boat reached the cog, the cloak was drenched and the feather hung limply across the pilot's face like a wet rat's tail. Now the most perilous part of his journey began because the deep swell tossed his boat's oars about like tinder sticks and threatened to smash them against the cog's hull. The pilot's position was not helped by his crew, all of whom deemed themselves to be captains shouting orders and hearing none, but despite their chaotic seamanship and alternating yells of anger and encouragement, he managed to slip the hoist thrown to him from *Morning Star* round his ample waist and allowed himself to be dragged unceremoniously aboard the cog like a sack of wet flour. Unaware of his lost dignity, he immediately began to issue orders to the English crew in execrable French but the mariners, most of whom had done this trip many times before, went about their duties with quiet efficiency which the pilot doubtless thought was the result of his natural air of command.

The reason for the haste was the tide which was nearing low water, and soon *Morning Star* was drifting towards the Lido channel on the beginning of the incoming flow. As soon as the cog entered the lagoon the waters calmed, the crew relaxed, and under the pilot's guidance they set a course towards the city. To Richard the sheer volume of water traffic seemed remarkable. Boats of all shapes and sizes scudded haphazardly back and forth across the broad lagoon. He could see fishing smacks, skiffs, rowing boats, heavy cargo vessels and crowded water coaches, but the ship that impressed him most had just left its berth near the customs house and was rapidly heading towards the cog indifferent to the opposition of the incoming tide.

Henry had seen it too. "What ship is that Captain?"

"If I'm not mistaken Henry, we are looking at a Venetian war galley, the bane of the Turks and the bulwark of Christendom against the infidel."

The sleek, low sided galley cut through the water like a shark, the bow wave almost obscuring its name, *Loredan*. Richard could clearly hear the chant of the bosun giving the rhythm to his oarsmen. What a contrast to the pilot's crew! The three banks of oars moved in perfect harmony, the blades entering the water with hardly a splash and the officers standing quietly at their posts watching the tubby English cog as a wolf might gaze at a well fed goat. As the two ships closed, passing less than a hundred feet apart, Richard saw the galley's bearded captain standing in front of the stern cabin. His royal blue cloak billowed behind him in the breeze created by the sheer speed of his vessel, and he was smiling broadly as he gave *Morning Star's* crew a cheery wave.

"He cuts a dashing figure," said Henry admiringly as *Loredan's* stern passed the cog's bow. "I wonder what's amusing him?" Suddenly *Morning Star* lurched to larboard tumbling the pilot across the deck, much to the amusement of the wily English mariners. Then the cog pitched just as violently back to starboard again but the rocking motion soon diminished as the wake from the galley faded away. The pilot ran to the cog's stern and let fly a torrent of Italian abuse, but this served only to add to *Loredan's* sport; ripples of laughter echoed across the water as the galley sped towards the open sea.

Richard loosened his grip on the beam rail and smiled, "That galley captain has got a sense of humour. I wonder who he is? Did you notice there were cannon on the bow and stern? I would not want to oppose her; she looks every inch the hunter."

"Aye," agreed Henry, "But those low beams would not suit our Atlantic rollers. She would not have survived the journey we've just been through."

Morning Star glided gently towards the straight between the island of San Giorgio and the Molo, the dock area at the entrance to the Grand

The Templar Legacy

Canal where most of the sea going ships berthed. The two English pilgrims could only stand and stare in admiration at the vista before them. Dominating the Molo was the Doge's Palace whose colonnaded wall ran parallel with the water front. The upper storeys contained dozens of decorative, arched windows which not only lit up the interior but also reduced the weight of the masonry bearing down upon the unstable sand beneath the foundations of the city. Richard had seen pictures of Venice before but they did not do justice to its splendour. Behind the palace, the domes of a large church or cathedral were visible, and Richard guessed this must be their meeting place, the Basilica of San Marco. To the left of the palace, two isolated columns heralded the entrance to the Piazza of San Marco, which was crowded with citizens going about their business. One of the columns was topped by a stone lion, the symbol of Venice, the other by a statue of Theodore patron saint of Venice until ousted by San Marco.

Extending from the Molo at regular intervals were wooden piers, along each of which small boats were moored. There were also berths directly alongside the water front for larger vessels and it was towards one of these that the pilot was guiding *Morning Star*, though the space available seemed hardly wide enough to accommodate the cog, When they were close to their berth, a rowing boat approached and one of its crew threw a line which was tied to the cog's prow. Then the rowers heaved on their oars and towed the English ship the final few yards to its berth. A second line was thrown from the dockside, which was attached to the stern, and *Morning Star* was carefully hauled in beam on by the dock workers, until her timbers almost touched the quay. Richard and Henry could stand on dry land at last.

It was noon on the tenth day of December in the year of Our Lord 1423.

The Basilica of San Marco made even the Doge's Palace look ordinary. Built by the Byzantines, who ruled Venice hundreds of years ago, the domed church epitomised the lavish expenditure on ecclesiastical art and structures favoured by the emperors of Constantinople at the zenith of their power. The basilica was a direct link to the culture and traditions of the late Roman Empire, the last vestiges of which still tried to oppose the irresistible advance of Islam in the east. The ornate, rounded arches and multi-coloured decoration were a striking contrast to the sombre, angular cathedrals of western Christendom. A beautiful fresco of the Christ blessing the fortunate citizens of Venice surmounted the main entrance, but just outside, priests were gathered to persuade their flock to part with money by selling them indulgences which would supposedly remove the fire of purgatory from them when their souls finally parted company from their bodies. At least some things don't change, thought Richard ruefully; even the Dunwich friars had started to use similar ploys since Father Simon had taken over from old Anselm.

Richard recalled his last visit to Dunwich Priory after he had left Hugh on that unsatisfactory day at the end of August. Anslem had also been worried about Hugh, who no longer visited him to be confessed. He had seen the change in the young Franciscan more than a year ago but Anselm was now too old to leave the priory to investigate for himself. But as Richard paused to admire San Marco's basilica he realised that Calveley Hall, though a thousand miles away, would never be far from his mind on this journey. It unsettled him; a traveller likes to think of his home base as secure, yet he had been forced to leave knowing that something was badly awry.

"Captain Calveley!" Richard, ashore at last, span round at the unexpected use of his name. Another black clad pilgrim approached him. "Captain Calveley, you are late. We have been waiting for you."

Richard could not recognise the face screened behind the black hood but the guttural, accented French identified the newcomer as Mamoun al Rashid, the Templar from the east. "We encountered storms and adverse winds," answered the Englishman. "We almost failed to get here at all."

"Then praise be to God even though the Grand Master is not pleased. Truthfully, you have not delayed us for there has been an unexpected problem. Last year we made arrangements with Doge Tommaso Mocenigo for the hire of two war galleys to take us to Outremer and back. Mocenigo accepted five per cent of our treasury which would have been paid on our return to Venice. Unfortunately Mocenigo died in April but his successor,

Doge Francesco Foscari, refused to honour the agreement. The Grand Master is due to reopen discussions with Foscari tomorrow. He told me that he wishes you to accompany him so that he has the benefit of secular advice."

"I should be pleased to," answered Richard, flattered that his presence should be considered of value.

"Until then," continued Mamoun, "we shall stay quietly in our lodgings in the German Quarter of the city. You will like them because they overlook the Grand Canal."

Richard and Henry followed the small, dark figure of Mamoun as he threaded his way through the crowded, narrow streets overtopped by tall buildings many storeys high. They crossed high arched bridges spanning the dense network of minor canals which criss-crossed the city, where they first saw the strange, high prowed gondolas, the main mode of transport in Venice. When they reached a road fronting onto the Grand Canal, a sudden violent belch from a nearby tavern followed by a series of stupendous farts and roars of laughter announced beyond any doubt that they had entered the German Quarter. Mamoun crossed the road and opened the door to a buff coloured, three storeyed house which, like almost all the other buildings in Venice, boasted more windows than walls. Inside the pilgrims entered a large room, which extended the full length of the building, where they were welcomed by their new comrades who openly wore the eight pointed red cross on white in the privacy of their own lodgings.

At the far end of the room, Richard saw a loathed figure skulking near the stairs to the next floor. "Keep that English Templar out of my sight," he whispered to Mamoun, "if you wish to prevent a repetition of the scene you witnessed in the Grand Master's tent."

"That will not be easy when we embark Captain Calveley," replied the eastern Templar, "but I will do what I can. In the meantime I ask you in return to exercise self control." The mild rebuke was not lost on Richard.

"What scene was that Captain?" asked Henry innocently.

"Never you mind Sergeant Hawkswood, let's find a bunk and get some rest."

* * *

II

The next day dawned sunny and pleasantly warm, for the chill northeasterly wind had veered to the southeast clearing the gloomy cloudbanks of the previous day. As well as Richard, the Grand Master chose Mamoun to accompany him for the audience with the doge and, as they approached the Porta dell Carta, the formal entrance to the palace, the Grand Master said,

"This will be a delicate negotiation. Observe the doge carefully, watch his face for reactions but say nothing unless I tell you to." The black cloaked pilgrims were stopped at the entrance by two tall guards clad in the characteristic platelet armour and open faced helmets of Venice, but upon presentation of a letter of appointment, they stood aside and allowed the pilgrims to enter. Inside a clerk met them and escorted them through the huge chamber where the Maggiore Consiglio, the Venetian equivalent of parliament, held its meetings. They followed the clerk up two flights of broad stairs and were left at the door to the vote counting chamber which was sometimes also used as an audience chamber. After an annoying wait of almost an hour, the door opened and the pilgrims were beckoned inside.

Richard's first and most abiding impression was light, light which flooded in through four large windows overlooking the Molo. He could see a multitude of mastheads bobbing at their berths and, at the other side of the lagoon, the island of San Giorgio. At the far end of the chamber, sitting on a plain wooden chair, was Francesco Foscari wearing the red gown and cap that marked his rank as the Doge of Venice. Standing either side of him like terrible, implacable angels were two Dominican friars clad in their all white robes. They stood motionless as statues, arms folded across their waists inside voluminous sleeves, with hoods pulled up over their heads almost hiding their faces. The man who had beckoned the pilgrims to enter also wore white Dominican robes but his head was uncovered revealing a broad, clean shaven face and close cropped, grey hair. The eyes were also grey, but cold as ice. He took his place standing behind Foscari and said in French,

"I am Father Pietro Cavalli. I shall be the doge's interpreter."

The Grand Master pointed to the other two Dominicans. "Our business is delicate and confidential in nature. We would prefer no witnesses."

After a few brief words with Foscari, Cavalli replied, "The doge agrees that this meeting may be granted the sanctity of the confessional. We are all therefore bound to silence at the risk of our immortal souls."

"Very well," said the Grand Master, rather too easily satisfied for Richard's liking.

While the old Templar described the background to the agreement with the previous doge, Richard observed Foscari. He was young for his rank, probably no older than thirty five, the same age as Richard and, but for a pronounced hooked nose, would have been a fine looking man. A strong, square jaw and alert brown eyes suggested a determined individual who would probably be a match for the Grand Master. Most interesting of all, from the slight changes of expression on Foscari's face and the occasional whitening of the knuckles as he tightened and loosened his grip on the arm of his chair, Richard became convinced that the doge understood all the words the Grand Master said before Cavalli translated them into Italian. Like a skilled market trader, he was giving himself time to gauge the quality of his opponent without revealing his own hand too soon.

When the Templar had finished, Foscari said through his interpreter, "I do not doubt your sincerity Grand Master, though I confess to being surprised at the continued existence of your Order. But you must understand that Venice's current interests lie on the mainland of Italy. The Turks are quiet at present and we do not wish to give them cause to resume war with us. Why do you not take a pragmatic approach and join your forces with the Knights Hospitaller? I am sure they would welcome you with open arms and together you can fight the infidel which, after all, was the reason your Order was brought into being in the first place."

That was rather like telling the Scots to submit to the English or the rabbit to embrace the stoat. Richard awaited the response with interest and the Grand Master did not disappoint. His voice quivered with anger. "What you suggest can never be! Despite the lies and false witness of a century ago, the Order of the Knights Templar is noble and without blemish. We do not need, nor have we ever needed, the support of the Hospitallers whose record of fighting the infidel, distinguished though it may be, is as nothing to ours. We stand or fall alone. Your predecessor gave us a commitment. I must insist you honour it."

Foscari's answer dashed the Templar's hopes. "I must not permit Venice to risk war with the Turks simply to satisfy the dreams of a long suppressed Order. I cannot help you." The proud Grand Master seemed to crumple. His hands shook and the blood drained from his face as his life's work collapsed before him.

Richard could stand it no longer, "Enough of this duplicity!" he said looking directly at Foscari. "Do you really believe the Turks will leave your empire alone while you concentrate on your petty squabbles in Italy?" Cavalli began to speak the words to the doge in Italian but Richard interrupted, "Do not trouble to translate Father Cavalli, the doge speaks French as well as you and me. All civilised men do."

Discomforted by the removal of his interpreter from the discussion, Foscari stalled for thinking time by asking Richard in French, "Where are you from?"

"England."

"What qualifies an Englishman to have opinions about Venetian strategy?"

"All Christendom knows Doge Mocenigo fought the Turks with success, but if you turn your back on them they will gobble up your empire in no time at all. The bully only understands strength, not reason."

"That is not reason enough to support your cause," said the doge truculently.

Richard raised an eyebrow. "Is it not? Well I will give you another one; it concerns honour. In England and France a pledge made by a king is binding on his successor. This is because kingship is a continuous office filled by individuals who pass it on from generation to generation. Consequently a promise made by a sovereign in his office as king must be acknowledged and honoured by his son. The office is greater than the individual. I know that every Doge of Venice is elected but even the petty, warring princes in Germany understand the concept and abide by it. Are your really telling us that the great Doge of Venice is a lesser man than the Elector of Saxony?"

Foscari and Father Cavalli lapsed into animated conversation in their own language. The priest seemed to be urging the reluctant doge into a course of action which displeased him. Meanwhile the Grand Master whispered, "I ordered you to be silent Captain Calveley."

"Do not worry Grand Master, this doge is no more than a glorified street trader. I know his kind. Leave him to me." The desperate Templar, realising that Richard was his only hope, nodded his approval.

After two minutes of magpie-like chatter with Father Cavalli, Foscari addressed Richard again, "If there is some way of ensuring your mission does not goad the Turks into attacking us, we may find a way to help."

Richard sensed he had broken through the doge's defences; it only remained to thrash out the terms. "The surest way of encouraging the Turk to attack you is to ignore him, but if that is your policy, so be it. We pilgrims will therefore travel under our own ensign. How would it be if we purchase a galley from you and hire a crew which will sail under the red cross of the Templars? If anything goes wrong no-one can blame Venice for our actions; we would be looked upon as simple pirates."

Foscari looked at Father Cavalli, who acknowledged the proposition with a non-committal shrug.

"Fetch me the naval ledger," ordered the doge. At a signal from Cavalli, one of the two motionless Dominican sentinels left the room and returned a short while later carrying a leather covered book which he handed to Foscari. The doge thumbed through a few of the pages and then, after a little thought, seemed to come to a conclusion. "I could sell you *Loredan* for five thousand ducats on condition you sell her back to me after your journey for three thousand."

"What about a crew?" asked Richard.

Foscari smiled. Now the bartering had begun in earnest, he was enjoying himself. "Paolo Dandolo is one of my best captains. He commands a veteran crew."

"How much?"

"Dandolo and his men will cost you three hundred ducats each month, or any part of a month that may be outstanding on your return."

"We may wish to select our own crew."

"All right then, two hundred and fifty ducats."

"Done," agreed Richard.

But the doge had not yet finished. "I shall still require the five per cent of your treasury agreed by Mocenigo. What is the estimated value?"

Richard had no intention of being drawn on this point but the Grand Master, thinking he was being helpful, said, "At least ten million ducats."

Foscari's eyes widened and he murmured, "So much!"

"It's only a rough estimate," added Richard trying to keep the irritation out of his voice. "We could all be disappointed." The Grand Master could just as easily have said one million ducats and reduced the commission in proportion; Foscari would have been none the wiser.

A strange look came into the young doge's eyes, the same look Richard had seen many times in Beccles market when a trader was about to engage in sharp practice. "One more thing," said Foscari, trying to make what he was about to say appear as an afterthought. "I have an envoy I wish to send to our great fortress at Nauplion in Greece. He might as well embark with you for it is on your route to Outremer."

Richard had no choice but to agree. "Very well we will take him. When can we expect *Loredan* and her crew to be ready for the voyage?"

Foscari rubbed his chin, "She will return from patrol in four or five days, then allowing for reprovisioning and so on, I estimate she will be ready to sail in one week. That will give you time to sign our agreement and arrange for the transfer of the purchase money including, say, three months crew hire in advance."

"Five thousand seven hundred and fifty ducats in all," said Richard.

The doge shut the naval ledger and handed it to Cavalli. "That concludes our business for today. Father Cavalli will be my agent in this transaction. Pay the money to him when you have it." As the pilgrims turned to leave he added, "And good luck with your enterprise, I suspect you will need it."

Once back in the piazza, Mamoun, a broad smile across his face, said, "You did well Richard. Our venture was foundering until you intervened. Is that not so Grand Master?"

The response was begrudging. "It is but where can we obtain the purchase money? We have less than a thousand ducats with us."

Richard asked, "Is there a Jewish Quarter in Venice?"

The Grand Master looked at him in horror. "I can have no dealings with Jews!"

"Why ever not? In my experience the Jews are generally the fairest businessmen you can deal with."

"But it was the Jews who martyred Our Lord Jesus Christ. He disapproved of money lending."

Richard's patience began to wear thin again. "Probably because he didn't need to borrow any. I expect he lived off charity instead."

The Grand Master's voice regained the edge of steel it had lost since his discomfiture in the Doge's Palace. "We are indebted to you for your help Captain Calveley, but that does not entitle you to be blasphemous."

Mamoun intervened, "With your permission Grand Master, I will accompany Captain Calveley to the Jewish Quarter. It seems to me that we sorely need to recover the business acumen of our predecessors as well as their wealth. Perhaps now is a good time to start learning."

As the three pilgrims walked slowly across the piazza, two pairs of avaricious eyes were watching them from one of the palace windows.

"Poor fools," said Foscari, "they are like lambs amongst wolves."

Father Cavalli smiled, "It was indeed an excellent bargain you negotiated Serenissimo."

"Hah! That was nothing Cavalli. I have something much more rewarding in mind. Bring Captain Spatafora to me."

* * *

III

In the afternoon Richard and Mamoun went to the Jewish Quarter which was located in the north of the city, the business heart of Venice. In truth there was nothing to distinguish the Jewish Quarter from any other foreign area of the city except for the occasional flourish of Hebrew script, a long dead language to the Jews themselves, above some of the shops, and the high standard of maintenance and decoration of the house fronts.

"You do not have the same difficulty meeting Jews as the Grand Master," said Richard as they strolled slowly through the bustling streets.

"Indeed no," replied Mamoun. "They are God's children as we are. My family dwelt in Outremer where Jew, Muslim and Christian lived contentedly side by side. Sometimes I think the Grand Master forgets that Jesus Christ himself was a Jew."

"Not an Englishman?"

"I'm afraid not Richard. England did not even exist then."

Richard laughed, "That would come as a shock to some of my compatriots, but pray tell me where exactly your forebears came from."

"Three generations ago my family owned land on the seaward slopes of Mount Carmel, but after the Turks destroyed Outremer we were forced to abandon our home and cross the sea to Cyprus, where we have lived ever since."

"Is that why you became a Templar?"

"Not really. There has always been at least one Templar in each generation of my family. This tradition was maintained even after the suppression of the Templars by King Phillipe the Fair of France. The suppression was never strictly enforced in Cyprus, which became the spiritual home of the Order once Outremer was lost, and even now there are more Cypriots in our company of pilgrims than any other nation except the French."

Richard's attention was drawn by a notice above a little shop which backed onto one of the smaller canals. The notice was unusual, for as well as being written in Italian, German and French, the owner had thought to add, as an obvious afterthought, an English version too. It read: 'Chaim ben Issachar, banker and provider of venture capital.'

Such originality deserved reward so Richard said, "Let's try our luck here. Perhaps ben Issachar might be bold enough to invest in a band of marauding pirates for a few months." They stepped inside the open door and entered a small chamber, at the back of which was a wooden counter stretching across the full width of the building. This, Richard guessed, was to give ben Issachar some protection against disappointed clients who regarded Jews as beyond Christian justice. The walls were painted in the yellow ochre colour so popular in Venice, and were adorned with paintings of numerous Old Testament epics. There were no chairs; the clients were expected to stand.

Mamoun picked up a small, brass bell near the entrance and rang it as hard as he could. Moments later, a door behind the counter opened and a young woman entered the room. She said a few words in Italian then, observing the blank looks on her customers' faces, she tried French. "Can I help you gentlemen?"

For a few moments neither man replied but just as she was about to try German, Richard stammered, "Er, are you ben Issachar?" He had never seen such an attractive woman. Her face was perfect, warm full lips, straight nose, unmarked skin and large eyes of the deepest brown that would melt any man. Her waist length hair was ebony black, her hands and fingers elegant and well manicured, but all this was as nothing when, seeing the wonderment in Richard's green eyes, she smiled and asked,

"Is something the matter?" That smile turned perfection into beauty and Richard knew he must keep himself on a tight rein in this woman's presence, but he could not help returning the smile as he answered,

"There is nothing the matter. It is just that I expected ben Issacher to be a man."

"He is. My father and I run this business as a partnership. I look after the day to day banking; he takes care of the venture capital."

Trying not to sound too disappointed, Richard said, "Then it is your father we wish to see."

The brown eyes glanced at Mamoun, then back at Richard. "First I need to know more about you. You are dressed as pilgrims but you do not have the countenance of holy men."

Despite his best efforts Richard found himself smiling again, "You are indeed perceptive. My companion is truly a pilgrim, I am not but we are both warriors. Our mission is secret and hazardous but, if successful, the rewards will justify many times the investment we ask you to make."

"Really?" said a male voice from the other side of the door. A short, portly man of about fifty entered. Long, disorganised ringlets of hair tumbled below a black cap framing his round, jovial face in grey curls and, although the orange and yellow striped gown might have been considered in poor taste in England, Richard noticed it was tailored in fine quality linen. There was nothing cheap about ben Issachar. He looked sidelong at his daughter,

"Cover your hair my dear." She went into the room behind the counter and quickly returned with her hair tucked neatly into a white bonnet.

Addressing Richard, ben Issachar said, "I am Chaim ben Issachar. Who are you and where are you from?"

"Captain Richard Calveley and I come from Suffolk in England."

"Ah, I have family in Ipswich. They live beside the northwest quay."

Richard frowned, "There is no northwest quay in Ipswich."

Ben Issachar smiled broadly, "Quite right my dear, just testing. You can't be too careful in my business. In fact a second cousin of mine runs a chandlers shop on the southwest quay."

"I believe I know it," said Richard. "Solomon's Ship Accessories."

"Yes! Yes!" beamed ben Issachar. "The world is getting smaller every day. I was there only two years ago to attend Solomon's son's wedding." Turning to his daughter he said, "Ruth, I think we can invite these two pilgrims into our humble dwelling while we discuss their proposal."

"Very well Father, provided they leave the weapons they are carrying under their cloaks in my care."

Richard and Mamoun handed over their daggers as requested and passed through a section of the counter which could be moved and locked from the inside. They followed the two Jews through an antechamber and entered a small, open courtyard which was sheltered on all four sides by ben Issachar's property. Coming from Cyprus, Mamoun was already familiar with courtyard style construction, but to Richard it was utterly charming. In the centre was a circular, brick lined pool containing fish of different shapes and colours swimming amongst water plants. Four small, square, raised herb beds were placed symmetrically around the pool providing a delightful fragrance and, on the south facing wall a huge, grape vine spread its branches in well trained abundance.

Ben Issachar pointed to some chairs near the vine and said, "Ruth and I spend many happy hours here cut off from the bustle of life outside. It's our sanctuary and good for the soul."

As he sat down Richard asked, "What is that delightful smell?"

Ben Issachar smiled, tapped the side of his nose, and pointed to a small, white flowering shrub. "That, my dear, is jasmine and here I can get it to flower twice each year. It can be made into an oil. The smell supposedly reinvigorates a jaded man if you understand my meaning. Rich Turkish men are said to use it to help them keep their harems well serviced."

"We have no such thing in England, but then we do not have harems either. One woman should be enough for a man."

"I agree Captain Calveley but alas my dear wife was called by Jehovah eight years ago. There is just Ruth and me now." Ben Issachar's eyes began to water as he added, "My Ann was too good for this world. I hope to join her soon."

"Father!" reprimanded Ruth, "You know mother would have disapproved of that sort of talk."

Richard said sympathetically, "My wife was also called Ann."

"Was?" enquired ben Issachar.

"She died nine years ago."

"I am sorry to hear it." Richard knew he should have said he had remarried but felt a strange reluctance to do so. He moved the conversation on to business and, after requesting and receiving an assurance of secrecy, Mamoun told the story of the Templar treasure and the venture that was being prepared to recover it.

Ben Issachar remained silent and expressionless, allowing the unlikely tale to be completed without interruption, but when it was finished he said reflectively, "As I recall, the Templars were no friends of the Jews."

"But that was more than a hundred years ago," acknowledged Mamoun. "Those were days of ignorance and violence in Outremer."

Ben Issachar raised a sceptical eyebrow, "Even so, we are not natural allies. You are both Templars?"

"No," answered Richard. "I am a captain in England's army in France."

"Then what is your part in this?"

"That, I regret, I may not tell you except that my presence here is at the request of the highest authority in England."

"And what precisely do you want from me?"

Richard said, "The new doge, Foscari, has refused to honour the pledge Mocenigo gave the Templars to recover their treasure. He is demanding money before we leave."

Ruth spoke up for the first time since the business discussion began. "It sounds to me that Foscari is showing laudable sense for a change."

"Quite so," agreed her father, "but let us hear what these gentlemen are offering."

It was obvious that both father and daughter were far from convinced; theirs was a partnership of equals. Looking from one to the other, Richard spoke in the deadpan voice he used in his farming days when negotiating in the Beccles market. "We accept that our venture must be deemed as high risk, therefore the reward should reflect that. We offer a tenfold return on your investment."

But ben Issachar was more than Richard's match when it came to negotiating. "That sounds like an offer from desperate men. How much are you asking for?"

"Five thousand ducats."

"Oive! That's more than my whole business is worth. How much of your own wealth are you putting into this venture?"

"One thousand ducats and our lives if necessary."

"And what collateral would we have?" asked Ruth as her father tried to recover from the shock of the request.

"The money would be used to buy the war galley *Loredan* for five thousand ducats" replied Richard, "and to finance the cost of the crew which is likely to be another thousand."

Ruth looked at her father. "So at worst, if the Templar wealth is not recovered we can resell the ship and be only a thousand ducats out of pocket."

"Only a thousand!" exclaimed ben Issachar. "Only a thousand she says! Don't tell me only a thousand."

"Father, that is the true investment against a potential return of fifty thousand. It deserves consideration." Richard noticed Mamoun was about to speak but signalled him with his eyes to remain silent. Now was not the time to mention the buyback arrangement with the doge which would mean the loss of another two thousand ducats.

"Would you like time to consider our proposal in private?" suggested Richard. "We could leave and return in an hour."

Ruth smiled her irresistible smile again. "That should be time enough for father to become accustomed to the idea." She looked Richard directly in the eyes as she spoke. There was none of that simpering, false bashfulness that afflicted so many women in Rouen. What an asset she will be, thought Richard, to some fortunate son of Israel when the time comes to wed. Beauty, humour, intelligence; she had everything a man could ever want.

Suddenly the smile turned into a laugh. "You are staring again Captain Calveley."

When Richard and Mamoun returned, a table had been prepared in the courtyard upon which three silver goblets, a plate of exotic sweetmeats and a jug of wine had been set, but to Richard's disappointment, Ruth was not there.

"I apologise for my daughter," said ben Issachar. "She has always been confident, forward even, but she means nothing by it."

Richard did not know quite what to say but Mamoun answered graciously, "Your daughter does you credit Chaim ben Issachar, and I suspect she is well able to look after herself. There is no need to apologise."

But when he replied, ben Issachar looked at Richard, not Mamoun. "I have sent her to our bankers to prepare the papers we will need. Perhaps she could have stayed here." It was more a question than a statement.

Richard was expected to respond. He said, "Neither you nor your daughter have cause for concern because of me. If I have been too open in my regard for her, it is only as an admirer of fine things, no more than that." But somewhere in the back of his mind a voice whispered, 'then why do you not say you are married?'

Ben Issachar, now reassured, poured out the wine. "Well my dears, it seems we have a deal, so pray tell me when do we depart?"

"We?" said Richard and Mamoun together.

"Of course. Ruth and I will be coming too. We must keep an eye on our investment."

"But a war galley is no place for you," gasped Richard, "and especially not for your daughter. There is no privacy, we may come across pirates; do you wish me to spell out the details?"

"Do not worry. I shall pay out of my own pocket for suitable quarters for Ruth to be constructed on my ship," ben Issachar emphasised the word 'my', "and is not *Loredan* one of the fastest galleys in the Venetian navy? Ruth has decided she wishes to come on this venture, and as my business partner she has every right. Do you think I would permit this if I thought she would be in danger? I have travelled to Cyprus on two occasions with no trouble at all; Outremer is only a little further away. The only condition I have insisted she obeys is that she remains aboard *Loredan* with me when we reach Outremer. That will be the dangerous part of the mission."

"But what about your business here?" asked Richard.

"I have associates who will look after it while we're away."

Richard looked to Mamoun for support but, to his surprise, the Cypriot Templar shared ben Issachar's view. "The Dalmatian pirates have nothing to threaten *Loredan* and Mocenigo destroyed the Turkish navy. There are many cases of bold Venetian women taking part in daring voyages. Ruth will be safe with us."

Perhaps, thought Richard but will she be safe from me?

CHAPTER FIVE

While Richard was making arrangements in Venice for the voyage to Outremer, events in Suffolk were taking a sinister twist. It was the first Sunday in Advent, a time of the year when people began to turn their minds towards Christmas. Father Hugh sat at the back of Saint Peter's, Holton waiting for the nine o'clock mass to begin. He was in good spirits. The depression that had afflicted him since Richard's unexpected visit had lifted, for things had improved considerably. The harvest was safely gathered in despite the late start, Luke Cotter had not reappeared and, best of all, Annie had taken Luke's dismissal surprisingly well. 'It's his own fault,' she had said when Hugh told her what he had done. 'You gave him every chance. If he's too stupid to see that, it's not your concern.' In fact after the event, she seemed to become warmer towards Hugh as if his show of strength impressed her. Perhaps that was why Luke had not come back asking for more money.

The bumper harvest had enabled Hugh to adjust the accounts quite easily to cover Luke's pay-off and now the immediate future seemed much brighter; he tried not to think too far ahead. He settled back into the carved, wooden seat as the parish priest, clad in fine vestments, walked to the altar to begin mass, and looked down at his own non-clerical garb. Deep in his heart he knew that his affair with Annie would have to end some time, but hopefully not for a good while yet. But living in a state of perpetual mortal sin was a concern for anyone, especially a priest. He recalled the words Father Anselm used when, as Prior of Dunwich, he concluded late night prayers by saying, 'Do not live in a state in which you dare not die'. It was a chilling thought. When the time came for the parting of the ways with Annie, Hugh knew that at least he would find some solace by being shriven of his sins and celebrating the sacraments again in a state of grace once more.

It was late morning when he returned to Calveley Hall. Heavy, grey clouds and a biting easterly wind threatened early snow, but there would be a warm fire waiting for him at the hall. He smiled at the thought as a flurry of small snowflakes brushed across his face. When he arrived he was greeted by his new foreman, Tom Riches, a typical Norfolk man who heard much and said little. He had fought alongside Richard and Hugh in Fastolf's company during the Agincourt campaign, but had to be invalided home with a head wound which had left a vertical scar down the left side of his cheerful face.

"Mistress Ann is here," said Tom as he took Hugh's horse. "She awaits you upstairs." He meant Hugh's chamber but did his best to be discreet.

"That's odd Tom, she never comes here on a Sunday."

"She seemed in some distress."

"Then I had better go to her at once."

Leaving his cloak thrown over a chair in the main hall, Hugh ascended the stairs three at a time not knowing whether to be pleased or worried. Tom, sad eyed, watched him go, knowing it would all end in tears. He, like the rest of Fastolf's Agincourt warriors, had developed a fatherly affection for their enthusiastic, young cleric but, being a man of Norfolk, he felt he should only offer advice if asked.

As soon as Hugh saw Annie he knew what had happened. Her pretty face was bruised and her upper lip was swollen.

"That bastard's hit you again!" he said angrily.

She quickly settled herself into his arms and whispered, "It's all right now. I feel safe here with you." At times like this Hugh always felt useless. Will Mullen was a violent man and whenever Annie arrived with cuts and bruises Hugh feared she was going to say her husband had found out about them. He tried to sound reassuring.

"What was it this time?"

"The drink again. He had too much last night and woke up this morning in a vile mood."

"How did you explain leaving him on a Sunday?"

"I said I was going to my sister's house in Saxmundham. He won't expect me back until tomorrow."

Hugh looked at the fire Tom had thoughtfully prepared in his chamber and sighed, "I think I will have to go to Halesworth this very day and have it out with Will."

"You'll do no such thing." Thank God for that! he thought until she added, "At least not yet awhile." That last remark left Hugh wondering. 'Not yet', what did she mean by that? But soon he became distracted by more immediate considerations as Annie's expert fingers began to unbutton his tunic.

It was past noon when their lovemaking ended. They sat together naked in front of the fire wrapped in a large, French bearskin, a trophy from the wars. Hugh looked dreamily into the dancing flames enjoying the closeness of his lover's body and avoiding deeper thoughts of the world outside.

Suddenly Annie turned, kissed him on the cheek and whispered in his ear "You're going to be a father, Father."

It took a moment for the remark to register, but when it did Hugh's stomach turned leaden. His contentment was shattered; the equanimity of the last few weeks just a naïve memory. He was horrified but he dare not reveal his shock to his lover. He wondered how he should react; pretend to be happy? Show paternal concern? God, he should have guessed this might happen! In the end he responded with the age old question men have used in these circumstances since time began. "Are you sure?"

"Certain," answered Annie, "and before you ask, yes it is yours."

"Are you pleased?"

"That depends on you." I thought it might, said Hugh to himself. "And what about you?" she asked. "Are you pleased?"

"Of course, wouldn't any man be?"

"I can think of one who might not be."

"Will?"

"He thinks I'm sterile. In ten years of marriage there has never been a hint of a child but now," she patted her smooth tummy, "this."

"So he's the sterile one."

"Yes, but he's so arrogant it wouldn't have occurred to him. He'll probably think the child is his. We'd better hope so."

"So you still make love then?" asked Hugh with a mixture of jealousy and relief.

"Not often but enough to cover your tracks if that is what you want." She was testing him; he knew he must be careful.

"That is not what I want. I am proud of you and our child but we must consider what is best."

Annie moved away from him slightly and said, "What do you mean by that?"

"First, how long have we got before it shows?"

"Well, I'm two months gone so I expect we have another two before Will starts asking questions." Two months! Is that all, thought Hugh. Two months to find a solution to the insoluble, but already he knew the choice was stark; either abandon the priesthood and admit the truth publicly, or abandon Annie who might in any event tell all out of spite. Facing the wrath of Will Mullen would be bad enough but, as Cotter had foreseen, what about the impact of all those valueless baptisms, marriages and confessions? It did not bear thinking about.

Annie saw the indecision written across Hugh's open face and had a good idea of what was going on in his mind. It was what she had expected but she was still disappointed. An outpouring of joy would have been too much to hope for, but even if Hugh was prepared to abandon the priesthood for her, she would have preferred the decision to be sourced from love rather than duty. This was a moment of crisis for both of them. She knew she was better equipped to face it than her unworldly lover; he needed her to help him to make up his mind. "Listen to me Hugh. You love me and you have just said you are proud of me. I feel the same about you and now I am carrying your child in my womb. It is what men and women are made for. The Church will not allow us to live openly together so now is the time to change your life and leave the priesthood. It's been done before."

"How can I support you?"

"You are a good steward and from what I hear, Richard Calveley would probably keep you employed here. If not, we do not have to stay in Suffolk. With so many knights away in France there must be plenty of work available for good stewards. I have some money saved to keep us going until you find something and I don't mind where we go as long as I am with you."

"But we could never be married. We would be living in sin and condemning ourselves to eternal damnation."

Annie had heard enough. She had tried to persuade him but she would not plead. Nor would she stay a moment longer with the man who was abandoning her. She got up and went over to the bed where her clothes lay scattered. "You and I cannot worship the same God. The love I bear for you Hugh could never merit eternal damnation, far from it. Certainly your precious Church would not approve, but who cares. Most of the Church's laws are made by emasculated men like-" she stopped short of adding 'you'.

Hugh asked, "What are you doing?"

"Going home to my husband."

"I thought you might stay awhile."

"I no longer want to."

"But we haven't finished discussing the future."

"There is no need for your so-called discussion. I already know you will take the easiest option which is to do nothing. Well I cannot afford to do that. I have a child to consider as well as myself. Have no fear, your secret will remain safe with me. Your bastard will grow up in another man's house never knowing its true father." Hugh put his head in his hands hating himself. He could find no words of mitigation; there were none.

Annie quickly got dressed but as she opened the door to leave, she looked back at her humiliated lover sitting alone by the fire and, despite her bitterness, felt pity for him. She did really love him. This would probably be the last time they were alone together; the parting ought not to be harsh.

"Hugh," she whispered. The Franciscan looked up with damp eyes. "I will try to make this easy for you. On Friday at noon I will wait for you at our usual meeting place by the river. If you do not come, I will know we have no future together and I shall tell Will he is to become a father. That gives you five days to make your decision."

Hugh answered, "Thank you Annie, I shall think hard."

"I know you will. I love you, good bye."

She shut the door behind her; she knew he would not come.

* * *

II

A month passed. Christmas was only a few days away and snow carpeted the Suffolk countryside like a soft, white blanket. The main roads were still just passable but no-one ventured out unless the journey was really necessary. This was a time for sitting by the fireside and enjoying the fruits of a good harvest. Father Hugh was still trying to come to terms with his return to celibacy, but the flame Annie had stirred in him could not easily be quenched. There had been no contact between them though Hugh had heard Will Mullen responded well to his wife's news, telling anyone who would listen about his prospective fatherhood as if no-one had had a baby before, and scotching gossip about his sterility. Hugh hated to think of Mullen making love to his own wife, the Franciscan was as susceptible to jealousy as any man, and he was far from sure he had made the right decision by remaining at Calveley Hall.

Annie had been right because in truth he had made no decision at all. Instead he had weakly allowed events to take their course hiding behind such excuses like 'living in sin' or 'eternal damnation', but all his instincts supported Annie's more pragmatic view of life and love. One thing was certain, his faith in the Church had emerged from this affair greatly weakened and his faith in himself was utterly destroyed. Yet though he did not now realise it, he would emerge stronger from the ashes of his love for Annie, a more complete and stronger human being than he had been before.

One way of helping the days to pass was to throw himself into his work. Hugh took advantage of the inhospitable weather to update the estate records which he had allowed to fall into arrears during the last year. He was sitting in his study, quill in hand and writing up his notes on the stock account when Tom Riches entered,

"Please excuse the interruption Father Hugh, but you have a visitor." Hugh's hopes were momentarily raised, only to be dashed as Tom continued. "He won't say what it's about except that it is of great personal interest to you, so I said I would find out if you would see him."

"What time is it?"

"Nearly three o'clock."

"A bit late in the day for visitors."

"Shall I send him away then Father?"

Hugh put down his quill and sighed, "To come here in this weather means I probably should see him. Tell him I'll be down in five minutes. I'll see him in the main hall, but stay nearby Tom, not all strangers are friendly."

Hugh need not have worried for the visitor was little more than a boy, seventeen at most. No doubt the more senior members of his household had delegated travelling in poor weather to him.

"Sit down lad," said Hugh. "A cup of mulled wine to keep out the cold?"

"That would be most welcome sir," answered the boy.

As he stretched out his hand to take the goblet, Hugh noticed his fingers were blue with cold. "Have you far to travel after your visit here?" he asked. "You are in no fit state for a long journey."

"That's all right sir. My master has business in Laxfield. I am to return there this evening; it's only seven miles." He drained the goblet and wiped his lips on his sleeve.

"Well then," said Hugh, "who are you and what is so urgent that you must travel in this awful weather?"

"My name is John Hopkins, sir. I am in service to Squire Calveley of Eastwell Hall."

"Geoffrey Calveley?"

"Yes, you know him sir?"

"Not personally, but I know of him." Like a startled rabbit, Hugh was suddenly alert. Geoffrey Calveley was a name from the past he did not care for. He had only seen him a few times and never spoken to him, but he was well aware of the part Geoffrey had played in Richard's troubles nine years before. "What does your master want with me?" he asked.

"He requests you to meet him tomorrow for lunch at the King's Head in Laxfield. He has matters to discuss of great interest to you."

"What matters?"

"He did not say sir except that he will tell you tomorrow."

Hugh was sure no good could come of a meeting with Geoffrey. In any exchange of wits or negotiation, Geoffrey Calveley was said to have few peers. The Franciscan decided that if he had something Geoffrey wanted, then whatever it was, he should do his best to hold onto it. He said, "I am not inclined to meet your master in Laxfield or anywhere else for that matter."

Hopkins, unnerved by the sudden menace in Hugh's voice asked, "Have I offended you in some way sir?"

"It is not you boy. Your master and mine are cousins but they are also enemies. Tell Geoffrey I will not meet him and to keep well away from here. You'd best be on your way now before it gets dark."

Hopkins stood up and turned to leave, but as he slung his cloak around his shoulders he turned back again and said, "Oh, I almost forgot. In the event of you not wishing to meet my master, I am ordered to mention the name Luke Cotter. I do not know if that makes any difference sir."

On the outside Hugh maintained an appearance of calm, but inside his guts heaved. He felt he needed to vomit but could not allow that to happen, not yet anyway. Luke Cotter and Geoffrey Calveley! By all the devils in Hell, what an unholy alliance! If Geoffrey had found out about Annie, Hugh faced utter ruin. Was that why Cotter had not returned for more money? Was he already in Geoffrey's pay? Surely even Cotter would not sink that low because by destroying Hugh he would publicly disgrace his own sister, and God only knew what the reformed Will Mullen would do to her if he discovered that the child in his wife's womb, his pride and joy, was not his. Geoffrey had assessed the Franciscan's reaction shrewdly. Hugh would have to know more.

"Tell your master I will see him tomorrow at Laxfield at noon, but I will not stay long nor will I eat lunch with him." Despite that last, defiant remark, the first bout of the impending confrontation had already been won by Geoffrey.

Hugh cantered into Laxfield a few minutes late. The heavy, grey skies were discharging their load and large flakes of snow sank gently to earth in the still, cold air. The village looked charming in its covering of white, which obscured the muddy, rutted tracks between the cottages and the heaps of manure needed by each dwelling to supplement its stocks of firewood during the winter months. Light shone cheerfully from braziers inside the King's Head, which was located conveniently near the church to quench the dry throats of the congregation after Sunday morning mass. Hugh's countenance was anything but cheerful as he drew rein and dismounted outside the tavern, handing his horse to a shivering stable lad who emerged from a snow covered shed. Tom Riches, who accompanied his master in case muscular support was required, did likewise and, as both men shook the snow off their cloaks outside the black oak door, Hugh said,

"I want to avoid trouble if possible Tom, so make yourself scarce but stay in hailing distance in case you're needed."

Tom patted the heavy, beech wood club hanging from his belt under his cloak and smiled, "Just call Father, and I'll be at your side."

The heat inside the tavern generated by a large fire in the inglenook and numerous sweating drinkers was overwhelming. Hugh was obliged to unbutton his cloak and undo the top buttons of his leather tunic. He looked across the pine settles but saw no sign of Geoffrey until he noticed a man standing alone at the far corner of the tavern waving at him. Holy Saint George! He's changed thought Hugh. The Geoffrey he remembered had been raven haired like his cousin, but portly. Now the hair was more grey than black and the figure had expanded considerably across the waist line and around the chin or, to be more precise, chins. The last time Hugh had seen Geoffrey was outside Ipswich court house when the magistrate had just ruled in favour of Richard as the legal owner of Calveley Hall. That was eight years ago. Geoffrey's face had been white with shock and anger; he had departed vowing to anyone who would listen, revenge on his cousin and on the man who had handled Richard's case in his absence. That man was Hugh.

"Sit with me Father Hugh," said Geoffrey affably. "A mug of ale perhaps?"

"Thank you, yes," answered Hugh curtly, "though I won't be here long." He sat down opposite Geoffrey separated by a roughly hewn pine table covered with years of poorly cleaned ale stains. Geoffrey nodded to the tavern keeper and the ale was placed in front of Hugh, smooth, clear and straight from the tap.

"I see you have brought Master Riches with you," mused Geoffrey. He pointed to two heavily built men sitting at the next table, "I too took similar precautions. Are you sure you won't take lunch with me? I understand there is roast pork for today's meal."

Hugh shook his head, "I only eat with my friends."

"Tut, such aggression and you a man of the cloth. I see you no longer wear your Franciscan habit." Geoffrey seemed to be enjoying himself.

"My garb is no concern of yours. Let us keep this meeting brief and to the point. Tell me what you want Master Calveley."

Geoffrey's brow furrowed. He liked to be called Squire Calveley as Hugh well knew. "My property of course."

"What property? You already have Eastwell Hall."

The affable mask slipped away. Geoffrey lowered his voice to a menacing snarl. "The property my cousin stole from me with your help, and I shall have it back whatever you say."

"Really," said Hugh in mock surprise, "and how do you propose to achieve that?"

Geoffrey smiled wickedly, "You shall achieve it for me my randy little popinjay."

It was then that Hugh had to face the sickening truth. Luke Cotter had broken his silence in the most devastating way possible. It now only remained to be discovered just how much had been said. Hugh's bluster sounded hollow even to himself as he replied, "I think you had better explain that remark Master Calveley."

Geoffrey gloated, "Ah, so I have your interest at last. Somehow I thought I might." He took a deep pull at his mug, allowing dribbles of brown liquid to run down his neck, and wiped his sweating face with his kerchief; he was squeezing as much pleasure out of this moment as he could. "I have in my employ a farm foreman by the name of Luke Cotter, and a right worthy man he is too, so much so that he has felt obliged to divest himself of some information that has troubled his honest soul for some time. You see, in my capacity as a magistrate he could be sure that the correct measures will be taken to remedy the situation."

"In other words you paid him."

Geoffrey ignored the insult, he was enjoying himself too much. "This information," he continued gleefully, "concerns a certain fornicating priest, a Franciscan no less! Now would you not agree that, as a magistrate, I am duty bound to inform the Church authorities?"

Hugh snapped, "Why do you not just tell me what you have in that devious mind of yours!"

But Geoffrey was not to be put off his sport. "And to crown it all, this Franciscan has planted his clerical seed inside the body of Cotter's sister who happens to be another man's wife! I have heard that Will Mullen, who currently labours under the misapprehension that he is to become a father, has turned over a new leaf. No longer is he the violent bully who beats his pretty little wife whenever he's sober enough to do so; far from it. Now he dresses smartly, shaves every day and even helps Annie with the household shopping, carrying home her basket from Halesworth market in case the weight puts too much strain on her. How sweet. What a shame it will be when he discovers the truth. I doubt Annie will live long enough even to spawn your bastard, Father Hugh."

"So what is stopping you doing your so-called duty!" demanded Hugh angrily.

Geoffrey returned to the affable approach he had used earlier. He took another pull of ale and shook his head sadly, "It does not have to be this way Father Hugh."

"Does it not?"

"The anger of those whose loved ones have died unshriven at your hands, the wrath of those who believe they were properly married by you, not to mention Will Mullen's violent retribution; all might be avoided."

"How?" said Hugh dully, knowing he was beaten. He had hurt Annie enough already. She seemed to have found some sort of contentment with Will. The thought of taking even that crumb of solace away from her was intolerable.

Geoffrey abandoned his mockery and became business-like. "In exchange for my silence, you will become my man until Calveley Hall is mine again. You will swear before a jury that you perjured yourself eight years ago because of threats to your personal safety from my cousin. You will say that the affidavit you presented to the court concerning my father's first marriage was a forgery and that you yourself never saw the marriage register in Calais. Thus my father's second marriage was not bigamous and, as his legitimate heir, I shall resume my rightful possession of Calveley Hall."

"I could do as you ask but you would still fail to recover Calveley Hall."

"Why?"

"The Calais priest saw the marriage register."

"He's dead now."

"The register could still be brought to court as proof."

Geoffrey smiled, "Then let it. The offending page no longer exists."

"That could be seen as an unlikely coincidence favouring your cause."

"It could just as easily favour Richard's. Without your support it could be claimed that he removed the page because the fatal marriage entry never existed. Any page within a year either side would have sufficed for his purpose."

Hugh paused for thought. Geoffrey had certainly prepared his campaign well, but he seemed to have missed the most important aspect; the other witnesses. For the first time the Franciscan took a drink from his mug as a flush of hope passed through him. "You seem to be unaware that there are two other people of unimpeachable character who also know of your father's marriage entry in the Calais register."

"You mean Sir Thomas Erpingham and Sir John Fastolf?"

"Well, yes," acknowledged Hugh, taken unawares by Geoffrey's foreknowledge.

"Sir Thomas is in his seventieth year and in his dotage now. He does not leave his manor, his memory is poor and confused. He could never give evidence in court."

"And Sir John Fastolf?"

"Aye, Sir John could be a problem if he's in England to testify, but he spends nearly all his time in France now."

"But Richard will surely call upon Sir John for evidence."

"My informants tell me that my cousin has left Rouen to go on a long journey. He will not return for many months. I expect you know more about this than I do." Hugh did not respond to the implied question so Geoffrey went on. "It does not matter anyway because I shall argue my case as the occupant of Calveley Hall."

"How can that be?"

"Having publicly acknowledged your perjury, for which I shall graciously forgive you, you will, as steward, hand over the property to me. My position will then be greatly strengthened for, as you know, possession is nine tenths of the law."

Hugh was horrified. "I cannot do that! Betrayal on such a scale is unheard of."

"You have no choice Father Hugh. In any event, you have already betrayed your master by using his money to pay Luke Cotter for his silence. Your judgement of Cotter's character was, to say the least, optimistic."

The Franciscan stared blindly into his mug of ale. The laughter and merriment in the tavern around him seemed at odds with his own wretched state. Geoffrey had cornered him. There was no escape. "Cotter has broken his silence once," said Hugh. "How can I be sure that even if I do everything you say, he won't break his silence again when it suits him?"

Sensing final victory at last, Geoffrey became the embodiment of concern. "Do not worry about Cotter young Hugh, I know his type. He would not dare to disobey me. Fear is a more powerful weapon than persuasion as you are now experiencing for yourself at this moment. I regret putting you through it but I intend to recover what is mine, and you are my means to that end."

"What about the staff at Calveley Hall?" asked Hugh. "What will happen to them?"

"Their positions will be secure. I shall employ all of them except Master Riches. I will even keep you as steward if you wish."

Hugh shook his head. "No, I shall return to Dunwich Priory. I have seen enough of the outside world. When will you take possession of the hall?"

"I am not an unreasonable man," said Geoffrey. "You may remain for Christmas. I shall take possession on the feast of the Epiphany."

"The sixth of January! So soon!"

Geoffrey frowned, the veneer of friendliness fast disappearing. "Then what date do you suggest?"

"Would you accept the first of February? That will give me time to get my affairs in order, bring the accounts up to date and so on. In all other respects I accept your terms."

Geoffrey was unsure. Much could happen in six weeks but it was a small risk compared to losing Hugh's co-operation. The meeting had gone remarkably well and de Groot had reported that the men in Fastolf's company, who were wintering in Rouen, did not expect to see Captain Calveley back in France again before midsummer. Geoffrey decided he could afford the extra time. "Very well Father Hugh, you have until the first day of February. At noon on that day I shall arrive at Calveley Hall and require a servant to be waiting for me with the keys to the house. I shall expect you and your baggage to be gone."

* * *

III

The Christmas of the year of Our Lord 1423 was a desperate time for Hugh. What a contrast to the previous Christmas! Then, his affair with Annie was fresh and new. Life, though dangerous, was exciting and full of promise. Even better, he had not yet heard of Luke Cotter. When he was a small boy his father used to say, 'Be careful, your sins will find you out'. But the young Hugh was never a wayward child; he saved that for later in life. His father and mother had died long since, but if ever he needed the benefit of loving, parental advice it was now. There was one person who could still fulfil that role, someone who might see a way out of the turmoil Hugh had created for himself so, before finally surrendering Calveley Hall to Geoffrey, he decided to visit Dunwich Priory.

By the Epiphany the snow had turned to brown slush and the roads were a little more passable. A steady, penetrating drizzle fell from the leaden skies which had not broken to reveal the sun for weeks. When he reached the bridge at Blythburgh, Hugh was soaked to the skin. He had diplomatically donned his grey, Franciscan habit again for this particular journey, but priestly robes were not designed for wet weather travel and the coarse grey cloth clung uncomfortably around his legs.

Hugh dismounted on the bridge and looked at the murky foaming water below. There were no other travellers about in such poor weather, so he could be alone with his thoughts as he stood beside the wet, wooden railing which was all that was preventing him from falling into the icy waters of Blythburgh mere. A few hundred paces behind him, the bell tower of the church of The Holy Trinity chimed ten o'clock. The church was being rebuilt with money from wealthy local wool merchants and was already being dubbed 'the cathedral in the marsh'. How insignificant Hugh felt in the presence of such a glorious tribute to Man's love of God. He stared dolefully into the eddying, snow fed torrent beneath him as a permanent solution to his troubles presented itself to him. Suicide was considered to be a mortal sin by the Church, but he was already condemned and you could only go to Hell once. At least it might save Annie, and it would certainly be more honourable than meekly handing over Richard's inheritance to Geoffrey. It would take guts, but if no solace was to be found at Dunwich Priory, Hugh resolved he would not live to see the end of this day. He had heard that drowning was the least unpleasant way of doing away with one's self, and certainly the easiest. He could never have used a knife on himself, and poisoning took too long.

It was late morning when he arrived at the priory. This was Hugh's first visit for almost two years and he soon noticed there had been a few changes. The simple wooden gate that used to provide access to the Franciscan enclosure had been replaced by an imposing wrought iron structure and, attached to one side of the priory, a new building had been constructed outside which was a sign reading 'Prior's House.' He tried to push open the gate but discovered it was locked. Hardly in the Franciscan tradition of welcoming passing travellers, thought Hugh. He noticed a bell sunk into the flint curtain wall and rang it loudly. A young novice emerged from the priory and walked slowly along the gravel path to the gate before unlocking it.

He asked in a supercilious tone, especially for one so young, "And who might you be?"

"I am Father Hugh."

The novice's attitude quickly became more respectful. "Father Hugh, I have heard of you of course. Father Simon was singing your praises only yesterday."

The gate was soon opened and Hugh said, "I am here to see Father Anselm."

"I am sure Father Simon will want to see you too. You should call on him first." Hugh did not need a novice to explain common courtesy to him, but he let the comment go unchallenged and allowed himself to be taken to the prior's house.

Father Simon was a short, dark, urbane man of about forty. Hugh thought he would look more at home in a City of London merchant's guild or the Inns of Court rather than a rural priory. He certainly spoke in a rich, mellow voice which was pleasing to the ear, and had that superficial charm essential for success in a big city. Around his neck he wore a jewel studded crucifix, which probably cost three year's pay for a labouring man, and unlike the rest of his brethren at Dunwich, his grey Franciscan attire was manufactured from fine, Flemish linen instead of roughly woven local wool. His quarters too were furnished with no thought for expense and Hugh concluded that Simon must have a private income to support his extravagant tastes. His chairs were padded, the stone floor was covered with artistically woven mats, and no doubt the pictures hanging on the walls were painted by some of the best artists of the day.

"Welcome Father Hugh," said Simon as he ushered him towards a beautifully carved oak chair beside the fire. "This is indeed an unexpected pleasure. I trust all is well at Calveley Hall?" What he really meant was 'Is my source of income from your master still secure?'

"All is under control at the hall," lied Hugh. "I see there have been some changes here since my last visit."

"There certainly have. The priory was in a poor state when I took over, but with good management and an improvement in our funds, thanks in part to your own efforts, I have been able to bring this place into the modern world."

The slur on Anselm's period of office did not please Hugh. He pointedly looked round the prior's chamber. "So I see."

"And what brings you here on such a miserable day for travelling?"

"I wish to be confessed. I am long overdue to be shriven."

"Of course, of course," acknowledged Simon, "the temptations of the outside world are much more immediate for you than the other brothers. I will personally hear your confession."

"Father Anselm is my confessor."

The prior frowned, "You seem not to understand, I am offering you a privilege. I am the personal confessor of William de la Pole, Earl of Suffolk."

Hugh was determined he would not open his soul to this man. "I thank you for the honour Father Simon, but Father Anselm has always been my confessor."

"But he is all but senile."

"Even so, it is my right to choose."

Father Simon stared unblinkingly at Hugh. His pale blue eyes were cold and his face expressionless as he tried to weigh up his itinerant subordinate, but even he could not deny Hugh the right to be confessed by whomsoever he chose. The warmth left his voice as he said, "So be it. I trust you will stay long enough to share lunch with us."

"Thank you Father."

"Good. It is helpful for the brothers to hear tales of the sinful temptations of the world outside the priory and how you manage to overcome them. It prepares them for their mendicant duties." If only you knew, thought Hugh as he left the prior's house and returned to the main priory building.

Anselm's chamber was on the south facing side of the priory where it had always been. It was his only concession to luxury for he loved the sun and, apart from the occasional goblet of good clairet, his physical needs were meagre. Hugh knocked once on the door and entered. The chamber was perhaps four paces square and contained only a bunk, a table with a few books on it, and two simple wooden chairs in one of which Anselm sat motionless beside the small window. His eyes were closed and his wise old face seemed at peace. For an uncomfortable moment Hugh thought he might be dead, but then the eyes opened and blinked. The voice crackled with age, "Who is there?"

"It's Hugh, Father."

There was a brief pause as the response sank in, then the old, slumped figure sat up and the voice suddenly became younger. "Hugh, welcome my son, welcome. I had not thought to see you again in this life. Actually, 'see' is hardly the appropriate word; I am little better than blind now."

Hugh sat on the rough, flint lined window ledge. "It is good to see you too, Father. Are you well?"

"As well as can be expected for a man in his eightieth year. The mind still works properly but the body is falling apart. I am so pleased you have come. Can you stay long?"

"I have told Father Simon I will stay for lunch."

Anselm nodded, "That should please him; he will be able to show you off as a fine example of Franciscan business acumen."

"He would have made a better banker than a friar."

"Now, now Hugh," scolded Anselm gently, "he does his best in the way he sees fit."

"But he is a poor substitute for you as a prior."

"Some might agree with you my son, but let us not waste precious time talking about our worthy prior. It is your news I wish to hear. News of those I care for is now my greatest pleasure."

Hugh sighed, "Not this time Father, I have got myself into a terrible mess and all of my own making. Retribution is imminent and others will suffer because of my wrong-doing. Before I make a final decision I thought I would speak with you. You are the only person I can turn to."

"What final decision?"

"The best thing for everybody now is for me to do away with myself."

Anselm leaned forward, his face wrinkled with concern. "But that would be a mortal sin my son. You would condemn yourself to everlasting torment."

"I already have."

There was a short silence as Anselm considered the gravity of Hugh's state of mind. Somewhere down the corridor a bell rang sounding half past eleven o'clock. The old Franciscan put his bony hand on Hugh's as a sign of reassurance and asked, "Would you like me to hear your confession?"

The outpouring of Hugh's torment took almost half an hour, and when he finally drew to a close the bell was ringing for noon. Anselm remained silent throughout. He understood the value of confession, which not only shrived the soul but also helped to unburden the mind, at least for a while, by sharing problems with another. Perhaps, he thought, I can still be of use to someone even in my dotage if I can save this troubled priest from taking the irretrievable step.

Hugh concluded his confession disconsolately, "I am sorry to have been a disappointment to you Father, especially after the faith you showed in me by allowing me to work outside the priory. I have become as wicked as men like Titus Scrope and Geoffrey Calveley instead of respecting the vocation of the priesthood."

"That is not so," replied Anselm. "You have sinned, there is no doubt of that, but you must not compare yourself with Scrope or Richard's cousin. Their sins are spawned out of malice whereas you have sinned out of weakness. Jesus understands the difference. He will forgive you if you ask him to and truly repent."

"I do."

"But you must also have the courage to live on and face the consequences of your actions. It is your duty."

"I am not sure I can."

"But you must. You have been weak. Now you must be strong and behave like a man. You have hidden depths; this is the time to draw upon them."

"What should I do? Whatever I touch seems to go wrong and now I am at the mercy of evil men."

Anselm rubbed his chin in thought. Unlike Hugh, he had seen much of the world before entering the priory and knew that problems often have solutions that are not obvious to those closely involved. "My son, if you remain true to God and try to be a little pragmatic, you may be able to extricate yourself with minimum pain to those you care for. My counsel is this. Firstly, you must not betray Richard by handing over his property to Geoffrey. He is your friend and benefactor and will readily forgive what you have done thus far if you are honest with him. Secondly, you must accept that however much you grovel before Geoffrey he will, after he has extracted all he wants from you, reveal your illicit love for Annie Mullen anyway. That is his spiteful nature. And thirdly, you must disappear for a few months. Sometimes it is better to do nothing, and the penance I shall give you will ensure you will be absent for a while."

"But I can't just leave Annie to face her angry husband alone, nor can I abandon Calveley Hall."

"You exaggerate your own importance my son. Tom Riches will be a very adequate substitute steward while you are away and, as for Annie, she will have to take her chances. It is unwise to be too sure about human reactions before they occur. Will Mullen may not behave as you predict."

"But if he does?"

"Then instruct Tom to offer her sanctuary at Calveley Hall. He can certainly provide protection for her, and the fact that you will not be there might ease the situation a little. I am sure that is what Richard would want you to do."

Hugh thought for a moment then said, "But I feel I would be abandoning my responsibilities."

"Then that rules out taking your own life does it not? My son, can you not see that at the moment you are the problem? With you out of the way, the difficulties you perceive surrounding you have a chance of resolving themselves."

"Then I will do as you say Father."

Anselm smiled, "Good, and although I cannot release you from your vows I can at least channel God's forgiveness into your soul. For your penance you will leave at once for the Priory of Saint Francis outside Paris for a two month retreat to learn from your behaviour during the last year and to gain the moral strength for the tasks that still lie ahead of you. I shall write a letter of introduction for you to take to the prior, and after your retreat you must visit Mary Calveley in Rouen. I have a present for her." The old Franciscan pointed to his bunk. "Under there you will find a book. Bring it to me."

Hugh did as instructed and brought a large, dust covered book bound in expensive, red leather and placed it on the table in front of Anselm. "It's very heavy Father."

"It's very controversial too. Open it."

Hugh brushed some of the dust off the cover and opened it. "A Lollard Bible!" he gasped. "It's all in English!"

"You see my son, you are not the only one who breaks the rules. This is the Bible which was the evidence that effectively condemned Mary for heresy. I secured it after her trial saying I needed it for research and to develop counter-arguments to Lollardy. Actually some of the English prose is quite beautiful. You recall how Mary and her followers treasured it?"

"I do Father. I also remember that you always had a certain regard for the Lollards. Is that not so?"

"True," agreed Anselm. "Although much of what they believe is heretical, devaluing the sacraments, public ownership of all property and so on, the torch they carry for the poor against the wealthy Church hierarchy struck a chord with many of us Franciscans except, perhaps, our current prior. I have always felt that the Lollards are honest but misguided children of Christ."

"What about women priests?"

"I do not recall Jesus saying anywhere in the Bible that the priesthood should be restricted to men only."

"Well, the Lollards are certainly closer to God than the Father Simons of this world."

The bell in the corridor outside Anselm's chamber rang for half past twelve. "Time for the midday meal," he sighed.

"Are you not coming Father?"

"I eat but once a day, in the evening. That is plenty for an old man. Come back after you have eaten and I will give you the letter of introduction for your retreat. I will absolve you now. Ego te absolvo ......"

* * *

IV

Geoffrey Calveley rode slowly back to Eastwell Hall, humiliated in front of his retinue. It was the first day of February in the year of Our Lord 1424 and, as promised, Hugh had left. But Tom Riches was still there and had driven Geoffrey off the property like a common trespasser.

"By all the devils in Hell," whispered Geoffrey to himself. "I shall have my revenge upon that Franciscan wretch. It's time de Groot started to earn his pay."

CHAPTER SIX

The eighteenth day of January in the year of Our Lord 1424 saw *Loredan* nosing her way out of the great, military harbour of Nauplion in Peloponnesian Greece. There was almost no wind beneath the clear, blue sky and the banks of her oars moved in perfect harmony back and forth as the sleek, low sided vessel headed into the Gulf of Argos. Anyone watching from the fortified island of Bourzi, which guarded the entrance to Nauplion, would have been in no doubt that *Loredan* was a craft designed and built for war. The thump of the bosun's drum giving the time to the rowers echoed across the dark, still water and sentinels stood quietly at their posts on deck like warriors from ancient Greece awaiting the call to arms.

Captain Paolo Dandolo, hero of many a skirmish with pirates and Turks, watched his crew, all freemen, heave at their oars from his position beside the helm. Slim, brown haired and the owner of a devastating smile, he seemed to Richard the epitome of the bold Venetian mariners who, almost single handedly, had stemmed the westward advance of the Turks since the fall of Outremer. Richard, who as a kindred spirit had quickly struck up a friendship with him, climbed up the steps to the quarterdeck and approached Dandolo. "Excuse me Captain, I cannot help but notice a change in the crew since we left Nauplion. Everyone seems more relaxed now."

Dandolo, who only spoke French with a heavy accent, pointed back to the fortress city. "What you say is true Captain Richard. This because we now leave behind the doge's spy in Nauplion. My men now feel they can talk freely without thinking about each word before it is uttered." The doge's spy, as Dandolo called him, was none other than Father Cavalli, the Dominican interpreter Richard had met at the audience in the palace. Cavalli created an ambience of fear which encircled him like a cloak, invisible yet tangible. Men instinctively gave ground before him as they might to a plague carrier, and their conversation was restricted to brief whispers in his presence.

Richard asked, "Is it usual for the doges of Venice to use priests as emissaries?"

"No, but Foscari's family always keep close links with Dominicans. They help him get elected despite death bed warnings of Mocenigo, the previous doge. This was bad for my family. Foscaris and Dandolos hate each other."

"Then why did the doge choose you to lead this voyage?"

Dandolo shrugged his shoulders. "I ask myself the same question. Every Venetian captain want to lead this voyage. Foscari has his favourites yet he choose me. Why? It make no sense."

Richard looked back at the massive fortress which stood guard over Nauplion on a huge spur of rock jutting out into the sea. The power of Venice was out of all proportion to its size. It controlled an empire yet it was still governed by a few squabbling families as it had been since its earliest days. That, he supposed, was part of its individuality. "How long will it take to reach Outremer?" he wondered aloud.

"Should be three weeks," answered Dandolo, "but it depend on weather. The Grand Master say go the direct route east from Crete to Cyprus, then southeast to Tyre and follow coast. He no want to go near Rhodes which means one less supply stop, so water must be rationed."

"That's all very well my dears," said another voice from the far side of the stern cabins, "but before he risks my investment he should speak to me." Chaim ben Issachar wobbled unsteadily into view along the larboard companionway. After two weeks aboard *Loredan* he had still not yet found his sea legs. He joined Richard and Dandolo by the helm. "And another thing, I understand there are Turkish galleys infesting the waters we intend to cross, but if we had called in at Rhodes we could have collected some Knight Hospitaller ships to escort us to our destination."

Richard said, "The last thing the Grand Master will do is ask for help from the Hospitallers. He would rather bow before the Sultan himself."

Dandolo was unconcerned. "Is no problem. *Loredan* can outsail any Turkish galley and since the year 1416 there has been no much trouble from them."

"Why? What happened in 1416?" asked Richard.

Dandolo looked surprised. "You no hear of Battle of Gallipoli?" Richard shook his head. "You English no hear much then. I hear of your Battle of Agincourt in 1415. Eight years ago Venice and Turks fight big sea battle off coast near Gallipoli. I was there as first officer aboard our flagship, *San Marco*. Was great victory for Venice and much glory for our leader, Admiral Pietro Loredan. This ship named after him. Since then not many Turkish ships venture south of Dardanelles."

"Do Turks make good sailors?" asked Richard.

"They, how you say, brave but raw. One day they will be strong at sea but still have much to learn."

"Your confidence reassures me Captain," said Chaim. He lurched and gripped the companion rail as *Loredan* met the heavier swell of open water. "I think I shall go and lie down for a while."

Chaim had been as good as his word concerning the cabin arrangements. In only two weeks he had managed to have the stern quarters completely rebuilt in the Venetian arsenal, where he had enough influence to put *Loredan* at the top of the refit list. There were four cabins at the stern of the ship, two starboard and two larboard, all leading onto a narrow corridor which ran down the middle of the living accommodation. Two of the cabins were occupied by Chaim and Ruth, one by the Grand Master and one by Captain Dandolo. Richard, Henry and the Templars were quartered on the foredeck under a canvas sale, along with the Venetian marines. The rowing crew ate and slept at their benches.

As they cleared the lee of the Arachnaion mountains, a strong westerly breeze developed. Even though *Loredan* was sailing due south, Dandolo was able to give the command to ship oars and use sail power alone, because the lateen rigged galley could sail closer to the wind than the square rigged cogs which plied their trade around English coasts. Richard decided to go forward and check all was well with Henry who he found talking to one of the Templars in his pidgin French, commonly referred to as 'Franglais' by the English soldiers in France, most of whom picked up a smattering of French after a year or two campaigning. Below, he could hear the relieved oarsmen chattering like magpies as he leaned against the starboard companion rail. He could not understand a word they were saying, but his military senses told him they all worshipped their captain with dog-like devotion.

As he looked back at the Greek mountains, he heard a voice which had become increasingly familiar over the last few weeks. "Richard!" It was Ruth. She had just emerged from her cabin and was bounding down the starboard beam deck towards him. "Isn't this wonderful! To feel nature drawing us along with such power! If I had been born a man I should have chosen a life at sea."

"I'm glad you weren't," smiled Richard, "but unlike your poor father you seem to be a natural mariner." She was pleased by the compliment and held his arm as they looked out at the grey waters of the Gulf of Argos together. Richard delighted in her company, as did everyone else aboard ship. To Chaim's utter despair she would engage even the humblest off duty mariner in happy chatter, avidly seeking to learn about everything around her. There was no evidence of her open friendliness being misinterpreted as something else, though this may have had something to do with Captain Dandolo's dire warnings about the consequences of misbehaviour. Ship's crewmen tend to be superstitious creatures and gradually the mariners decided that Ruth brought good luck like a ship's talisman. While she was with them all would be well.

But there was nothing simple or immature about the eighteen year old Ruth, she was just irrepressible. Her curiosity and enthusiasm stemmed in part from the sheltered life she had led, even as a businesswoman, which being a daughter of the Chosen Race required. Chaim's decision to bring her on this voyage had been frowned upon by his Jewish peers, but he had claimed it was Ruth's right as his business partner. He also wanted her near him, for in her his wife lived on.

Richard kept telling himself that Ruth treated him no differently to anyone else aboard *Loredan,* but she did seem to seek his company more frequently than most. Unlike her father, she had never been to England and was eager to hear about the distant, northern land at the western tip of Europe. Her only previous experience of North Europeans was with the German community which traded in Venice in large numbers. Their main topic of conversation was usually related to bodily functions, particularly the access and egress of food and drink, but Richard's stories of the characters living in rural Suffolk and anecdotes of the non-violent aspects of military life brought a refreshing change. They found they laughed much together, always a warning to those who care to listen, of deeper emotions lurking not far away.

* * *

II

Loredan made good progress before a friendly wind which backed northerly once she cleared the mainland of Greece. In less than a week landfall was made at Crete, and in another ten days she reached Cyprus where her dwindling water supply was replenished and her crew spent a day relaxing in Nicosia, Mamoun's home town. All seemed set fair for the last stage of the journey to Pilgrim's Castle, which was an easy two day voyage to the southeast, but on the first day out of Nicosia and almost within sight of Outremer, disaster overtook them.

It came out of the north without warning. They had left the cloud behind and were sailing under a clear, blue winter sky. Richard and Henry stood on the foredeck straining their eyes for their first glimpse of Outremer when a shout from the crow's nest interrupted them. They looked back across the larboard quarter expecting to see a Turkish galley but there was nothing. Captain Dandolo began giving orders with uncharacteristic urgency, the rowers closed their ports and some of them ran to the masts and started to lower the sails. One of the ship's officers left Dandolo and began running along the starboard companionway towards the Templars gathered on the foredeck, but before he reached them the squall struck.

To a landsman there was no warning, no sudden shift in the wind, and had it not been for the sharp eyed lookout who saw the change in the sea on the larboard quarter, *Loredan* would have been swamped at the first onslaught. Sadly, the time for preparation had been insufficient. The squall smashed into the side of the galley beam on. The main sail spar became stuck in the rigging and all who had been unprepared, like Richard and Henry, were hurled to the deck. One of the Templars was swept overboard by the sheer fury of the blast. The noise was terrifying as the storm shrieked around them like a multitude of howling spirits. Richard wriggled across the heaving, wet deck and grabbed the base of the foremast while those around him desperately strove to find something firm to hold onto or be pitched into the violent sea as huge waves began to break over the ship. The wind seemed to be striking them from all directions at once. Richard glanced up at the sky, now almost obscured by spray, and saw that the mainsail rigging, which seconds before was occupied by six or seven mariners, had now been swept clear. Dandolo had been given no alternative but to order the men up the rigging. To allow the heavy mainsail spar to remain unsecured would have been even more dangerous and at least the brave crewmen had cut the spar free before being devoured by the voracious sea.

To his right Richard saw the heavy, oak water barrel, which was still three quarters full, begin to shift ominously as it pushed against the wooden framework which held it in place. There was nothing he could do. Another huge wave pitched *Loredan* into a deep trough, the framework snapped and the water barrel tipped over and rolled across the deck, crushing two prostrate Templars before smashing through the companion rail and disappearing into the sea. On his left Richard could see Henry hanging on grimly to one of the deck bolts which were used to steady the cargo.

"Worse than anything we saw on *Morning Star* Henry!" he shouted.

"Aye Captain, I'm not sure we'll get through this one!"

Richard looked back at the quarter deck where Dandolo had taken personal charge of the helm and called back to Henry, "If anyone can get us through this it's Paolo Dandolo. All we can do is hold on and pray!"

Dandolo was forced to run before the squall; there had been no time to turn and face into it. The mountainous sea threatened to engulf the ship as each new wave broke across her, but *Loredan's* timbers were seasoned and well sealed; she would not give in easily. Each time she plunged into a trough it seemed to the inexperienced eyes of the Templars impossible that the bow would be able to lift rapidly enough to breast the crest of the next wave, but all the mariners knew the real danger lay behind. With a following sea the threat of being overwhelmed from the stern was ever present and even the most skilful captain needed luck as well as judgment in such conditions. The rowers sat at their benches, drenched and knee deep in water and, after a few minutes at the helm, Dandolo began to feel *Loredan* was no longer breasting the waves quite so well. Her bow was beginning to cut through the wave crests rather than riding over them; the increasing weight of water in her bilges was pulling her down. She was beginning to founder.

Then, almost as quickly as it had arrived, the squall died away. It had lasted barely half an hour, but the danger was not quite over. As Richard got unsteadily to his feet to survey the devastation on *Loredan's* deck, he heard the sharp crack of splitting timbers. He was momentarily confused, for the pitching of the vessel had disorientated him and his balance was affected. Suddenly he was grabbed round the waist and hurled across the deck like a helpless straw doll. His shoulder struck the larboard companion rail but, as he looked back dazed and dizzy to find out what was happening, he saw the foremast top plunge to the deck exactly where he had been standing. The heavy, splintered pine mast would undoubtedly have killed him. The Templar, who had risked his own life to push Richard to safety, got slowly to his feet.

Richard gasped in surprise, "Scrope!"

The bony, grey bearded face broke into a rare smile, "Aye Captain Calveley."

"But why? Why save the life of the man who has sworn to kill you?"

Titus answered, "My life means nothing to me."

"No man wants to die."

"That is not so, but I would prefer to live a little longer to continue reparation for the things I have done."

"You can never compensate for your past Scrope. God may forgive you, though I doubt it, but I shall not."

"Then perhaps Captain Calveley, you will consider this little incident a small amelioration for the enormous evil I have done you. While I live I shall continue in like manner." He turned and joined the rest of the Templars, who were gathering on the foredeck. Richard tried to be unimpressed by the quiet dignity which now seemed to emanate from Titus Scrope, but just at this moment it was difficult.

The squall cost the lives of seven crewmen and two Templars. Two more Templars were seriously injured when the heavy water barrel broke loose and could take no further part in the Grand Master's venture. Captain Dandolo called a conference to discuss what to do next while the crew bailed out water, cleared damaged spars and rigging from the deck and began emergency repair work on the broken companion rail and leaking timbers. Four people sat with the captain in his small cabin. Chaim, in his capacity as owner, insisted on being present, and the Grand Master and Mamoun represented the Templars. Richard was not quite sure why he was there except that the Grand Master had asked him to attend.

Dandolo opened the conference by explaining what had happened. "No-one ever really know this sea. In these waters squalls strike without warning, often near mountainous coasts. The only good to come from this one is it push us towards where we want to go. I think Outremer now just over horizon."

"Excellent!" exclaimed the Grand Master who was sitting opposite the captain with his back to the door, "then we are only a day or two from our destination."

Dandolo shook his head, "Wait minute please before you say that. *Loredan* is badly damaged. One more storm only half as bad as the one we just go through will sink her, and only God know what happen if we meet Turkish galley in our condition. We, how you say, lamb to slaughter."

"Then what do you propose?" asked Chaim whose prime concern was his investment.

"We go back to Cyprus and repair damage in Nicosia. Is good dock there. Should have all we need to make *Loredan* seaworthy again."

The Grand Master frowned, "How long Captain Dandolo?"

"Three, maybe four weeks."

The captain's answer did not please the Templar. He turned to Mamoun, "What is the feeling amongst the brothers?"

"They are much shaken by the storm Grand Master. Their only desire at present is to walk on firm ground again."

Dandolo became impatient. "If we no go back to Cyprus nobody walk on firm ground again. Is winter now; many storms at this time. We must go back."

But the Grand Master would not be thwarted. "Captain, I understand your concern but this ship is chartered to me -"

"With my finance," interrupted Chaim.

Ignoring the Jew, the Templar continued, "Can you not find the materials you need in Outremer? Surely there are trees you could cut down for masts and spars on the flanks of Mount Carmel?"

Dandolo answered, "Is no that simple. Some damage is below the waterline. We must have dock for that. Even if we could find materials we need in Outremer, it will take much time to cut out, shape them and prepare them before repair work can begin on *Loredan*. What happen if Turkish galley arrive or another storm break while we refit? Apart from that, we cannot use fresh cut wood; is too green. Must have seasoned timber, must go back to Nicosia."

Grim faced, the Grand Master said, "I must insist."

But Dandolo would not be moved. He stood up and said, "I command here."

In frustration, the Templar turned to Richard, "You have said nothing yet Captain Richard. What is your view?" This was the first time he had used Richard's Christian name. It showed how desperate he was.

Richard replied, "There is a way both of you can be satisfied but it will involve some risk."

"Not to my ship I trust," said Chaim.

"No, only to the Templars but at least their mission will not be delayed. If Captain Dandolo will sail the extra day to Pilgrim's Castle, we will be able to disembark and then he can return to refit in Cyprus while we secure the treasury. When *Loredan* is seaworthy again, she can return with all speed and pick us up."

Mamoun raised his eyebrows, "You are suggesting cutting ourselves off from escape in a hostile land for three weeks?"

"Four," interjected Dandolo.

"Surely that is madness?"

"It is risky," agreed Richard. "I do not know Outremer, but I would guess there will only be local levies stationed where we are going. We are not expected, and with luck we will be far away before any first line troops arrive from Antioch or Damascus."

"And if we do meet trouble," said the Grand Master enthusiastically, "Pilgrim's Castle is protected on three sides by water. There are still thirty eight of us including Captain Richard and his sergeant. We could hold the castle long enough I am sure."

Dandolo, who was also warming to Richard's suggestion, added, "And I will strain every muscle to finish refit quickly. I will return in not less than three and a half weeks."

"Then we are agreed," concluded Chaim. "Next stop, Outremer!"

* * *

III

In the early morning after the conference aboard *Loredan,* a cry from the lookout announced land. At first, all that could be seen from deck level were white, flat clouds just above the horizon on the starboard bow, but soon a dull, pale grey shape came into view which Dandolo declared was Mount Carmel. He was delighted for this meant that despite the storm, his navigation had been accurate. Pilgrim's Castle lay only a few miles south of Carmel but the captain decided to hold off until sunset to avoid ships using the busy port of Haifa, just six miles north of the great Templar castle. There was no need to declare one's presence earlier than necessary. It was the ninth day of February in the year of Our Lord 1424.

It was while *Loredan* lay hove to that Richard, who was leaning against the stern companion rail watching seagulls squabbling over scraps thrown overboard from the ship's kitchen, heard raised voices coming from Chaim's cabin. He entered the living quarters and knocked on Chaim's door.

An irritated Jewish voice called out, "Who is it?"

"Richard Calveley."

"Come in then." As Richard entered the cabin, an exasperated Chaim said, "Perhaps you can talk some sense into the girl. She no longer seems to respect her own father's wishes!"

Ruth stood opposite Chaim, red faced and pouting as might a small girl who has been sent to bed early for being naughty. She was distractedly winding and unwinding a tress of long, black hair around her forefinger and looking fixedly at her feet. Richard was captivated and felt a sudden desire to gather her into his arms and console her even though he had no idea what was causing the rift with her father. He tore his eyes from her and asked,

"What is the problem?"

Chaim pointed angrily at his daughter. "Problem! Problem! That is the problem my dear. Richard, you have a daughter do you not?"

"Yes."

"Then would you knowingly allow her to walk into danger?"

"Of course not, but what has that got to do with Ruth?"

"Well might you ask. My darling daughter has decided she wants to land with the Templars at Pilgrim's Castle while our ship refits at Nicosia. Can you imagine that! Not only would she be unattended amongst nearly forty men, but she risks being captured by the Turks if they turn up sooner than we think. Goodness only knows what they would do to her. It doesn't bear thinking about."

Ruth looked at Richard instead of her father and pleaded, "This is the only chance I shall ever have of treading upon the soil of my homeland, the land Jehovah gave to the Jews. You would not deny me, Richard, would you?"

"It is not my choice. I do not believe you have anything to fear from the Templars but we simply do not know where the nearest Turkish troops are. We are hoping we will get a month's grace before they can gather a force together, but we cannot be sure. I would not let my daughter go."

Ruth's dark eyes moistened and Richard felt as if he had betrayed her. "There you are!" exclaimed Chaim. "You should listen to Richard even if you ignore your own father."

Ruth replied quietly, "I thought Richard would have understood. Mother would have."

"You leave your mother out of this. You always use her when you want your own way."

"She would not have denied me the chance of seeing our homeland."

Chaim, now thoroughly exasperated, said, "Homeland! It's only rock, soil and water like everywhere else." But deep down he knew as he spoke, he did not mean it. Love of the Promised Land was too deeply ingrained in him, as in all Jews, but love of his daughter was stronger still. His voice softened, "My darling daughter, for all we know the Turks could even be waiting for us. Our preparations in Venice might have been seen. There are many spies in the city."

"Perhaps there is a compromise," suggested Richard. "When we reach Pilgrim's Castle, Mamoun can, with the Grand Master's permission, land first to carry out a thorough reconnaissance. Unlike the rest of us, Mamoun will be able to speak to the local people without raising suspicion. If he finds out all is well, and there are no Turks nearby, I see no reason why both of you should not disembark for a few hours while we unload our stores and equipment. At least then you can say you walked upon the Promised Land."

Chaim frowned, "To walk upon the land of our forefathers for only a few hours may create a longing in me that does not at present exist."

"Then if you choose to stay aboard the ship, I will give you a personal warrant for Ruth's safety for the few hours she goes ashore."

Ruth smiled. At least she was happy with his offer but Chaim was still troubled.

"You still have doubts Chaim?" asked Richard.

"Well yes. You see there is something that has puzzled me from the start. You all seem to assume you will be able just to walk into your great castle unopposed, yet in Christian lands such a place would not remain unoccupied for long."

"I agree and I too asked the same question, but Mamoun's answer convinced me that the castle will be empty. It was built by the Templars who always regarded the sea as friendly. Christian ships dominated the sea lanes; the threat came from the land. Consequently, the main strength of the castle's fortifications lies in its landward defences. Although the seaward side is naturally protected by steep cliffs, little effort was put into fortifying it against maritime attack. In that respect nothing has changed. The Turkish attempt to become a power at sea was beaten off by the Venetians. To the Turks, the sea remains a hostile place, so there would be little point in occupying a castle which is open to the sea and shuts off what is, from a Turkish point of view, the friendly land."

Chaim nodded, "Well in that case I suppose I might permit a short visit as long as Ruth stays under your direct protection Richard. She must return to the ship in good time for the voyage to Cyprus."

Ruth embraced her father. "You're wonderful. I love you!"

Chaim beamed, "Just like your mother, always getting your own way in the end. But I look to you Richard to make sure nothing goes wrong."

Before Richard could answer, Ruth detached herself from Chaim and threw her arms around him. "And thank you Richard, I promise I'll behave." Richard's senses were suddenly a riot of delightful confusion. This was the first real physical contact between them. Her body was soft but firm as she pressed against him; the exotic fragrance of her perfumed hair seemed to make his head spin. She nestled against his chest for a second longer than was wise, especially in the presence of her father. Richard did not know what to do with his hands, but realising this pleasure must not last too long, he placed them round her narrow waist and pushed her gently away. Just before he withdrew his hands he gave her a brief, almost unnoticeable squeeze so that only she would be aware of the fleeting moment of affection, but when he looked into her dark, smouldering eyes he understood that the affection was returned in full measure. To have her to himself for just a short time while *Loredan* was being unloaded was something he anticipated with a mixture of fear and excitement, fear for letting down Chaim and his own wife Mary back in Rouen, and excitement, he supposed, for the same reason. But for now he must ensure Chaim did not change his decision as a result of his daughter's uninhibited behaviour.

Richard read the renewed doubt in Chaim's mind and tried to reassure him. "Youthful exuberance Chaim, that is all. Nobody aboard this ship takes Ruth's friendly way as anything more than that."

Ruth laughed, "Stop worrying Father. Richard will take good care of me. You know that."

Chaim looked skywards and shrugged, "I suppose so."

* * *

IV

Loredan approached the coast out of the setting sun. Her ensign had been lowered and, to a shoreline observer, she would have appeared as an unidentified silhouette bearing towards Haifa. Richard stood amidships watching the oars dip rhythmically in and out of the still, black water creating little whirlpools of foam as the blades pulled the ship towards the shore. There, sombre and dark against the green, wooded slopes of Mount Carmel, stood Pilgrim's Castle whose grey walls topped the steep cliffs of the peninsula where they had been built more than two hundred years before.

"Doesn't look the most welcoming place," said Henry who was standing beside his captain. "I would prefer not to be the first person to enter."

Richard was untroubled. "Don't worry Henry, you won't have to be. The Templars are positively eager to get into the place. They see it as one of their spiritual homes."

The Wiltshire sergeant spat into the sea. "It's the spiritual bit that worries me; restless Templar ghosts eternally wandering about the battlements seeking out new victims for their hatred."

"You are no lover of the Templars, Henry?"

"Their lives are dominated by a lust for revenge upon all those they feel have injured their Order in the past. I do not speak French as well as you Captain, but I understand enough to listen to their talk. Do you realise that as soon as the Order has been officially reinstated by us, the Grand Master intends to lead another crusade to capture Jerusalem?"

"I am not surprised by that but it will fail."

"Well I am only a humble sergeant," said Henry, "but even I understand the Holy Land is lost to Christianity. If I can see that surely the Grand Master can?"

Richard sighed, "I wish it were so, but fanaticism is no respecter of intellect. Once its icy claws grip the soul, there are few who can shake it off."

"It is not the Grand Master's demise that bothers me but the fate of the humbler folk who follow him. He will lead them to their deaths."

"Take comfort Henry. At least I shall not allow him to lead us to ours."

Mamoun, who had been put ashore the night before, returned with an encouraging report. As expected, he found the castle deserted, but there was still a plentiful supply of sweet water thanks to the winter rains which drained into large, stone lined cisterns built deep underground, well below the foundations. Posing as a traveller, he had visited the nearest town, a sordid collection of smelly, mudbrick dwellings lining the main coast road. There he learned that no-one ever went near 'The Great Castle in the Sea' because it was said to be haunted by vengeful souls of the fearsome Christian warriors who lived and died there during the jihad of Malik al Ashraf, the sultan responsible for driving the western barbarians back into the sea. In the time available to him, Mamoun had been unable to discover the location of the nearest Turkish troops, but the Grand Master was sufficiently confident to proceed with the landing without delay.

By the time *Loredan* had dropped anchor fifty paces off the gently shelving coast the sun had set, radiating a warm afterglow of crimson and purple in the western sky out at sea. Above, a waxing moon cast a hard, silver light which would assist the landing, now restricted to a single rowing boat; the storm had destroyed the other one. There was no time to lose for Captain Dandolo wanted to be well clear of the shore by dawn, preferably out of sight below the horizon. Isolated pinpoints of light scattered along the dark coast indicated dwellings from where the landing could easily be observed by unfriendly eyes if a delay were to prevent it being completed under cover of night.

Most of the Templars were already ashore when the rowing boat returned to the ship to collect Richard and Henry. The two Englishmen helped to hand down forty heavy crossbows and thousands of iron bolts before clambering down the rope ladder which hung over *Loredan's* beam. The boat was already crammed because in addition to the weapons, there were six burly oarsmen and a coxswain already in it. But they were obliged to squeeze tighter still when another small, black cloaked, hooded figure climbed down the ladder and wriggled into the stern next to Richard. It was Ruth. Richard had decided it was not necessary to mention her brief visit ashore to anyone except Henry. The Grand Master would certainly have objected, and in any event the trip would last only an hour, or at the most two. Dandolo would be weighing anchor shortly after that.

The rowing boat sat low in the water almost gunnel deep, but the sea was calm and the oarsmen knew their craft. Richard thought back nine years to the landing at Harfleur when Fastolf had been the first man ashore leading Henry V's invasion of France. Then, the waves had been five feet high and many a knight had received a good soaking. In such conditions *Loredan's* overloaded rowing boat would have foundered in seconds.

The landing stage was on the southwest side of the castle's peninsula and, as the rowing boat rounded the last rocky buttress, a spectacle greeted Richard which remained with him for the rest of his life. Towering above them, perhaps a hundred feet high, was the black mass of the cliffs which overlooked the landing stage. Along the cliff tops the moonlight picked out the regular blockwork of the castle walls and, climbing diagonally upwards from the sea towards the walls, were about forty flickering points of light which stood out in the darkness like tiny beacons. Richard guessed these were torches illuminating the path linking the castle to the sea, but it was the singing which etched itself more than anything else into his memory. A deep, plainsong chant rolled out of the darkness across the water towards them. It was the Te Deum, traditionally sung by Christian warriors at moments of triumph, and now the Templars were singing as they worked, celebrating their arrival at Pilgrim's Castle. Richard had heard it many times before, but never like this. The rich deep voices seemed to come at him from all directions as they echoed around the cliffs and out on to the sea. He felt the pores in his skin open, for only now did he sense, at least a little, the spiritual strength that drove these extraordinary men forward. He would never understand them but he could not help but admire them.

Ruth felt it too. "Richard," she whispered, "how was it that such terrible, fearsome men were beaten by the Muslims?"

"There were never many of them. How could there be, for such men are few and far between. Even at the height of their power, the military orders numbered no more than two thousand or so. The rest of the Christian soldiers were little more than a rabble, but the Templars and Hospitallers gave them the cutting edge they needed to win for many years. Yet the armies of Saladin and al Ashraf counted their numbers in tens of thousands; they were sure to conquer in the end."

"Do the Templars hope to return here, permanently I mean?"

"They say they do but they are blind to reality. The world has passed them by. No-one can turn back time, no matter how much one desires it. If ever the Templars manage to muster another crusade it will only end in failure as most of the others did. I hope for their sakes it never happens."

The prow of the boat bumped gently against the landing stage and the crew and passengers disembarked to begin unloading. Richard, Ruth and Henry were each handed a burning torch by two Templars who were stationed at the water's edge, checking in the arrival of their cargo. In the darkness neither of them noticed Ruth's relatively short stature. Her elegant female shape was well covered by her voluminous pilgrim's cloak and so, like Richard and Henry, she was allocated two heavy crossbows to carry up to the castle. As one hand was already carrying a torch, it was necessary to sling one of the crossbows over the shoulder and carry the other under the free arm. Together they weighed about sixty pounds, more than half Ruth's body weight, but that did not prevent her leading the way, albeit a little unsteadily, towards the stone stairway which had been cut into the living rock when the castle was built.

"By Holy Saint George," whispered Henry, "that young lady has hidden strengths but she'll never climb to the castle under that load."

"I think she might," answered Richard, "but a little discreet help will not go amiss." Henry handed his torch to Richard and ran forward to take some of the weight off Ruth's slight frame by placing his free hand under the shaft of the crossbow she was carrying over her shoulder without her realising it. They climbed more than a hundred steps before Richard stopped counting. Occasionally they would cross with singing Templars on their way down the steps to collect another load. The warrior monks had already cast aside their pilgrim cloaks to reveal their white tunics with the eight pointed cross as if to say, 'We have come home.' In the moonlight the cross looked black but whenever Richard's torch briefly lit up a passing Templar, the cross shone blood red, a colour that was to become all too common before this venture was over.

They entered the castle through a small sally port in the southern wall which led to a rectangular courtyard where the stores and provisions were being gathered. By now Ruth was almost staggering under her burden, despite Henry's unseen help, but she still managed to complete her mission handing both crossbows to another Templar who said, "The Grand Master will be holding a ceremony of thanksgiving at daybreak in the church. It will be followed by a chapter meeting, full ceremonial you understand."

The forms and ceremonies of the Knights Templar meetings were a long held secret. All sorts of rumours used to circulate about their strange and, some said, blasphemous rituals which was the main reason given for their suppression by the French King Phillipe the Fair. Richard was sorely tempted to use his pilgrim's disguise as a means to gain entry to the chapter meeting but it was futile to think he could get away with it. Instead he turned to his two companions and said, "The night is well advanced and the ship will be leaving soon. I will take Ruth outside the castle perimeter to whatever lies beyond so she can say that she really did walk upon the soil of Sion. The rock of Pilgrim's Castle hardly counts."

To his disappointment, Henry did not take the hint and accompanied them through one of the open gates and across the moat to the outer wall where they passed through yet another gate which had not been shut for a hundred and thirty years.

Outside the land was rough pasture, more or less like any pasture in arid lands, but Ruth fell to her knees and kissed the ground. She seemed to be breathing heavily, labouring almost, and for a moment Richard wondered if the climb had taken too much out of her, but then he realised she was weeping and once again he felt an overwhelming desire to gather her into his arms. Unfortunately Henry was sticking to them like a leech. The Wiltshire sergeant had no intention of being left alone amongst men who made him nervous in a castle he was convinced was haunted. Richard had not the heart to send him away, and he knew that to do so would be tantamount to declaring publicly his feelings for Ruth. He was also well aware that Henry, like the rest of the men in Fastolf's company, held his wife Mary in great esteem so he was forced to accept that his hopes of spending a little time alone with Ruth would be thwarted. Perhaps it's just as well he thought, and at least my promise to Chaim won't be threatened.

He looked up at the eastern sky and saw a slight greying in the black, star-studded velvet canopy.

"Ruth," he said, "we must hurry. Dawn is not far away and Captain Dandolo will be leaving soon."

She held out her hand to be helped to her feet but just before their fingertips met, the gallant Sergeant Hawkswood stepped forward to support her. "Allow me Miss. That climb up the stairway must have taken its toll. Even my legs are aching from it."

"Thank you Sergeant," replied Ruth wistfully.

"Henry Miss, just call me Henry." At that moment Richard could easily have called his sergeant a few things. 'Gooseberry' was the first word that came to mind, but that thought was unworthy for there was no man in England more good hearted than Henry Hawkswood.

They parted on the landing stage with Henry still in attendance. In the darkness Richard could not see Ruth's eyes, but as he helped her into the rowing boat her hand squeezed his; at least she shared his disappointment. He said, "Give my regards to your father. I regret you could not have longer ashore but we shall see you again in a few weeks."

Ruth spoke softly, "Sooner than that I shouldn't wonder."

Neither Richard nor Henry gave that remark a second thought.

The Templars worked with remarkable speed and before the sun's red rim appeared above the eastern horizon, they had already cleared the large, pillared hall that was to be their accommodation during their stay. It was next to the octagonal church, a shape characteristic of many Templar churches, and a replication on a small scale of the original Templar church in Jerusalem. At Pilgrim's Castle the church had been built almost in the centre of the precinct and, as the Templars filed in for their ceremony of thanksgiving, Richard and Henry made their way up to the battlements to watch the sunrise.

When the great red disc finally appeared in the east, the landscape was flooded in warm, friendly, red light which lifted the spirits of the two Englishmen. For Henry it drove away all the malevolent ghosts that wandered through the corridors of the castle, while for Richard it provided a kind of spiritual communication with Ruth who, he was sure, would be watching the same sunrise from the deck of *Loredan*.

He bent down and picked up a small bag he had brought with him from the ship. "Cast away your pilgrim's cloak Henry. I have something here you can wear in its stead. The Templars shall not be the only ones to bear the colours of their Order." He took out two white surcoats each emblazoned with the red cross of Saint George, the mark of the English at Agincourt and many battles since. Although the same combination as the Templar colours, the Saint George cross was larger and simpler, without the double points at the end of each bar. As soon as they put on their surcoats Richard and Henry felt strengthened. Instead of nondescript pilgrims, they were Englishmen again with that tradition of invincibility that went with being English.

Now they could face whatever perils that lay ahead, or so they thought until a female voice behind them said, "I decided to stay."

CHAPTER SEVEN

"God's blood!" swore Richard as he spun round to see Ruth standing there. "What's happened! Why are you not on the ship?"

She raised her chin and looked him defiantly in the eyes ready for any criticism that might be directed at her. "I changed my mind," she said simply.

"But I saw you get in the rowing boat. I saw it leave the landing stage!"

"There were a few more loads to be brought ashore after that. I came back with one of them."

Richard looked despairingly out to sea but *Loredan* was already hull down below the horizon. "Chaim," he groaned. "My promise to your father; he must be distraught."

A little smile plucked at the corners of Ruth's lips. "My father will not know yet. I made a point of seeing him as soon as I got back to the ship. Your promise is discharged."

"But you didn't tell him you were going to return to the castle."

"Of course not. He would have locked me up otherwise."

Another unwelcome thought reared itself up in Richard's mind. He asked no-one in particular, "But what will the Grand Master say?"

Henry, who was far less put out than Richard by Ruth's unexpected appearance said, "It seems to me he can say what he likes. It will make no difference, and from the way Mistress Ruth helped unload those crossbows, I'd say we have an extra pair of useful hands with us."

"Thank you Henry," acknowledged Ruth with an elegant little bow of the head. "I wish Richard was as pleased to see me as you are."

Stung by the contrast between his mean criticism and Henry's generous welcome, Richard smiled broadly, "Of course I am pleased to see you. We will face the wrath of the Grand Master together."

Ruth had taken the opportunity to change her attire during her brief return to *Loredan*. She now wore loose fitting mariners trousers and a lightweight, Turkish style chainmail shirt which came down almost to her knees. The mail hood was thrown back so that her raven hair hung freely about her shoulders and, at her side and wedged into a platted leather belt, was a small dagger. Unlikely to prevent a wild Turk having his way with her, thought Richard, but at least she's made a good attempt to obtain practical clothing during the short time available to her.

Ruth recognised Richard's appraising look. "Will I do?" she asked.

He laughed, "You will never make a Templar but who would want to be one anyway. You certainly pass our muster, is that not so Henry?"

"Aye Captain, Mistress Ruth is welcome in my troop any time."

"Then let us get the audience with the Grand Master over and done with."

They had to wait until mid morning before the Templars emerged from their church but the interview, when it came, lived up to expectations. It took place in a small chamber, which had been cleared for the Grand Master's private use, leading off the large pillared hall. As well as Ruth and the two Englishmen, Mamoun was present which was all to the good because he was always a moderating influence on his master. The torrent of abuse levelled at Richard was as vitriolic as it was colourful. Richard was even obliged to put a restraining hand on Henry's shoulder when he noticed the characteristic frown on the Wiltshire sergeant's broad brow which was usually the prelude to violence.

"I hold you entirely responsible for this mess Captain Calveley," concluded the Grand Master, white faced with rage, "and as such I have no further use for your services nor those of your sergeant. Henceforth you will be confined to the castle where you will ensure this... this... this woman," he almost spat the word out, "will remain invisible to the brothers."

This was not at all to Richard's liking. He had always intended to be present at the discovery of the Templar treasure, indeed it was his duty to the Duke of Bedford to be there. Until now he had remained calm before the Grand Master's tirade but now he felt his anger rising at the prospect of being excluded from the climax of the journey. He spoke quietly, restraining himself with difficulty. "I had no idea the presence of a woman would cause you so much discomfiture. Women are also God's creation. Did you not have a mother?"

"Women were created for the temptation of Man!" responded the Grand Master, visibly shaking with anger.

"Are you saying women are the Devil's creation? That is not what we read in the Bible." This comment was greeted with an ominous silence. Richard wondered if he had pushed the Templar too far; he was thousands of miles away from the protection of English law and he recalled the Grand Master's threat at their first meeting of the ultimate penalty for defying him.

But the argument was not yet over because support came from an unexpected source. Ruth, confident and bold, was not overawed by the angry man standing opposite her. "Grand Master," she said, "you presume too much. Need I remind you that without my father and me, you would still be stranded in Venice!"

"Ah, so your father approves of your actions does he? He authorised you to impose yourself on us?"

"I did not say that."

"Then you are here without his permission," said the Grand Master dismissively. "Do you not at least owe him the obedience every good daughter should give to her father?"

"As a daughter yes, but I am here as a business partner. In our business my father and I are equals. I do not need your permission to watch over our investment."

"Your investment is sailing away to Cyprus and you are hindering our ability to pay back the loan."

Ruth in turn raised her voice. "Allow me to be the best judge of how to run our business. I do not have the impertinence to tell you how to run your gaggle of emasculated virgins." The Grand Master's mouth opened and closed like a stranded fish. Richard, delighted with Ruth's spirited fightback, cringed as he waited for what must come next, but before the irate Templar could find the words he wanted, Mamoun intervened,

"Grand Master, permit me to make a suggestion." A cursory nod authorised him to continue. "Our numbers are not great for the task ahead of us, yet we must watch the roads to Damascus and Jerusalem for it is from those great cities that the enemy will come. Tomorrow I shall buy some horses for the four scouts who must watch out for us. Two will ride down the coast road towards Jerusalem and the other two will travel inland towards Damascus so that we will get at least two days' warning of an approaching army from either direction. Perhaps Mistress Ruth and Sergeant Hawkswood would take the inland route thus enabling more brothers to be freed up to help with the removal of our treasure." God's balls! thought Richard, why did he not suggest Ruth and me? All that time we might have had alone together.

The Grand Master said nothing so Mamoun continued, "I estimate that two days' ride should take Mistress Ruth and Sergeant Hawkswood as far as Nazareth, a holy place indeed, where they can wait on events. If all goes well we will call them in once our treasure is secured." Ignorant of Richard's affection for Ruth, Mamoun thought he was helping by sending away the object of the Grand Master's anger while at the same time keeping Richard available for the treasure hunt.

Somewhat mollified by Mamoun's proposal, the Grand Master replied, "Three shall go to Nazareth. The woman must not be alone with a Christian man. Send Brother Titus with them."

Now it was Richard's turn to vent his wrath. "Never! You might just as well set a rat to guard the cheese. You don't know his history!"

The issue was not very important to the Templar and, seeing the green fire blazing in Richard's eyes, he decided another confrontation was unnecessary. "Very well, if it means so much to you I will send someone else. However I was thinking of the protection of the Christian from the Jewess."

"Was not Christ a Jew?" said Richard. The Grand Master shook his head feigning sadness at Richard's stupidity, but the more perceptive Mamoun sensed the Englishman's anguish and wondered.

* * *

II

Pilgrim's Castle was a mighty fortress. Built after the fall of Jerusalem, it incorporated all the knowledge gained from a century of castle construction which the Crusaders had developed to compensate for their meagre numbers. There was a pleasing symmetry about it. Its mighty triple walls cut off the end of the peninsula it occupied and the massive middle wall, its main defence work, was augmented by a moat and three towering gate houses. Behind the middle wall, the inner wall was strengthened by two tall donjons, both of which would have to be captured before the castle finally fell.

Inside the walls was a pleasant array of halls and courtyards centred round the octagonal church. Although he was never to see a Templar chapter meeting, Richard did look inside the church after the audience with the Grand Master and was astonished to see how different it was from the churches he was accustomed to in the west. Instead of having the altar at the far end of the apse, it was placed in the centre of the church with the seating facing inwards around it. The octagonal walls were simple, and uncluttered with the ornate sculpture so typical of western churches, emphasising that it was people not buildings that constituted God's church.

Unlike most of the Christian castles in Outremer, Pilgrim's Castle was never captured but simply abandoned in an orderly manner after the fall of Acre when the Templars realised all was lost, at least for the time being. It was with some trepidation that the forces of Mohammed eventually entered the castle and, although they plundered it of all portable valuables, they did not deem it necessary to destroy it now that the Christian knights had abandoned their last toehold in Outremer. For this reason the latter day Templars were able to make the castle habitable again quickly. All the stonework and main beams were still in place, and there was little more to be done than clearing away a century of dust and superficial mess before they could settle comfortably into their new home.

On the fourth day after the landing the Templars were ready to embark on the next stage of their venture. Mamoun, a natural plunderer, had scoured the nearest villages and returned with six bony horses and a score of donkeys. The horses would have shamed even a beggarly Scottish knight and the awkwardness of the donkeys was a marvel to behold but, concluded Mamoun, they did not like working for Christians, which was particularly galling because he had paid for them instead of stealing them. The ghost of the great Saladin would have smiled if he was watching.

The scouts departed first. "Look after her well Henry," said Richard as he held the bridle of his sergeant's horse.

Henry, a born infantryman, wobbled unsteadily in the saddle and looked nervously at Ruth who was clearly at ease on horseback. "I'm not sure who'll be looking after who Captain," he replied. "It's a good few years since I travelled on anything but my own two feet." The third member of the party was a middle aged, humourless knight from Avignon, the Sieur de Graveson who understood no English. Henry had nicknamed him 'Laughing Boy' because he never smiled but Richard comforted himself by reflecting that de Graveson would make a perfect chaperon for Ruth; there could be no immodesty in his presence.

It was late morning when the Grand Master led his men across the moat and through the south gate of the outer wall into the open land beyond. He rode the best of Mamoun's horses while the rest of his little company trudged on foot, each man accompanied by a donkey. The Grand Master had prudently decided that there should never be less than ten men guarding the castle which left only twenty four, including himself, to secure the treasury. Richard attached himself to the middle of the column, trying as best he could to keep out of the Grand Master's sight. Everyone was wearing black, pilgrim's cloaks again, which not only hid the eight pointed cross but also gave some protection against the cool, onshore breeze. But if the Templars had hoped that obscuring their identity would somehow delay the nemesis in store for them, they were to be proved sadly mistaken. The Turks had sentinels spread all along the coast of Outremer to warn of pirate raids. News of the re-occupation of Pilgrim's Castle was already in Damascus.

The land outside the castle had once been cultivated by servants of the Templars of old, but it had fallen into disuse since the Muslim conquest. Since then, generations of grazing goats had reduced this once fertile area into sandy scrubland. Even now, the first sound Richard heard as the Templars headed south was the tinkling of goat bells when a group of mangy, brown and white creatures scattered into the scrub to avoid these unfamiliar humans. The Grand Master led his men in a direction parallel with the shoreline across sand dunes held in place by coarse tufts of grass. The going was hard because their feet sank ankle deep in soft sand. The normally sure footed donkeys baulked on the unstable, undulating slopes and tugged on their leading reins. Richard wondered how much more difficult the return journey would be when they were heavily laden.

After three hours of twisting ankles and cajoling obstinate donkeys, the Templars at last turned inland and the ground became easier. They left behind the unstable sand and climbed onto firm soil underlain by the white limestone of Outremer. Soon they entered the wooded foothills of Mount Carmel where tall Tabor oaks, and stately cedars and pines flourished in the relatively wet climate along this part of the coast. Once in the woodland, the tension Richard sensed amongst his companions seemed to ease; they no longer felt so exposed to hostile eyes and a few of the brothers began to chat to each other until silenced by a stentorian word of reproof from the Grand Master. They followed a stony goat track for about an hour along which the aroma of wild garlic hung heavy in the air; Richard could never smell garlic again without thinking back to that silent march through Carmel's woody foothills.

The protective woodland suddenly came to an end as if an unseen hand had drawn a line along Carmel's slopes beyond which the trees should not go. The Grand Master and Mamoun stopped to consult a small, yellow piece of parchment while the remainder of the column took a welcome rest. Stretching out before them was the vast pale mountain. Although not especially high, Carmel was many miles long and looked to Richard's eyes like a huge baker's loaf. Scattered along the slopes were many dark cave mouths one of which, he assumed, was their destination. He hoped the Grand Master's map was accurate, otherwise the search could take weeks and still end in failure. The ground immediately to their front hardly rose at all and formed an arid, thinly soiled plain a few hundred paces wide before the land resumed its upward trend once more. A grazing herd of long horned ibex took flight as their acute sense of smell picked up the new arrivals. Richard marvelled at their elegance as they athletically bounded over the boulder strewn ground with an ease that suggested they were only travelling at half speed.

The thin layer of cloud, which hung over Carmel like a white fleece, started to break up and permit the sun to bring some cheer to the men in black as they continued their march along the forest eaves, but after only a few minutes a halt was called again. This time the march did not resume and some of the Templars sat down beside their donkeys and soon fell asleep. No-one seemed to wonder what was causing the delay; the faith in the Grand Master was absolute. This faith was not shared by Richard and eventually he decided to risk bringing himself to the Grand Master's attention in order to satisfy his curiosity.

The scene that met him was not encouraging. The Grand Master and Mamoun had left the forest eaves and walked out a little distance into the open plain. They were about a longbow shot away, agitatedly looking from side to side. Mamoun pointed to something in the distance but the Grand Master shook his head and referred to the parchment he was holding. Something had gone wrong, so Richard left the column to join the two distracted Templars who were so pre-occupied they did not notice him approaching until he hailed them from a few paces away. The Grand Master quickly handed the parchment to Mamoun who furtively hid it in his cloak.

"What are you doing here Captain Calveley!" demanded the Grand Master. "Brother Mamoun and I are discussing confidential matters."

Richard answered, "It may be of interest to you to know that I am a military surveyor in the Duke of Bedford's army. The making and understanding of maps is one of my trades. I may be able to help you if you'll let me."

The Grand Master hesitated but Mamoun quickly accepted the offer. "It seems that some of our reference points have disappeared. We cannot identify the third point of the triangle." He brought out the parchment again, looked at the Grand Master who nodded his approval, and handed it to Richard. The parchment was only six inches by six and the ink upon it had faded to a rusty brown. The map was clearly not truly surveyed because even the supposedly straight lines had been drawn freehand, yet there was no indication of dimensions which meant that the reference points were critical. The map showed the ridge of Carmel below which was drawn a simple triangle, each apex being marked with a cross, but there was no writing except for the seal of Guillaume de Beaujeu, the Grand Master who hid the treasure one hundred and thirty three years before.

The Templar Legacy

Richard looked at the terrain ahead of him which was uneven. As well as being covered with a scree of boulders, there were numerous dried up river channels which criss-crossed each other in no particular pattern indicating that at one time the mountain had seen much more rainfall than now. Elsewhere small peaks of bedrock up to twenty feet high stuck up through the scree like islands in a sea of boulders. With only the map as a guide, the task of finding the Templar treasure seemed impossible.

Richard looked at the map again. "When we first met you said there are some words that go with this map which are passed down through each generation of Grand Master. What are they?"

Years of instinctive secrecy had made the Grand Master recoil at the thought of speaking the words aloud to anyone but Mamoun. He said, "Can you not help us by just looking at the map?"

Richard's patience with this awkward, irritable man began to wear thin again. "What good is a secret if it tells you nothing? Your men have followed you out here convinced of your infallibility, but unless you let me help, you will fail them at the last and most important obstacle. Now are you going to tell me or not?"

The Grand Master considered remonstrating at Richard's disrespectful tone but thought better of it. But nor could he bring himself to utter de Beaujeu's words so he just said, "Mamoun?"

The Cypriot Templar did not hesitate, "The words are these; 'The base of the triangle shall be marked by a Templar cross carved in two stone peaks. The third point, the place of the treasure, shall be found by standing at each cross and stretching a line in the direction of two piles of loose rocks twice the height of a man which I have built in haste. Each line should be stretched towards the furthest pile so that the lines will cross. Where the lines meet, dig there.'"

Richard asked, "What have you found so far?"

"We have found the two crosses," answered Mamoun. "That was easy. There is one just behind you, and another over there." He pointed to a small rock pinnacle standing proud of the ground around it a short distance away."

"What about the piles of rocks twice the height of a man?"

Mamoun shrugged, "They are gone. Heaps of piled stones will not last like solid rock. Years of weathering and occasional heavy storms must have swept them away."

"I suppose de Beaujeu thought our Order would return quite soon," said the Grand Master. "He could not have anticipated a gap of over a century."

Richard was not so sure. "It is difficult to believe that de Beaujeu would have hazarded the entire accumulated wealth of the Knights Templar to two hastily built piles of rock." He held the map up to the watery sunlight. It was thin and not quite opaque, so the sun illuminated it from the back. He caught his breath, "That's interesting."

"What is?" asked Mamoun and the Grand Master together.

"There is another symbol on this map but it is so faded I did not notice it before. It is the mark of an angle of a quarter circle shown at the place where we are now standing. It is sometimes called a right angle."

"What has this right angle go to do with our search?" asked Mamoun.

"It might just be the answer to the riddle. We may not need the stone piles at all. I think de Beaujeu anticipated the loss of the stone piles and has given us another way to find your treasure. A right angle is the angle made where the sides of a perfect square meet. It might mean nothing, it might mean everything. We can soon find out. Have you brought measuring lines with you?"

"Yes, we have two," replied Mamoun.

"What are the gradations?"

"De Beaujeu's paces."

"How quaint. Be so good as to measure the distance between your two Templar crosses. We will soon know if my instinct is sound or not."

Mamoun ran back to the other Templars and within a few minutes the measuring line was in position. De Beaujeu must have been a small man because the span of his paces was barely two thirds that of Richard's. Each pace was marked by a knot in the hemp string and every fifth knot was stained red for ease of counting. The string was pulled tight by eight Templars, four at each end, and Mamoun walked beside it counting the knots.

"Exactly forty," he announced when he returned to the Grand Master and Richard.

The Englishman smiled broadly, "Excellent!"

"Is it?" said the perplexed Grand Master.

"I believe so. Have you ever studied mathematics?"

"Certainly not! Mathematics is a base art unfit for knights of God. Our intellectual pursuits are confined to philosophy, religious instruction and languages."

"I doubt de Beaujeu would have shared your opinion. As a boy I was taught mathematics by the Franciscans at Dunwich Priory. They had a copy of a book by a scholar called Euclid who lived during Rome's imperial power. He collected all the wisdom of the ancients and put it into a treatise which has survived the dark times that separate us from the distant past. Thanks to Euclid, I believe we have before us a three, four, five triangle."

Both Templars looked blank. "Will this three, four, five triangle help with our search?" asked Mamoun.

"Certainly it will. If the base of a triangle with a right angle in it is forty paces, then the other two sides must be thirty and fifty paces long. It is a simple law of geometry."

The Grand Master said, "I am still unclear. What should we do now?" For the first time since the row over Ruth, his voice had lost its menace.

The entire expedition was in the hands of the Englishman. Richard knelt down and cleared a flat piece of ground to demonstrate his theory with the point of his dagger. First he cut a straight line,

"This is the base of the triangle between the two crosses. We know it is forty de Beaujeu paces long. Now you must cut two measuring lines, one thirty and the other fifty de Beaujeu paces long. Fix one end of the thirty pace line to the cross where we now stand and have one of the brothers walk towards Carmel with that line until it is pulled tight. Then have another brother start from the other cross with the fifty pace line and walk towards the brother who is holding the end of the thirty pace line. The aim must be to meet but without crossing so that the two ends of each line just touch each other. That will close the triangle and will be the location of your treasure." Richard sheathed his dagger with a flourish; he was well pleased with himself.

"And that is where the future of our Order lies," whispered the Grand Master in wonderment.

"More or less," said Richard, "but we must allow for some measuring error. When we close the triangle we should use that point as the centre of a circle ten de Beaujeu paces in diameter. Our search will be rewarded within that circle."

Getting the ends of the thirty and fifty pace lines to touch while still tight was not as easy as Richard made it sound because of the uneven ground, and the sun was well advanced in the western sky before the triangle was finally closed. Richard himself marked out the error circle but now that the moment of truth had arrived he began to have doubts. What if, after giving the Templars so much hope, they found nothing? It was always possible that a measuring error could have been made when de Beaujeu first set out the original triangle all those years ago, but that excuse would do nothing for Richard's reputation if they failed now. He had taken the entire success or failure of the venture upon himself, but he took some comfort from the configuration of the ground within his error circle, for a dried out stream channel about eight feet deep passed through the middle of it. A hidden cave mouth might easily be lurking behind one of the scree covered slopes.

The Templars threw off their black pilgrim's cloaks and each was allocated a segment of the circle to search. Very soon they were hard at work clearing the loose rock that blanketed the sides of the dry river channel. All Richard could do now was to watch and wait.

* * *

III

An hour passed. A blood red setting sun cast a warm glow as it touched the western horizon, turning Carmel's light grey mountainside into a pale pink. The Templars, their long shadows mirroring their frenetic activity, were trying to conclude the search before nightfall. Richard kept telling himself that it would take many more hours to cover the ground properly, but as the minutes passed he could not ward off a growing sense of unease.

Suddenly a bright eyed, young Flemish Templar who was working close to the edge of the error circle, called out, "Grand Master! I have something here!" Everyone immediately stopped what he was doing and ran to see what the Fleming had discovered. When Richard arrived the Grand Master was already on his knees thanking God for there, carved upon a newly cleared, smooth face of white limestone, was another eight pointed Templar cross. For a short while the strict discipline of the Knights Templar was shed and, except for the Grand Master who remained on his knees, all of them danced and capered under the evening sun like children at a birthday party.

Mamoun came prancing up to Richard and slapped him on the back, "Well done my friend. You and your three, four, five triangle have saved us all! We shall forever be grateful to you."

Richard smiled, "And to Guillaume de Beaujeu's foresight. He was a credit to your Order. Now we must hope no-one has been here before us."

Mamoun frowned, "Unlikely Richard but you are right to be cautious. We have not found the treasure yet, and when we do we still have to get it back to France."

Richard thought to himself, I think you mean England, but he said nothing about that for the present.

The sun had just set and the Templars spent the twilight hour clearing the area round the carved cross. What had appeared to be a section of virgin rock forming the side of the river channel turned out to be a large, round, wheel shaped stone nearly five feet in diameter. The cross was in the centre of the stone wheel and the base was slotted into a groove so that it could, with enough effort, be rolled to one side. No-one doubted that it covered the entrance to a cave.

The Grand Master's stentorian voice brought discipline back to the Templars, "We will wait until morning before we enter; it is now too dark to see what we are doing. After one hundred and thirty three years of waiting, one more night will make no difference." There were sighs of disappointment but the brothers obediently left the rock wheel untouched and prepared for the night. Richard overheard the Grand Master say to Mamoun,

"There must be no mistakes. If it really exists I shall be the one to find it."

The next day dawned cloudless. When Richard woke up, the Templars were already moving silently around the little camp on Carmel's stony flank. He sat up, rubbed his shoulder where the uneven ground had dug into him through his cloak, and stretched his long limbs. Today, the fourteenth day of February, would not only determine the fate of the Order of the Knights Templar, it would also decide the outcome of ninety years of war between England and France. But the Englishman would have to be patient because, even today, the Templars would not be deflected from their rigid morning routine of silent prayer and plainsong.

About eight o'clock everything was ready. The brotherhood was gathered in front of the rock wheel with Richard standing a little behind them; this was after all, their great moment. The Grand Master gave the command to start. Four of the burliest Templars gripped the wheel, which Richard estimated to be at least two tons in weight, and at a signal from Mamoun heaved together. The wheel began to move along its groove remarkably easily; de Beaujeu's stone masons had done their work well. After a single, complete revolution the wheel came to a halt where the groove ended and behind it, exposed to the light of day for the first time in more than a century, was de Beaujeu's cave. Some of the Templars coughed as a pungent, throat tightening smell came from inside.

"Bats," said Mamoun wrinkling his nose. "The smell is caused by their droppings but although unpleasant, it does no harm." The Grand Master was handed a bitumen capped torch from which a flame burned brightly, and then crossing himself, he entered the cave. He had to stoop, for the entrance was only the height of a ten year old child. Very soon the light from his torch was gone, as if the earth had swallowed him up, and after a few minutes some of the anxious brothers began to mutter, concerned for their leader's safety. Mamoun stepped forward and peered into the darkness, but almost immediately the light reappeared in the cave mouth reassuring the brothers that all was well. Seconds later, the Grand Master emerged from the darkness carrying a long silver tube, the mid section of which was cut away and replaced by heavy, old fashioned glass. He stood at the mouth of the cave, eyes glazed in that state of euphoria sometimes generated by religious mystics, and smiled broadly and uninhibitedly in the way of a child who sees its mother again after a long period of separation.

"I have it!" he proclaimed. "I have it! Everything is as de Beaujeu left it, even this." He held up the silver tube and through the glass Richard could just make out a piece of dark, weathered wood. "Yes my brothers," continued the Grand Master, "this is a piece of the True Cross!" Almost as one the Templars fell to their knees gasping in awe. The only laggard was Titus Scrope, who exchanged glances with Richard before following the example of his brethren. Both Englishmen were thinking the same thing; there were enough relics of the True Cross in the world to build a dozen warships. The original was supposed to have been captured by Saladin after his great victory over the Crusaders at the Horns of Hattin near the Sea of Galilee, though even the provenance of that cross had already been questioned by some. Chivalrous man that he was, Saladin eventually returned the cross to the Christians, after which it disappeared from history.

Richard had never been an admirer of relic worship which was increasingly tightening its grip on the Church. He regarded himself as no more or less pious than the next man, but the rivalry that now existed between some parishes in England concerning the quality of their relics was morbid in the extreme. Who could possibly care whether or not Saint Anthony's leg bone was more holy than Saint Swithin's teeth? The clerics seemed to think that the better the relic, the bigger the congregation. Perhaps they were right but to Richard it did not matter. Still, now was not the time to mention such heretical opinions, so he dutifully knelt down with the rest.

"Consider my brothers," said the Grand Master, raising his voice in religious rapture, "the very body of Our Lord Jesus Christ actually bled and died against this simple piece of wood I now hold before you. You will all be permitted to touch it in recognition of the service you have given to our cause." Two of the Templars actually wept at the prospect, overcome with emotion, but Richard found himself thinking of Hugh. What would he have made of all this? Still more worrying, what was it that had stopped him coming on the venture of a lifetime. He would have loved all this. Richard determined he would return to Suffolk as soon as possible to solve the mystery surrounding Hugh. But then he remembered Ruth; perhaps Hugh could wait a little longer.

After the ceremonial fingering of the True Cross, in which Richard took part despite his misgivings, it was time to examine the contents of the cave. He was the last to enter. Once inside, the narrow cave quickly opened out so that even Richard, who was the tallest in the company, was able to stand upright. The cave was well illuminated because the Templars had wedged burning torches every few paces into natural fissures in the rock. Richard's shadow flickered against the cave wall like a huge black goblin, and as the tunnel began to descend he cast a nervous glance back at the daylight behind him; he had never liked enclosed spaces.

The Templar Legacy

After a descent of about forty paces, the walls narrowed again so that both his shoulders brushed against them. He could feel beads of sweat running down his brow and knew he would be unable to go much further in these tomb-like conditions. Then quite suddenly, the walls disappeared and he found himself walking into a large, cavernous chamber where the rest of his companions had already gathered. Torches had been placed in the walls, and in the flickering yellow light he could make out a roughly circular chamber which was thirty or more paces across and at least twenty feet high. Scattered across the rocky floor in no particular order were scores of chests and boxes of all shapes and sizes which seemed to have been dumped in a hurry. Some had just been thrown on top of each other and none were even locked. Richard pictured de Beaujeu's Templars feverishly working against time as the Muslim army of al Ashraf was massacring the inhabitants of Acre, only a day's march from Pilgrim's Castle. Mamoun had explained that de Beaujeu was forced into these desperate measures because he had no way of knowing if the Venetian fleet, which was supposed to evacuate his men, would actually turn up. The relationship between Venice and Outremer had always been based on convenience rather than comradeship, and the doge's fleet had not hurried to save the Christians in Acre. In the event the Venetians arrived, but too late; de Beaujeu died with most of his men manfully fighting al Ashraf's overwhelming forces to the last, but not before they had managed to hide their treasury. In the end only a few remained to be rescued from Pilgrim's Castle.

Some of the chests had already been opened by the Grand Master's men and Richard walked to the nearest to look inside. It was almost large enough to hold a full grown man yet it was full to the brim with glistening Venetian gold ducats, thousands of them. Slowly he put his hand into the chest and picked up one of the coins which shone a fiery, almost liquid yellow in the torch light. He half expected it to be cheap gilded alloy but it was too heavy for that. He turned it over and saw the head of Doge Jacopo Contarini and the date of A.D. 1279.

"Yes my friend," whispered Mamoun. "They are all genuine. Come and look at some of the other caskets."

As well as ducats, there were English marks, French livres and coins of silver and gold from all over the known world. Richard never believed until now that there was so much gold in existence. Quite apart from the coins, there were ingots, bars, torques and plate as well as statuettes, goblets, and a host of other items which were finely wrought by craftsmen, so it was difficult to know if some objects were more precious for their artistry than the intrinsic value of the gold from which they were made. Elsewhere there were chests overflowing with fabulous jewellery, some of which looked suspiciously Christian, not in the Latin style perhaps, but more akin to the ornate Byzantine work which flooded into Europe after the sack of Constantinople by the warriors of the Fourth Crusade. Clearly not all the plunder from that disgraceful event got as far as Europe.

At the far end of the chamber Richard saw many more chests still unopened. He turned to Mamoun, "There must be more bullion in here than in the combined treasuries of England, France and the Holy Roman Empire."

Mamoun agreed, "I think you could add a few more countries to that list. Our valuation of ten million ducats was ridiculously low."

"But the only real value lies in how much of this we can take away. There are many tons to be moved and not much time. All these chests will have to be part emptied before those half starved donkeys you purchased can carry them."

"Then let us make a start," smiled the Cypriot, "and make sure your pockets remain empty while you're about it."

The Grand Master organised the great task in shifts so that everyone took turns guarding the castle and transporting the treasury, but despite working all the hours of daylight the cave was still more than half full after eight days. Worse still, the pace of the work began to slow down as men and donkeys became exhausted. The chests were stored in the main donjon of the castle and guarded night and day by four Templars. But on the morning of the twenty third day of February, events took a dramatic twist.

On that day it was Richard's turn to be part of the castle guard. Mamoun and the Grand Master were at the cave supervising the loading of more bullion chests, so discipline in the castle had eased a little and no-one noticed the three riders approaching along the Damascus road until they were within hailing distance.

One of three hailed the castle in English, "Open the gate!" Then remembering who he was shouting at, Henry Hawkswood used his best French, "Ouvrez la porte! Quickly!" The three dust covered riders galloped into the open area between the outer wall and the main moat, which had been cleared by the Templars shortly after their landing from *Loredan*. Richard's heart leaped as he recognised Ruth, who rode between Henry and the Sieur de Graveson, but there could only be one reason to account for the evident speed with which the scouts had returned from their observation post at Nazareth.

Any lingering doubts were dispelled when Henry saw Richard. "Captain, the Turks are coming!"

——————◆◆◆◆◆◆——————

CHAPTER EIGHT

"How far away and in what strength?" asked Richard, as he steadied Henry's horse while the Wiltshire sergeant dismounted.

Henry wiped some dust from his brow. "I counted about five hundred Captain, moving this way quickly in an orderly column. We are not going to be dealing with local levies; the troops I saw are front line warriors."

"They are well mounted too," added Ruth as she slipped neatly from the saddle. "I estimate they could be here by tomorrow night. The outriders could even get here by tomorrow morning."

Impressed by Ruth's assessment, Richard asked, "How can you be sure the Turks are heading this way? Perhaps they are just out on exercise."

Henry shook his head. "Unlikely Captain. They had siege equipment with them, mangonels, ladders and so on. We shadowed them past the turn-off to Jerusalem but they kept going towards Haifa. I can go back and watch what they do at Haifa if you wish. It's possible they could head north to Acre but I can't imagine why they would do that."

"No thank you Henry, we need every man here now. I am sure you're right about the Turks' intentions. I must send a warning to the Grand Master. Much has happened since you left."

They were speaking in French for Ruth's benefit, so the Sieur de Graveson understood every word. He was still in his saddle. "Do you command here Englishman?" he asked pompously.

"Unofficially."

"Ah, I see," said the French Templar, as if he had made an important point.

Henry briefly relapsed into English, "It's all right Captain. Laughing Boy is fussy about his honour, but he's good hearted really. Just humour him a bit."

Richard put on an air of formality. "With your permission Monseigneur?" De Graveson nodded his acknowledgement and Richard tried not to smile as he began to ask him for advice. "Monseigneur, since you left we have found de Beaujeu's treasury. More than half our men are engaged in transporting it back to the castle. I propose to send a messenger to recall them at once."

"Naturally," agreed de Graveson. "Is there anything you wish me to do?"

"I know you have just had a hard ride, but if we provide you with a fresh horse perhaps you would care to accompany the messenger so you can see for yourself the treasure before it is resealed?"

"Indeed I would. I shall leave immediately." De Graveson dismounted and Richard quickly ordered one of the garrison to bring a fresh horse and accompany him to de Beaujeu's cave. As they watched the two Templars trotting through the south gate on their bony steeds, Ruth said, "That was well done Richard. De Graveson will follow you to Hell and back now." She lowered her voice so that none could hear, "And so will I if you ask me."

The Grand Master and his men returned at nightfall, by which time Richard had already organised much of the defence. The crossbows were strung and oiled and each had been allocated fifty quarrels, those nasty little iron bolts that had even more penetrating power than the one yard ash shaft of the English longbow. The chainmail hauberks were laid out and prepared for their users, and piles of large stones had been placed along the battlements to be hurled down at the besieging enemy. The heavy wooden doors in the outer wall and the portcullis in the main wall had been repaired and could be opened and closed, no easy task considering they had not been moved since the castle was last occupied, and finally a sight that warmed every Templar's heart. Richard had arranged for their flag, the eight pointed red cross on white, to fly from the top of the main donjon.

After the evening meal, the Grand Master decided to call a council of war which was held in his private chamber. Richard, Mamoun and the Sieur de Graveson, who was the next most senior Templar, were asked to attend. The discovery of de Beaujeu's treasure had changed the Grand Master. The pervading bitterness and overwhelming arrogance were gone. It was as if light had at last entered his grey soul after a lifetime of wasted years. The purpose of his life seemed about to be fulfilled; now there was a brightness in his eyes which made him seem ten years younger. His attitude towards Richard had also changed as his opening remarks clearly demonstrated.

"My brothers," he said. "Although there is still at least half of de Beaujeu's legacy in the cave, we have now secured enough to fulfil our destiny. The cave has been resealed and we will, in time, return at the head of a conquering Christian army to recover what is left. But now our primary task is to return safely to France with what we have. For this reason I intend to put Captain Richard in command of all military operations. He is experienced in matters of war, I am not, and I believe our best chance of success lies under his leadership. I will, of course, remain in overall control but for the purpose of battle I will put myself under his command." This proposal was immediately approved by the other two Templars, after which the Grand Master addressed Richard directly,

"Well Richard, you have more than anyone else ensured the success of our mission so far. Will you accept?"

Richard was surprised, flattered and bemused all at once. It was of course a great compliment to have the Grand Master of the Knights Templar place himself under his command, but accompanying this honour was an almost child-like faith that by doing this all would be well. In fact it was more than likely they would all be dead in a few days' time because Dandolo had only been gone two weeks. He knew the Venetian captain would do all in his power to return quickly but the Templars could not expect rescue for at least another week. But as an experienced commander, Richard knew how important it was to maintain morale, so the naïve belief in his leadership had to be nurtured.

"I accept," he said quietly.

"Excellent! Then what do you propose we do now?"

"I have already thought much about our position which, although perilous, is not without hope." The Grand Master nodded his agreement; this was just what he wanted to hear.

Richard continued, "Our most important asset is time, and we must create enough of it to hold out until Captain Dandolo returns. Also we must take no risks and suffer no unnecessary casualties. Cold, common sense soldiering will get us through this. We want no heroics. We are outnumbered twelve to one based on Sergeant Hawkswood's estimate of the Turkish force, so we must exploit the natural strength of Pilgrim's Castle to help balance the odds. We will not make a serious attempt to hold the outer wall, it is too low and unprotected by a moat, though we can use it to slow the Turkish attack. Even a few hours could prove vital in the end."

"But we are by nature horse soldiers," said de Graveson, "All our training is centred on cavalry warfare."

Mamoun sighed, "Have you looked at our mounts? Would you have us go into battle on bony ponies and donkeys?"

"But the Sieur de Graveson has a valid point," said Richard, trying to maintain harmony. "We still have at least one full day before the Turks get here, so let us use it wisely in siege defence training and crossbow practice. Each of us must be able to shoot a minimum of two bolts a minute before the battle starts; forty bolts every thirty seconds will give the Turks something to think about. We must avoid close quarter fighting for as long as possible, but it may well come to that before this is over. Our main weapon will be the crossbow, so the sooner we learn how to use it well, the better."

Richard paused for a moment thinking wistfully of the archers in Fastolf's company. Forty English longbow men could hold the castle without difficulty against five hundred enemies. They were trained to release a one yard shaft every ten seconds, some could even shoot a second arrow before the first had reached its mark. Two bolts a minute was considered a good rate for a crossbow but even that was ambitious because none of the Templars had ever used one.

Trying to keep his voice calm, de Graveson asked, "If the worst should happen, will we ask for terms? I am of course thinking of the younger brothers who still have their whole lives ahead of them." One look into his grey eyes revealed he was thinking about an older brother too.

The Grand Master understood and spoke softly, "That would be pointless Henri. You know the traditional fate of Templars captured by the Turks is beheading. At least it is quick. No matter what promises the infidel makes, he does not regard them as binding unless they are given to another Muslim. Surrender means certain death but that will not happen; Captain Richard will make sure of that."

De Graveson's frightened eyes turned to Richard begging for reassurance. He had to give it because fear, especially when seen in older men, is highly contagious. The best cure was action.

"The Grand Master is right," agreed Richard. "We will certainly hold out until *Loredan's* return. I have in mind a surprise welcome for our Turkish friends which should give us an extra day's grace. I should be pleased Monseigneur if you would accompany me as my second in command.

* * *

II

Mustafa Akurgal was feeling pleased with himself. As Governor of Damascus, he had had the foresight to place watchers along the stretch

The Templar Legacy

of coastline under his control, and now his strategic brilliance had been rewarded. In truth, he admitted to himself as he sat outside his campaign tent sipping lime juice chilled with snow from Mount Hermon, the precaution was orientated towards his cousin and suzerain, the Sultan of Egypt who envied the power of his northern vassal but even so, Mustafa was not one to miss the unexpected opportunity that now presented itself to him.

Everyone had heard of the fabulous Templar treasure which even the great al Ashraf had failed to find, but if recent reports reaching him were anything to go by, a Templar expedition had arrived to retrieve it; why else would these Christian warriors risk their lives to re-occupy the deserted castle on the coast? Now at last it seemed that the treasure would see the light of day again, and Mustafa himself would be the instrument to recover it for the followers of the Prophet Mohammed, blessings be upon him. He had to move quickly, for not only must the Christians be destroyed before they could escape, but Mustafa knew he must assume that the Governor of Jerusalem was also likely to hear what was happening around the old Templar castle and would doubtless send an expedition of his own. This was glory Mustafa was not prepared to share and fortunately the best warriors in his army happened to be in Damascus when the exciting news arrived. Normally they would have been on the northern frontier watching the worrying expansion of the Ottoman Turks, or in the south keeping an eye on the Governor of Jerusalem.

Like himself, Mustafa's troops were mostly Mamelukes, descendants of freed Circassian slaves, who ruled a huge empire from their base in Egypt. To the ignorant Christians they were simply 'Turks' or 'Saracens' but that was like describing a Knight Templar as a simple man at arms. Mustafa's chest swelled with pride as he watched his tall, blue eyed warriors setting up camp for the night outside Haifa. He clapped his hands. Selim, his second in command, appeared at his side as if by magic. Mustafa was respected rather than loved by his men.

"Ah Selim, are all the pickets set for the night?"

"Indeed Blessed One."

"The men seem to be in good spirits do they not?"

"The prospect of fighting the unbelievers encourages them. They feel they are marching for the Prophet himself, blessings be upon him."

"And to make themselves rich," added Mustafa wryly.

Selim smiled revealing a row of broken, yellow teeth, "It is as you say Blessed One."

"Tomorrow we shall reach the Christian castle. I will hold a council of war with my officers then. Tonight they may rest but I shall want an early start in the morning. We have, at best, four days before the meddlesome Governor of Jerusalem arrives to claim his share of the spoils. The business must be concluded before then."

Selim bowed, "The castle shall be in your hands two days from now, and you shall have all the Christian heads to send back to Damascus as a tribute to your greatness Blessed One."

"Let us hope so Selim, let us hope so."

It was two hours before dawn. The sky was at its darkest and a chill wind blew in from the sea. In the Mameluke camp all was quiet and some of the sentries, tired out by the rapid march from Damascus, had fallen asleep. It should not have mattered because they were in friendly territory with nothing to fear. Suddenly Mustafa awoke and sat up on his campaign bunk listening. Years of living amongst the higher echelons of Mameluke society had sharpened his senses, for the threat of the assassin's dagger was ever present. He quickly rose from his bunk, put on a robe and opened the flap of his tent. Both sentinels outside were fast asleep, a fact which lodged itself in Mustafa's excellent memory, but something else was wrong. He took a deep breath. Burning! He could smell burning! Just as he raised the alarm, an orange flame leaped into the air from the baggage train area, panicking the horses nearby. Someone had cut free the tethers because the terrified animals began to stampede, flattening tents, crushing sleeping soldiers and galloping in all directions. The camp was in total confusion enabling the flames to take hold amongst the wooden supply wagons unhindered. Within minutes the entire siege train, so laboriously hauled all the way from Damascus, was in ashes, and the horses were scattering far and wide throughout the countryside around Haifa.

The cost in Mameluke lives caused by Richard's night time raid was not great. Four sentries had been quietly dispatched so that the Templars could gain access to the baggage train and picket lines, and another three lives had been lost in the stampede. But Mustafa Akurgal's anger required more victims, for not only had he lost his siege train, he had also lost a precious day. That was how long it took to round up the horses and commandeer enough timber in Haifa to make siege ladders.

When the Mamelukes marched out of camp a day late, they filed past the grisly remains of Mustafa's victims. He had executed the six sentries who survived the Templar raid by impaling them on sharpened wooden stakes to serve as a lesson to his men, but there was a seventh corpse recognisable by its death grin of broken, yellow teeth. Poor Selim had discovered that Mustafa Akurgal was just as ruthless with his officers as with his men.

* * *

III

The Templars put their extra day to good use strengthening the defences and preparing more surprises for the Turks. Richard and Henry took a break from the work and stood on the fighting platform on the outer wall watching the Templars labouring below them. The flat area between the middle and outer wall was to be the main killing ground if all went to plan.

"It's amazing what an effect a success, no matter how small, can have on the hearts of men," remarked Henry as he wiped some of the sweat from his arms. "Those there Templars seem to think they're on a church outing; they're chattering like magpies."

"I must admit, I've never seen them more cheerful apart from when we found de Beaujeu's treasure," agreed Richard. "Our little victory at Haifa was a heady tonic for them. They think they're invincible now."

"Well that's all to the good Captain; they performed well but many are untested in real battle."

"That's true enough. There is something boyish about them which is probably caused by abstinence from women, but I do not doubt their courage or determination. It's only their inexperience we need worry about."

Henry wrinkled his nose and sniffed the air, "What's that savoury smell?"

"It's Ruth's cooking. The Grand Master has even softened towards her. He has agreed to allow her to cook for our little army."

"Thank Holy Moses for that!" laughed Henry. "I've had quite enough of that Templar swill we've been trying to eat. Death no longer seems quite so attractive."

A call from one of the lookouts further along the fighting platform drew the Englishmen's attention to three riders approaching from the northeast. The other Templars stopped what they were doing and ran to the outer wall; the Turks had arrived. The main force was still some miles to the north, but three scouts had been sent forward to reconnoitre Pilgrim's Castle and assess its state of readiness. They advanced as close as they dared and halted beside a small pile of innocuous looking boulders not realising their significance. Because of the inexperience of his troops in handling crossbows, Richard had ordered ranging markers to be placed at fifty yard intervals from the castle as far as three hundred yards away. The three Turks had obligingly drawn rein exactly beside the two hundred yard marker,

Richard turned to his sergeant, "Who is our best marksman Henry?"

"I am," said the Wiltshireman modestly, "but I'm only the second best in all."

"I don't understand you Sergeant Hawkswood."

"You asked for our best marksman, but our best crossbow user is a markswoman."

"You let Ruth use a crossbow?"

"I insisted," said a female voice from behind them. Ruth had quietly left her cooking and come to join them when the lookout raised the alarm. "If you think I am going to sit quietly over cooking pots when the fighting starts, you are very much mistaken."

"But Ruth, it is not seemly," objected Richard.

"Nor is what those Turks will do to me if they manage to break into the castle." Richard glanced at the Grand Master, who was standing nearby, for support but he just shrugged. Never had a man changed so much, so quickly as he.

"Very well then," said Richard, "take a shot at the middle fellow of the three on the tall grey horse."

Ruth picked up one of the crossbows, which were laid out on the fighting platform below the parapet, and attached the windlass with the ease of a veteran. Then she wound back the drawstring until it slotted into the metal notch which was held in place by the trigger mechanism. Removing the windlass, she loaded a quarrel and put the crossbow to her shoulder, steadying her aim by resting her elbows on the battlements. Then, while still in the shooting position, she adjusted the range finder to two hundred yards and took a deep breath. She exhaled, but only when her body was utterly still did she pull the trigger. The steel tipped quarrel hissed through the air with almost no trajectory. A second later the Turk on the grey horse was bowled out of his saddle as neatly as a skittle at a summer fair. His two companions scattered but he lay still, shot through the heart. The Templars cheered wildly and Ruth acknowledged their praise with a smile, but in truth she was shocked. Until now war had been a game and the dead Turk just a target, but a mother had just lost her son because of her. The reaction set in immediately; she felt sick. Reason dictated that she should kill as many Turks as possible, but all she wanted to do was get away from the scene as quickly as she could.

Sensing her distress, Richard asked, "Ruth, are you all right?"

"Yes thank you, but I think I shall return to my pots and pans for a while."

Richard had seen this reaction in raw troops before. He tried to comfort her. "Do not worry, it will be much easier next time. You have more than earned your place in the front line." But such words of encouragement, even from Richard, were ill timed. She hurried back to her cooking to be alone.

Akurgal's army arrived in the late afternoon watched by the Templars from the castle walls. The Turks pitched their camp a respectful six hundred yards away, well beyond crossbow range, and doubled the number of pickets. There would be no more opportunities for surprise nocturnal visits. They made an impressive sight. All were clad in white, loose fitting trousers and long, white surcoats which were gathered at the waist by a leather belt that supported a heavy scimitar. They were lightly armoured with just a small breast and black plate and an open faced helmet, which had a rim above the eyes to shade them from the dazzling Outremer sun. On top of the helmet was a spike, which added to the height of the tall Muslim warriors, whose martial bearing impressed the Christians mightily. But by the time the tents had been erected, the horses fed and watered and the sentinels posted, the sun was setting; the assault would not come until the morrow.

The twenty eighth day of February dawned grey and still. During the night a sea mist had rolled inland and shrouded Pilgrim's Castle in a damp, cloying cloud. Richard stood on the outer wall swearing quietly to himself because the mist would give the attackers a huge advantage. He could not even see his one hundred yard range marker; the Turks could approach the walls to within almost a spear throw in perfect safety. He looked along the wall at the silent Templars. The jollity of the previous day was gone and all stared intently into the mist in front of them. They numbered thirty nine including Ruth who stood beside him, yet the walls were more than a hundred paces long. All the familiar pre-battle sensations came flooding back to Richard. Although he was now an experienced soldier, some might even say a veteran, his stomach always felt uneasy and his mouth dry at times like this. The waiting was the worst. He knew he would be all right when the battle started but this time he had Ruth to consider. If things went badly, what should he do about her?

A shout broke the heavy silence and the two lookouts, who had been stationed within sight of the Turkish camp, came running back out of the mist to the transient safety of the outer wall. Some of the younger Templars began to fidget and there was much nervous throat clearing and coughing.

"Mark your man well. Aim low." The reassuringly, bad accented French was spoken by Sergeant Hawkswood, who was walking behind the Templars on the fighting platform steadying strained nerves in the time honoured manner of English sergeants. "Look to your front, range seventy five yards. Remember your training and all will be well." The calm Wiltshire voice exuded confidence, which seemed to transmit itself to the young Templar on Richard's left, who even smiled as he adjusted the sight on his crossbow.

The gates in the outer wall had just been shut behind the returning lookouts when a blood chilling voice rent the air, "Allah Akbar!" The cry was taken up by hundreds more and then, appearing out of the mist like a wave of white and silver, came Akurgal's Mamelukes. The bearded warriors trotted at a steady, experienced pace to ensure they reached the wall as one but still with enough energy to give a good account of themselves. Some of them carried scaling ladders, others fascines, the rest brandished scimitars. All called for Allah's blessings upon them.

Sergeant Hawkswood shouted, "Shoot!" Thirty nine quarrels hissed from their crossbows bringing down about ten of the attackers, but the Turks never faltered, supremely confident in a quick victory. Henry's voice, powerful though it was, sounded thin and puny against the oncoming roar of "Allah Akbar!" and when he gave the order to shoot for the second time, the white and silver tide had almost reached the wall. This time nearly half of the wicked iron quarrels found targets, but the result was no more effective than a castle of sand blocking an incoming sea. Seconds later, the first scaling ladder slapped against the wall. Richard could already see that the outer wall would be overwhelmed at the first rush; he had hoped to fend off the first attack at least, but the bravery of the Turks and the dense mist put paid to that.

"Back to the middle wall!" he shouted. "Back! Back at once!" There was just time to hurl back a ladder which appeared in front of him, before Richard leaped from the fighting platform to follow the Templars across the open space between the outer and the middle wall. This had to be done carefully, avoiding the numerous patches of fresh earth that pockmarked the ground.

Although there were only fifty paces between the two walls, the heavy chainmail hauberks and crossbows slowed the retreating Templars, so the leading Turks were able to climb to the top of the outer wall while Richard's men were still filing across the drawbridges of the three tall gatehouses in the middle wall. A hiss of air brushed past Richard's right ear and the Templar in front of him suddenly jerked rigid, dropped his crossbow and clutched desperately at his back where a white feathered arrow had embedded itself between his shoulder blades. Richard ran forward to try and support him but the Templar was already dead and toppled head first into the moat. The old fashioned hauberk was no defence against modern archery. More arrows whistled past.

Richard fled across the drawbridge and into the gatehouse where Henry was waiting for him. "Hot work Captain. Are you all right?" asked the sergeant as he signalled the drawbridges to be pulled up and the portcullises lowered.

"Yes thank you Henry. Our losses?"

"Just the man you saw in front of you. Everyone else is here."

"And Ruth?"

"I've just seen her climbing the steps to the fighting platform."

"Good. You look after the northern section of the wall; I'll take the southern. God go with you Sergeant."

"And you too sir."

The middle wall, the main defence of the castle, was forty feet high, nearly twice the height of the outer, and protected by the moat. Unfortunately the moat was half filled with generations of debris, there had not been enough time to clear it out, so it was no longer the obstacle it once was. There was one gatehouse in the middle of the wall and one at either end where it met the rocky cliffs. The gatehouses were even taller than the wall and beyond the range of Turkish scaling ladders, which meant that the assault would have to be concentrated on the wall itself, north and south of the central gatehouse.

Just as Richard reached his place on the fighting platform beside Ruth, a roar went up from the jubilant Turks as they swarmed forward from the outer wall to resume the attack. The mist was beginning to lift to reveal in the clear light of day the forty five paces between the outer wall and the lip of the moat, where the next phase of the battle was about to take place.

"Range twenty five yards. Shoot!" shouted Henry, whose voice carried easily across the full length of the main wall. A ragged volley of quarrels felled only a few Turks because some of the Templars did not have time to complete loading their crossbows before the order came. Oh for the longbow, thought Richard again as he was about to pull the trigger of his crossbow, but before he could do so, the target suddenly disappeared from view. His second Turkish surprise was beginning to take effect.

The extra day gained from the night raid outside Haifa had been spent digging man traps in the killing ground. Large holes eight feet deep, hidden with a thin mat of dried twigs and topsoil were randomly scattered between the moat and the outer wall. The Templars had worked like demons to prepare ten of them. Each pit had sharpened stakes lining the base with the points facing upwards, and the screams that emerged as the Turks tumbled headlong into them told of their terrible effect. The leading ranks wavered but the pressure from their comrades pressing from behind pushed them forward until all the deadly traps had been sprung.

Despite this setback, the boldest of Akurgal's men still managed to reach the moat and hurl their fascines into it. The fascines were made of wood weighted with large stones and were intended to fill the moat with dry causeways so that scaling ladders could be put in place. But the impetus of the assault was gone and many of the fascine bearers lay impaled in the death pits. As the Turks hesitated, the Templars rained down a deadly shower of quarrels from the battlements. The brave Muslims started to back away like a broken wave receding from a rocky coast. No orders came to help them for all of the first wave officers had been killed. Then suddenly they ran. The Templars cheered and fired into the backs of the fleeing enemy until they disappeared behind the cover of the outer wall.

"Cease shooting!" shouted Henry, "And well done all!"

It took a moment or two for the defenders to appreciate their victory. The attack had begun badly for them with the ominously quick loss of the outer wall, but the man traps had turned the tables. They stared disbelievingly at the carnage in front of them. Amongst broken ladders and abandoned fascines, at least twenty five Turkish bodies lay in the incongruous poses of death between the two walls, and possibly double that number were impaled in the death pits. Time seemed to have slowed down during the fighting, but it had lasted only twenty minutes from beginning to end. In that short period, Mustafa Akurgal had lost almost a fifth of his men killed, or wounded so badly that they could take no further part in the battle. Just two Templars had fallen, both to Turkish arrows.

But Richard knew it would not be so easy next time. The man traps, the last of his surprises, had now been sprung, the odds were still ten to one and there was no sign of *Loredan*. They had gained valuable time and his men were in good heart, but the worst was yet to come.

* * *

IV

All was calm until noon. The mist had lifted and the Templars sat quietly on the fighting platform keeping their heads down, lost in their own private thoughts. To look over the battlements was to risk instant death because the Turks would immediately respond with a volley of arrows. Richard had used the pause in the siege to alter his battle plan a little by forming a small tactical reserve under Mamoun's command, which could counter any breakthrough the Turks might make. The reserve consisted of only five men because he dare not take any more from the front line. Now short, sharp words of command could be heard coming from behind the outer wall as the Turkish officers drew up their men for the second assault.

Richard gently nudged Ruth who was dozing with her head nestled against his shoulder. "Listen carefully," he said.

Ruth's eyes opened and stared blankly at him for a moment as she tried to adjust to her unfamiliar surroundings. "Are they coming again?"

"Soon."

She sat up and stretched. "I was dreaming I was back home in my garden. You were there too."

"Really?"

"I think you were my husband and the small child picking grapes from the vine was our son." She looked away as if she had said too much.

Richard put his arm round her and squeezed her gently. "A prediction perhaps?" It was a dangerous thing to say, but in a few hours or less they would almost certainly be dead so what did it matter?

She looked back at him, her dark eyes shining, and smiled, "I hope so." A son! What Richard would not have given for a son! He was already blessed with a beautiful daughter; a son would have completed the purpose of his life, and if it could not be with Mary then perhaps with Ruth?

He quickly drove such fanciful thoughts from his mind. "Now when the Turks get their ladders in place, as they surely will, I want you to go back to the donjon and wait until the fighting is over."

"But I would rather stay with you."

"No," said Richard firmly. "You have done well so far but the close quarter work that is to come requires the strength of a man. If you remain here you will hamper me because I shall be distracted for fear of your safety."

"Then promise me if things go badly and our defences are broken that you will return to the donjon before the end comes. I would have us die together."

Richard nodded, "You have my word on it." It was the first time death had been mentioned between them.

A single cry of "Allah Akbar!" pealed from behind the outer wall. It was answered by hundreds more, but above the din Henry Hawkswood's stentorian tones reverberated. "Take your posts! Look to your front! Mark your target well!" Richard remembered these same orders being given on that mad, wild October day at Agincourt, nine years before. The odds seemed just as impossible then. Perhaps there was still a little hope. The Templars stood up, crossbows at the ready, as the Turks swarmed across the outer wall again. Akurgal's marksmen took the opportunity to launch a final volley of arrows over the heads of their advancing comrades. A gurgling sound on his left briefly drew Richard's attention away from the attack. The young Flemish Templar, who had discovered the entrance to de Beaujeu's treasury, stood staring at him with an expression of surprise across his face. He was still gripping his crossbow in his right hand while scratching at his neck with his left, but there was nothing the Englishman could do. A white feathered arrow stuck out from the Fleming's throat where a thin trickle of dark red blood oozed through his fingers. His eyes rolled upwards and slowly, he toppled forward off the fighting platform into the courtyard below.

Although the man traps had been sprung during the earlier attack, they still served a useful purpose by breaking up the Turkish line into separated, concentrated groups which formed ideal targets for the crossbow men. When, on Sergeant Hawkswood's command, the Templars loosed their first volley, the slaughter was terrible but Akurgal's brave warriors did not waver. Clambering over their fallen comrades, they soon reached the moat and, despite the rocks and arrows being hurled at them, they threw their fascines into it and created the firm bases needed for the scaling ladders. The first ladder was put into place on Richard's right, but before a Turkish foot could step on to it, two Templars dislodged it and sent it crashing sideways into the moat. More ladders were placed against the wall, only to be hurled back, but now a second wave of Turks advanced in the wake of the first and halted just behind their comrades. The newcomers were archers; there were about a hundred of them. Within seconds of their arrival they commenced a deadly close range arrow storm which swept clean the top of the castle wall and forced the defenders to cower below the protection of the battlements. The escalade was imminent.

Richard abandoned his crossbow, picked up his shield and drew his long, broad bladed English sword. "Ruth, go now," he said quietly.

She kissed him gently on the cheek. "Remember your promise," she whispered, and was gone.

Henry, calm as ever, shouted, "Escalade imminent! Make ready!" Rasps of steel answered his command as the Templars drew their swords, the true weapons of knightly chivalry. Crouched below the battlements in those last few seconds, Richard found time to admire the professionalism of the Turks. To look over the battlements would be suicidal, which meant the escalade could not be opposed until the arrow storm was lifted for fear of hitting its own side. However, he decided that the commander was not worthy of his men because if he had sent the archers forward first, he might have saved the lives of the twenty or so warriors who had just fallen to the Templar crossbows. It was almost as if the Turkish commander had acted in haste. The arrow storm suddenly stopped; a spiked helmet appeared above the battlements. The final act was starting.

The old crusader cry of "Deus Vult!" meaning, Let God's will be done! resounded from the battlements as the Christians stood up to trade blows with the Muslims. With one mighty sweep of his blade, Richard decapitated the Turk who had appeared in front of him. A jet of bright red blood spurted across his white surcoat from the headless body which still gripped the top of the battlements. Before he could dislodge the ladder, the body was pushed aside by the next Turk who immediately followed his comrade to Paradise. Richard took a quick look along the wall. He could not see beyond the central gatehouse but on his side there were already at least ten ladders in place full of Turks eager to wash their scimitars in Christian blood. If the assault was equally ferocious on Henry's side of the gatehouse, the defenders would inevitably be overwhelmed.

The next Turk to face Richard managed to land a blow with a small axe which glanced off the side of his shield. Richard thrust the point of his sword into his enemy's throat. He could smell the foul breath as it escaped from the neck but before the body fell back into the moat a cry on his right heralded a new threat. Here de Graveson was clutching at his face as a huge, ebony skinned Turk clambered over the battlements wielding a reddened scimitar. Blood pumped through de Graveson's fingers and dripped onto the grey, stone fighting platform. With a howl of victory, the Turk raised his blade to deliver the killer blow. Richard was forced to leave his post to parry the downward cut. The power of the blow sent a shudder up Richard's arm, almost knocking his sword out of his hand, but at least the helpless de Graveson had been saved even though he would probably never see again. But the sheer bulk of the Turk enabled him to push Richard away from the Templar and, out of the corner of his eye, the Englishman could see more Turks crossing the battlements from the ladder he had been blocking before going to de Graveson's aid. Pilgrim's Castle was falling!

Richard crouched down low, as if beaten, and took another blow from the huge Turk but this time on his shield. From this position he was able to thrust his sword upwards into his opponent's groin, an attack only the most alert warrior could fend off. The confident Turk was too slow and the sword buried itself in his soft, nether parts. Richard could only withdraw his blade slowly from the cloying, punctured flesh and, with a howl of agony, the Turk toppled backwards over the wall and into the moat.

Now Richard was fighting desperately. Three Turks advanced on him from the left and already another had crossed onto the fighting platform on his right in the wake of the large warrior he had just dispatched. For a split second he hesitated, wondering which way to face, but the odds were suddenly improved when Mamoun smashed into the rear of the three, leading his tactical reserve of five picked swordsmen. Richard launched a fierce assault on the Turk to his right and quickly finished him by thrusting the rim of his shield into his throat, another trick he had learned on the battlefields of France.

The counter attack unnerved the next Turk who baulked as he was about to leave his ladder and cross over the battlements onto the fighting platform. Mamoun appeared at Richard's side and together they pushed the Turk, ladder and all, sideways so that it slid down the wall taking the adjacent ladder with it. All of a sudden the immediate threat was gone.

Richard, almost exhausted and breathing hard said, "Mamoun, you are a most welcome sight,"

The Cypriot Templar smiled, his white teeth contrasting with his olive brown, unshaven face. "You seemed to be doing well enough my friend. Perhaps you will join us now that this section of the wall is secure?" The fighting lasted another ten minutes. Mamoun's reserve plugged the gaps as they appeared and one by one, the scaling ladders were thrown down and their occupants cast into the moat. The final admission that the escalade had failed came when the Turkish archers resumed their withering arrow storm to give their comrades cover as they retired behind the safety of the outer wall.

The surviving Templars collapsed where they stood on the fighting platform in the last stages of exhaustion. Some sat with their backs to the battlements staring blankly ahead of them, others lay full length amongst the dead and wounded, resting their aching bodies so that it was impossible to tell at a glance who was dead and who still lived. A few tried to patch up wounds received in the fighting, but none of the others had enough energy to help them yet. But even amongst the carnage, Richard could not help smiling when he saw Henry. The smile, in part, stemmed from seeing that his sergeant had got through the escalade completely unscathed, but it was the contrast in post-battle behaviour between the wily English sergeant and the divinely inspired Templars that amused him most. Whilst the Templars rested and thanked God for their survival, Henry, following the instincts accrued through years of campaigning, was calmly plundering the Turkish corpses for items of value.

"Anything interesting Henry?"

"I can't understand it Captain. These bodies are almost barren. It's like looking for a virgin in a brothel." Typical of his breed, the English sergeant was more concerned about quality plunder than glorious victories. The fact that one usually preceded the other was incidental.

"Perhaps," suggested Richard, "they leave their valuables in their camp when they fight instead of carrying them on their persons as we do."

"Holy Moses! That's a tall order; it means trusting your camp followers! We could never do that. Maybe we could launch an attack on their camp when Captain Dandolo gets here?" Richard at once felt humbled and honoured by the simple faith his sergeant still had in him. To Richard it was obvious they would succumb to the next assault, but the thought of defeat had not even entered Henry's mind as long as Captain Richard was in command.

It was time to take stock and decide what to do next, but before an assessment could be made of their plight, Mamoun called from the central gatehouse, "Richard, look at the outer wall. The Turks are signalling to us."

A three hour truce was negotiated to enable the Turks to collect and bury their dead. Richard and the Grand Master argued for a longer period, but this was rejected, and once more Richard gained the impression that the Turkish commander was racing against time. Unknown to the Englishman, Mustafa Akurgal had just received a report that the Governor of Jerusalem was only two days away and marching on Pilgrim's Castle with a thousand men at his back. Richard and the Grand Master agreed that they should not report an offer of honourable surrender made by the Turks back to their comrades. Both knew it was a ruse to winkle them out of their lair, but the offer might disturb some of the defenders if they knew about it.

Watching the Turks carrying away their dead and injured provided a useful headcount for the Templars. Richard's best estimate of the reduced Turkish strength was three hundred and thirty fit men plus some walking wounded, but despite their heavy losses the odds had swung back in their favour. Almost all the surviving Templars carried wounds to some extent and nine had been killed. Now only twenty six were in a fit condition to continue the fight, two of whom, the Grand Master and Titus Scrope, were well advanced in years. It was clear that defending the castle's main wall was no longer possible. Richard would have to think of something else.

* * *

V

There was still more than an hour of the truce left. Knowing what would happen when the next assault came, Richard left the wall and walked back to the donjon where he had decided the Templars would make their final stand. He had told the Grand Master he wanted to make sure all was ready for the donjon's defence, but that was not the real reason for going. He climbed the broad, stone steps that led to the great rectangular tower and pushed open the massive, wooden door which, due to the iron studwork reinforcing it, was still as strong as on the day it was installed. Bolting the door behind him, he ascended the narrow, winding stairway which led to the first floor, gaining some comfort from the knowledge that the Turks would have to fight their way up it before the donjon finally fell.

The steps opened out into a large room, the full width of the building. It was crammed with de Beaujeu's treasure and the stores which the Templars had transferred from less defensible buildings within the castle. Richard paused, looked round and pocketed a handful of gold ducats, a necklace and some other small items of value, then called out, "Ruth, where are you?" There was no reply so he climbed another flight of winding stairs which took him to the donjon's upper floor. She was there, peering out to sea through one of the narrow arrow slits.

She turned and saw him. "I hoped you might come," then frowning she added, "Richard you're wounded."

He touched the caked blood above his right eye. "It's nothing, barely skin deep."

"Let me see." She tore a piece of cloth from the bottom of her white sailor trousers and dipped it in a water butt which, apart from the Templars' bedding and a few personal items, was the only furnishing on the upper floor. He bent down so she could wash his wound with the damp cloth. The fighting had exhausted him, but the closeness of her body and the perfume in her hair made him realise he still had some energy left. Suddenly he recalled the scent in Chaim's courtyard garden in Venice; Ruth's hair smelt of jasmine, the aphrodisiac used in the harems of Turkish sultans to improve their virility according to Chaim. This could be no coincidence; he knew Ruth must want him as much as he wanted her. He put both hands on her narrow hips and held her firmly. Normally such a bold gesture would be unthinkable but these were not normal times.

"Ruth," he whispered.

She stopped working on his wound but did not try to step back from his strong but gentle grip. "Is the end close?" she asked, looking into his eyes which always became even more green at times of deep emotion.

"I believe so."

"Then hold me." He pulled her to him kissing her raven black hair as he did so.

"Do you love me Richard?" she asked starkly. He understood that she also sensed time consuming formalities must be dispensed with.

"Yes," he answered simply, "you already know I do." She looked up at him and their lips met. It seemed the most natural thing in the world, almost as if the decision was somehow out of their control. Richard lost all sense of time. That perverse human ability to find happiness in the midst of war and destruction reasserted itself yet again.

At last the kiss ended and Ruth, smiling as if they had a lifetime ahead together said, "If I must die today, I want to leave this world as a woman not a girl. There seems no point to have lived otherwise." Gently, Richard unstrapped her belt and removed the light chainmail surcoat. Then he unbuttoned her linen shirt and drew down the incongruous sailor trousers until she stood naked and beautiful before him. Her skin was a little darker than his pale English skin, and her breasts fuller than he had expected from such a slim frame. She showed no shyness and looked him straight in the eyes waiting for him. He unstrapped his heavy, mail hauberk and soon he too was naked, his tightly muscled body towering over hers. They kissed again, a passionate lovers' kiss, then lay down on some blankets to release weeks of pent up desire. Ruth, daughter of Chaim ben Issachar, would not meet her maker as a virgin.

Afterwards they slept in each other's arms, but only briefly, and when they awoke Richard guessed the truce was nearing its end. He whispered, "Ruth, I must return to the wall."

"Just a little longer my darling."

He did not need persuading and settled down under their grey blanket for a few precious minutes. "I hope I did not hurt you." He said.

She stroked his quiescent manhood, "You did a little the first time, but that was only to be expected. I did not think you would be so large, but after that it was wonderful. I hope I did not disappoint too much?"

"You were more beautiful than anything I could imagine."

"You still love me then?"

"Of course I love you."

Peter Tallon

"I have loved you ever since I first saw you," she said thoughtfully, "but both our faiths would condemn us for what we have just done. Yet all my instincts say it was right and proper."

Richard propped himself up on his elbow and smiled, "God would not have made men and women as they are if he did not intend them to make love. What we have done is to follow the nature he has created in us. It has harmed no-one." But as he uttered those last few words he thought of Mary. She would not have agreed. Her love and devotion for him had been ill rewarded, but at least she would never know, and he would be dead before the day was out anyway. He would have to plead extenuating circumstances if they met in the next world, but that presupposed he would get to Heaven which was, he thought, extremely unlikely.

Ruth saw the change in his eyes and sat up alarmed. "What is it? Have I done something wrong?"

He shook his head, "Of course not, I am just saddened by the parting that must shortly occur."

"God will forgive us. He will understand and we shall soon be together again in Heaven. I shall look forward to meeting your first wife." But not the second, he thought wryly; perhaps the other place will be more peaceful for me.

He reached over to his hauberk and felt in one of the side pockets. Then he drew out the jewel encrusted, gold necklace he had taken from the treasury on the way up from the floor below. "Take this," he said. "Under the circumstances I'm sure the Grand Master won't mind and de Beaujeu can't complain. War is unpredictable and it is possible you may survive the battle to come. The Turks may spare you and, if so, you must have some means of looking after yourself. I do not know its worth, but it must be many hundreds of ducats."

Ruth took the necklace, admired the ornate workmanship of woven gold into which large coloured stones were set, then handed it back to him. "Richard, I do not wish to become breeding material in a Turkish harem.

I would rather you end my life when the time comes. I know you will do it quickly and as painlessly as possible."

"I cannot do that. There is no such thing as a fate worse than death. Other captured women have survived and even flourished in Turkish society and, who knows, you might eventually be able to buy your freedom. Where there is life there must always be hope." He could see she was not persuaded. He placed the heavy, gold necklace over her head and let it rest round her shoulders. She flinched as the cold metal touched her flesh.

"It looks beautiful on you," he said. The bright yellow of the gold contrasted fascinatingly against the dark red of Ruth's nipples, still swollen from their lovemaking. He pulled her gently towards him and kissed both of them. Then they made love again.

The deadline for the end of the truce came and went. Back on the wall Mamoun spoke to the Grand Master. "Shall I go and call Captain Richard? The Turks could attack at any time."

The Grand Master's old, grey eyes glanced up at the donjon, then he shook his head sadly, "No, leave him be. A fleeting moment of happiness should not be judged too harshly. Richard will be here when we need him, you can count on that."

* * *

VI

Had Mustafa Akurgal known how few Templars were left, he would have come straight away but he could not afford another reverse. Even his bold Mamelukes were beginning to ask if Allah had decided against them. The next assault had to succeed so Mustafa decided to abandon a few vital hours and use the cover of night. The moon was only half full but still cast enough light to allow his warriors to avoid the man traps. This time Mustafa himself led them into battle.

There were no battle cries of Allah Akbar as they advanced through the killing ground, no exhortations to glory by their officers. Instead the Mamelukes advanced silently with cold determination to break the Christian resistance at last. They reached the moat unscathed. Mustafa nervously looked up at the massive battlements, which seemed to him in the moonlight like a row of huge, jagged teeth waiting to devour all who dared enter, but still no reaction came from the defenders as the scaling ladders were put into place. He was one of the first to climb over the battlements and onto the fighting platform where his men had come so close to victory earlier in the day. Now it was abandoned. For a fleeting moment Mustafa wondered if the Templars had somehow slipped away unnoticed, stealing his treasure from under his nose, but his fears were soon put to rest by one of his officers who pointed to the donjon.

"There is a light over there Blessed One. Shall we attack?"

"Yes, but first bring fire."

The Turks had captured the main body of the castle but it would not finally fall until the donjon was taken. Mustafa knew it would be a tough nut to crack. Although he diverted some of his men to begin searching the rest of the castle, he was certain the treasure would be held in the donjon. His best option would be to smoke the defenders out, but the use of fire would create enough light for those nasty little crossbow quarrels to find yet more targets before the siege ended. He said a short prayer to Allah, asking to be the first to wash his scimitar in Christian blood.

Richard watched the dark, stealthy shadows enter the courtyard with mixed feelings. He knew he had made the right decision to abandon the main wall, but having spilled so much blood defending it, he felt a sense of failure yielding it without a fight. But to remain there would have ensured disaster, for when the wall fell the defenders would inevitably have been split into isolated groups which the Turks could round up and finish off with ease. Now at least, the Templars were still united and fighting as a cohesive unit; the Turks would pay dearly for their victory.

As soon as the burning torches appeared, Henry gave the order to shoot. Pinpointing targets in the half-light was not easy, but the screams and groans which greeted the first volley confirmed that at least some of the quarrels had struck home. Richard had ordered the donjon door to be doused in water in anticipation of Mustafa's tactics, but as soon as the heaps of tinder and brushwood, which the Turks laid against it, caught fire his pre-emptive action caused little delay. Soon, grey wisps of smoke floated ominously up the winding stairs into the first floor of the donjon wrapping themselves round the Templars' ankles like sinister, ghostly vipers. Then the sound of cracking timber warned that the massive door would soon collapse and open the way for the Prophet's bloodthirsty hordes.

Triumphant shouts of "Allah Akbar" echoed round the donjon walls as the Turks began to scent victory at last. The Templars edged towards the stone stairs, ready to sell their lives dearly. Richard looked across the room at Ruth who saw him and smiled. Then he turned away for the last time and shouted, "Sergeant Hawkswood to me! Follow me down the stairs; we'll give those screaming bastards something to think about!"

Realising, at last, that even Captain Richard could not save them now, the Grand Master called out, "Be of good cheer my brothers! Christ is looking down upon us. We are doing his work and shall be in Paradise with him this very day!"

The exhortation was greeted with silence and Titus Scrope muttered, "Why does Christ make his work impossible to do? It's almost as if he wants us to fail."

"Perhaps," answered Mamoun sombrely, "we do the Devil's work, not God's."

The donjon's door fell inwards, dissolving into myriads of incandescent splinters which pulsated up the stairs in fiery clouds. Richard and Henry waited half way up and braced themselves for the final act. A minute passed, then another, but no Turks came. Perplexed, Richard looked at Henry but the Wiltshire sergeant just shrugged. Then suddenly they heard a single shout above the noise of the burning donjon door. Others soon followed but there was something different about them. For a moment there was confusion in the donjon, but then a vulgar Venetian oath reverberated round the courtyard heralding wild cheering and shouts of "Avante! Avante!"

Captain Dandolo had arrived!

CHAPTER NINE

It had been almost nine years since Hugh last saw Mary, but the woman who opened the door to him was even lovelier than he recalled. The short, trim figure and long fair hair reminded him of Annie Mullen, not that he needed reminding; he thought of her every day. The two month retreat at the French Franciscan priory had been restful, but it had done nothing to purge his love for Annie who would now be six months pregnant with his child. But as he stood on the doorstep of Richard's house in Rouen with a large parcel under his arm, he understood the wisdom of Father Anselm's advice which had taken him away from Calveley Hall before he sank into even deeper trouble.

"Father Hugh! What a wonderful surprise!" beamed Mary as she ushered him into her house. "This is so unexpected." She sat him in a chair in the front room reserved for important visitors and said, "It's past noon. Have you eaten yet?"

"I don't want to be any trouble…"

"Nonsense!" interrupted Mary. "Joan is playing with a friend but she'll be back soon. We can eat together then." She stopped talking and looked intently at the man who, nine years before, had played an important part in Richard's desperate gamble to save her from a heretic's death. "Is all well with you Hugh? You look different."

"How so?"

Peter Tallon

"Older and sadder, without that boyish bubble you used to have, if you see what I mean. Perhaps you are just tired after your journey?"

Mary's perception touched the spot in Hugh which started him talking. He talked and talked, telling her everything the way he had done with Father Anselm in the confessional. But telling Mary was different. Her adoration for Richard gave her a more direct understanding of how Hugh had got into his difficulties than Anselm could ever have.

Long before he had finished, Mary was sitting beside him holding his hand and whispering between sentences, "Poor boy, you poor boy." Although their ages were similar, there could have been a complete generation between them as Mary almost mothered the sad Franciscan. Her powerful, heartfelt sympathy brought tears to his eyes, and occasionally he was obliged to stop and gather himself before continuing lest he risk openly weeping in front of her.

When at last he came to the end Mary said, "Thank God for Father Anselm. It was he who brought Richard and me together, and now he has prevented our dearest friend from doing away with himself."

Hugh smiled sardonically, "I don't suppose I would have had the guts to do it anyway."

"Be that as it may, your arrival here is fortuitous. It also makes more sense of a letter I received from Tom Riches two days ago. In it he says that Cousin Geoffrey has applied to the courts for a hearing to put his case for the return of Calveley Hall to him. Tom does not say what the basis of the case is, he probably doesn't know, but it must surely relate to the validity of Geoffrey's father's first marriage."

Hugh replied, "We know Robert Calveley's first marriage to Blanche was genuine because four of us saw the marriage entry in the parish records, but at my recent meeting with Geoffrey he told me the record no longer exists."

"Then we must check. The marriage took place in Calais did it not? Tom Riches has asked to meet me to decide what we should do, but as you know I cannot risk returning to England where I am a convicted heretic and a fugitive from the law. I shall write back to Tom telling him to meet us both in Calais. He will need guidance; you may have to return with him and face whatever personal retribution awaits you in Suffolk."

Hugh always knew he would have to go back but he had hoped for a little more time so that local memories would be less fresh. But to allow Tom to handle complicated legal matters alone would have been unfair, so Hugh agreed. "I'm sure you're right Mary but the first thing we must do is check the Calais marriage register. Geoffrey may be bluffing."

Hugh picked up the large parcel he had brought with him and handed it to Mary. "Father Anselm sends you his best wishes and gives you this to remember him by."

Mary started to unwrap the parcel but as soon as she saw the red leather binding she knew what it was. Now it was her turn to weep, but with tears of joy. "The Lollard Bible!" she sobbed. "How did Anselm come by it?"

"After your trial he claimed it saying he needed to research the Lollard heresy in order to prepare good theological counter-arguments. In fact he believes the English prose is quite beautiful."

Mary held the book to her breast and said quietly, "Anselm knows what this means to me. Although there are no Lollards in France for me to worship with, he always understood and respected the strength with which I hold to Lollard beliefs, especially reading the Bible in English so all may hear the unedited words of Our Lord."

"There are many in the Catholic Church who would not disagree, at least amongst the lower ranks of the clergy."

"I will send a letter of thanks to Anselm and Tom can take it back to Dunwich after we meet him in Calais."

"I will go back with him," said Hugh. "Anselm is now almost blind so he will need someone to read your letter to him. He certainly won't want the present Prior of Dunwich reading it to him."

The back door of the house was flung open with a crash, and a moment later a pretty ten year old girl entered the room. The last time Hugh saw Joan, she had been a small child less than two years old. Despite her youth she was now almost as tall as Mary, and the large green eyes that looked at, or rather inspected him, were familiar.

"My word," said Hugh, "you're the very image of your father." He could have torn out his tongue for speaking without thinking. Obviously Joan could not resemble her stepmother, but Mary was the only mother she had known. He stammered, "Oh I did not mean, er -"

Mary quickly put him at ease. "That's all right Father Hugh. Joan knows that her blood mother went to Heaven when she was just an infant."

"But you are my mother now Maman," squeeked Joan as she put a long arm reassuringly around Mary's shoulders.

"I know dear. Do you remember Father Hugh?"

"No," answered Joan with the disarming frankness of her age.

"Father Hugh is your father's oldest friend," said Mary. "They have had many adventures together."

Mention of the friendship with her father created an immediate reaction in Joan. She quickly became more interested in the grey robed stranger. "Have you fought many battles against the Frenchies together?"

"Quite a few," replied Hugh casually. "I can tell you many stories about your father. He is a brave and noble man." The green eyes lit up. Hugh was accepted.

"But not too many war stories," warned Mary. "Joan has quite enough martial instincts already."

"Will you be staying with us long?" enquired Joan eagerly.

Hugh looked at Mary who said, "Joan and I would like you to remain here until the time comes to meet Tom in Calais unless you have more pressing matters."

"All that awaits me is a friar's cell in Dunwich, which is not a prospect I relish. I would be delighted to enjoy your kind hospitality and," he added for Joan's benefit, "I am sure I can recall at least once a day an adventure involving your father."

The letter from Tom Riches was not the only correspondence to reach Rouen from England during that chill early spring of 1424. Had Hugh arrived at Mary's home just a day earlier, he might never have reached Calais, let alone England, for while he was entering the city by the west gate, Henk de Groot was leaving by the south gate. The Fleming had received new orders from Geoffrey requiring him to abandon his watch over Richard's house and head southwards. But the chilling end to his orders read thus:

..... and when you have carried out my instructions, I want you to dispose of Father Hugh, the defrocked Franciscan who acts as my cousin's steward at Calveley Hall. This is not vital to my plans but will afford me personal satisfaction. I shall reward you generously when I have proof of his demise.

* * *

II

Seven weeks passed before the journey to Calais began, seven of the best weeks of Hugh's life. During this time he got to know Joan well. Although still tender in years, she had already developed her father's dry sense of humour and eagerness to learn. Mary was an excellent teacher and ensured Joan studied regularly, but there were new subjects such as philosophy and England's place in world history which Hugh could bring to widen the range of Joan's education. He kept well clear of religious matters because of Mary's Lollard background, but he felt that glorifying England was necessary to help Joan maintain her sense of nationality. After all, she had never visited her homeland since leaving it as a small child and her first language was French. Consequently her sympathies did not lean towards the English as much as Hugh would have liked. When he tried to explain why the great English king, Henry V invaded France, Joan had simply asked if the English had sought the views of the French before crossing the sea. Such ideas were dangerous.

But despite Joan's indifference towards the English cause, she devoured Hugh's stories about Richard's campaigns and adventures. As soon as her father was involved, she became an avid supporter of England, and at these times Hugh could not help but exaggerate a little until he was caught out when retelling the story of the battle outside Eu, in which he himself took part. Joan had smiled and asked innocently,

"Last time you said there were three hundred French at the battle; now you say five hundred. Had you been drinking church wine?"

Although Joan inevitably acquired many of Mary's assertive opinions and attitudes, there were moments when Hugh saw a quiet grace about her, a natural noblesse as the French would call it, which neither Mary nor Richard possessed. At these times Hugh felt sure he was looking at the hereditary influence of Ann Calveley. He had never met her, and Richard seldom mentioned her, but when he did it was with barely restrained passion. Hugh occasionally wondered if Mary realised how much her husband still loved his first wife, but whether she did or not, there could be no doubting how much she loved him. If Annie Mullen had displayed the same single minded devotion towards me, he thought, I might have abandoned the Church and started a new life with her. But then a voice would surface from his subconscious mind saying, such devotion must be earned. What did you do to deserve it? And have you already forgotten about her fearsome husband, big Will Mullen?

Mary and Hugh met Tom Riches at the Gloucester Tavern in Calais on the twelfth day of June. Calais was full of establishments with English names but the town remained determinedly French. Joan had elected to stay in Rouen with friends rather than travel to Calais, for summer came early that year and it was already unseasonably hot.

As the three travellers sat in the tavern watching the stallholders in the market place setting up their wares for the day, Tom outlined how much progress Geoffrey had already made. "He has convinced the Justice of the King's Peace that he has a viable case. The date for the hearing has been set for the second day of August. Geoffrey is claiming that his father, Robert, never actually married Blanche and so his marriage to Maude in 1477 was not bigamous. This would legitimise Geoffrey and so Robert's estate would revert to him."

"What about the record of the first marriage?" asked Mary.

"Geoffrey says that if it ever existed it must have been a forgery," said Tom, "and of the witnesses who claim to have seen it, Sir Thomas Erpingham's memory has long gone, Captain Richard is an interested party and you Father Hugh…" Tom hesitated.

Hugh sighed, "Do not spare my blushes Tom. Tell me what is being said."

"Well Geoffrey is putting it about that you are a lecher and a liar, so any evidence you may give cannot be believed. There is certainly much ill feeling towards you in East Suffolk Father Hugh."

"I shall nevertheless return with you and face whatever comes my way. It is the least I can do."

Tom looked doubtful. "It may not be safe Father."

"I must take that chance. You cannot be expected to fight a legal battle alone Tom."

"Then it would seem," said Mary, "that if the marriage record no longer exists, much will depend on Sir John Fastolf as the only credible witness to its existence."

"I assume he is with the army?" asked Tom.

Hugh nodded, "Yes, somewhere southwest of Rouen. You will not have heard that the French have been joined by a large Scottish army north of the Loire. The Duke of Bedford is scraping together every man he can so he is hardly likely to allow one of his best commanders to leave at such a critical time in order to appear as a witness in some obscure legal hearing in Suffolk. Much will depend on the attitude of the magistrate. I would not rule out the possibility that he may be corrupted, or at least influenced, by Geoffrey who is a magistrate himself."

"That would be typical," agreed Mary, "but surely even a corrupt magistrate would not dare to order Calveley Hall to change hands without Sir John's evidence?"

Hugh rubbed his chin thoughtfully as he recalled his last meeting with Geoffrey. One thing was certain; Geoffrey would have anticipated any weakness in his case and done something about it. "We cannot count on the good will of a magistrate," mused Hugh. "It might be argued that we have had plenty of time to gather our evidence, wherever it must be sought. At the very least we should obtain a sworn affidavit from Sir John saying that he saw the entry in the marriage register, but that will mean we must travel to the army in time of war."

"I could find a reliable person for that task," said Mary confidently. "I have many French friends in Rouen who can pass through the countryside in greater safety than an English traveller."

The church bell of Our Lady of Calais chimed nine o'clock and the shops that lined the market square began opening their doors for another busy day's trading.

"Mary, let us hope visiting the army will prove unnecessary," said Hugh finally. "If the marriage record still exists in the parish register then Geoffrey's case falls apart. The parish priest should be up and about in his church by now. I hope he'll be more co-operative than the objectionable creature who was there last time I was here."

Father Chadwick was far from objectionable. On the contrary, he was delighted to receive any visitors, for such occasions were rare events in his lonely life in Calais. He had to admit to a slight feeling of disappointment when he discovered that his three visitors had not come seeking spiritual guidance, but that was more than compensated because one of them was a beautiful, fair haired lady of great intelligence and another was a Franciscan friar, an Order that Father Chadwick had long admired.

"So you wish to see the marriage register for 1375," he said, trying to make the visit to his little presbytery last as long as possible. "Well that should be easy enough." He led his visitors to the small store room that adjoined the presbytery, pulled out the heavy, calf skin register for 1375, and handed it to Hugh.

The Franciscan sat down at a desk beneath a small window and opened the register. "I do not remember the exact date of the marriage but I know it was in May," he said as he carefully turned the yellowed pages. The others crowded round him as he ran his forefinger down the May pages; there were many entries because May was always a popular month for marriages. He reached the eleventh of May at the bottom of the left hand page, but when he looked at the right hand page, it began with the eighth of June; there was a gap of almost a month. On close inspection, the edge of the lost page could just be seen where it had been neatly cut away close to the binding.

Hugh sighed, "So Geoffrey is not bluffing. The page covering the critical date has been taken." He turned to Father Chadwick. "Can you recall this ledger being removed or looked at by anyone last year? If so can you describe that person?"

Chadwick shook his head. "I have been parish priest here for eighteen months, and in that time no-one has asked….." his voice trailed away and his eyes lit up. "But I can at least tell you when the page was stolen. Last summer someone broke into the presbytery by smashing the door to splinters while I was out. Although I searched and searched, nothing seemed to be missing, but now I'll warrant we have found the reason for that mysterious crime."

Mary looked up from the damaged ledger. "So it is as we thought. Our case stands or falls on Sir John Fastolf."

"Aye," agreed Tom. "It looks like a journey to the army will be needed after all. Sir John is the only witness left who the magistrate will listen to. Everyone else is dead, infirm or discredited."

A depressed silence settled upon the little gathering as Father Chadwick returned the ledger to its place. Anxious to be helpful, he led them back to the presbytery and asked, "Is there no-one else who can help you? Someone you may have overlooked?"

"I regret not," answered Hugh. "As Tom says, the other witnesses in our case cannot be used unless -" he suddenly stopped. The others looked at him as the hint of a smile brushed across his lips.

Mary touched his arm. "What is it Hugh?"

"It's just possible that Father Chadwick has stumbled upon something we've all forgotten; the most obvious witness of all." He turned once again to Chadwick who was becoming more confused by the second. "Father, when I was here nine years ago a certain Blanche Calveley resided in the convent next to this church. We were told she was old and frail and too ill to make a journey to England. I suppose she would be about eighty now if she still lives. Is that possible?"

Chadwick beamed, "Blanche is still with us. Is she relevant to your quest?"

"Not so much relevant as vital," answered Hugh. "May we see her?"

The parish priest shuddered; he avoided Sister Blanche as much as possible. She was a full generation older than the other nuns in the convent and lived in self-imposed, brooding isolation from her companions. She had a particular dislike for men, which tended to be reserved for poor Chadwick who, as parish priest, was obliged to visit her occasionally. "Is it really necessary?" he asked hesitantly.

The other three answered as one, "Yes!"

The Convent of Our Lady was a modest, single storeyed building located in a corner of the church compound. The mother superior, a buxom, red faced woman of about forty, who seemed to Hugh more like a barmaid than a nun, greeted the young parish priest with a less than platonic smile,

"John! How good to see you!" She gripped the slim priest in her beefy arms and kissed him on both cheeks. Then releasing him, her brow furrowed as she noticed Mary. "Have you brought me a new recruit John?"

"I'm afraid not Mother Superior, I am here on secular business. My companions wish to see Sister Blanche."

"Sister Blanche! They're welcome to her. I cannot imagine anyone wanting to see that miserable -"

"Mother Superior!" interrupted Chadwick before the expletive could be uttered.

"Well you know what she's like John. Your friends would be doing us all a favour if they take that miserable cow away with them."

"I must charge you to control your tongue," said the embarrassed priest.

The large mother superior suddenly became kitten-like before Chadwick's masterful order. She almost fluttered her pale, ginger eyelashes as she cooed, "Oh John, what would we do without your strong leadership. I hope you will hear my confession before you go. I've been having trouble with carnal thoughts."

"Not again," muttered Chadwick under his breath as they entered the convent.

The mother superior waddled officiously in front of her visitors and opened the door to the convent reception room. The plain white walls and small windows reminded Hugh of Dunwich Priory, and he reflected grimly that his own future lay in the monastic estate.

"Wait here," said the nun, "and I will bring Sister Blanche to you." She soon returned accompanied by a small, stooped figure whose black nun's raiment hung upon her like a shroud. The mother superior tried to steady the small nun as she slowly and stiffly lowered herself down onto a hard, wooden chair but the help was ungraciously waved away. Yet Hugh could see at once that though the body was frail, the mind was still alert. Small, dark, insect-like eyes scanned the visitors with predatory interest, and the thin lips curled scornfully when she saw Hugh's grey Franciscan robes. For a moment the face, old and yellow though it was, seemed familiar to Hugh but he was certain he could not have met this woman before.

"That will be all Mother Superior," said Chadwick. "I shall call for you when we have finished."

"Very well John, but you can see that Sister Blanche is advanced in years and tires easily so do not detain her long, bless her." She scowled at the old nun and left the room.

Chadwick opened the interview. "Sister Blanche, my companions have travelled far to see you concerning an important legal matter in England. There is every possibility that a miscarriage of justice is about to occur, but you may have the knowledge to prevent this happening." The dark, spider eyes remained unmoved, so the parish priest contented himself with introducing the other three and then handed over the interview to Hugh.

The Franciscan quickly outlined the essence of the case and ended by saying, "I apologise if I have reopened old wounds, but I am sure you can see that your marriage to Robert Calveley is central to the matter. If you would dictate to me a statement confirming when and where the marriage took place, and Father Chadwick countersigns it as an independent witness to your words, Richard Calveley will retain his property and Geoffrey's shameless attempt to take it from him will be foiled."

Throughout Hugh's account of the case, Sister Blanche remained silent, giving no hint of what she was feeling as the subject of her humiliation by Geoffrey's father was brought up again after so many years. Robert, a fine looking English warrior, had swept her off her feet but he very quickly tired of married life and deserted her after only two years; a common enough story in wartime. She had been considered quite fair when she was young, but almost half a century enclosed in a convent had turned her into a shrivelled, bitter old woman. Even her own father was no support after Robert abandoned her; all he did was complain of the extra mouth to feed and pack her off to a nunnery when he realised he would never recover the dowry from the spendthrift Robert.

Blanche spoke at last, her voice crackling like the snap of dried out twigs. "Tell me more of this Geoffrey."

The question surprised Hugh, who was eager to get on with the statement, but such a vital witness would have to be humoured if needs be. "Geoffrey Calveley, Robert's son by his bigamous wife, has risen to high office in the county of Suffolk and through marriage has acquired an estate north of Ipswich called Eastwell Hall."

"Just like his father," said Blanche. "Does he have children?"

"Yes, he has a son."

"And what is your interest in all this? Why should it concern a grey friar?"

Again Hugh was disconcerted by the directness of Blanche's question. He gathered his thoughts before answering. "I am Richard Calveley's steward."

"Ah, I see." The tight lips widened into a smile of contempt which revealed a few long, yellow teeth. "You are here on behalf of your employer?"

"Yes."

"And if Geoffrey was your employer you would no doubt be saying similar malicious things about Richard."

Hugh bristled at the insult to his integrity. "No, Geoffrey has already asked me to work for him but I refused."

"How noble of you; did he not offer enough?"

Mary, usually so calm and thoughtful, found herself intervening on the hapless Hugh's behalf. The Franciscan did not know how to respond, but there are some things women may say to each other that cannot be uttered by men. "Because you failed to keep your husband you believe that all men are of similar ilk to Robert Calveley. My husband is made of sterner mettle and so is this Franciscan. If you will not help us just say so and we will leave now."

Blanche raised two thin eyebrows and smiled her scornful smile once more. "Your passion does you credit my dear, though whether it is genuine or contrived I cannot tell. I have already decided I shall not write the statement you require. Instead I will come to England with you and testify in person that I married Robert Calveley. I have often wondered what my husband's homeland is like. After a lifetime in a convent I think I am entitled to a little freedom before I die. Do you not agree?"

This was far more than could have been hoped for. Hugh looked at Chadwick. "Would the mother superior object?"

"I think she'd be delighted."

"Tell me about the second wife," ordered Sister Blanche, "the bigamous one."

Hugh replied, "She married Robert in 1377. Maud was given a good dowry by her father because she was no beauty, but Robert must already have plucked her virgin flower because Geoffrey arrived less than three months after the wedding. It surprised everyone because Maud managed to conceal her pregnancy so well."

"Where did the birth take place?" asked Blanche.

"I am not sure but certainly not in Suffolk. Such things, you understand, must happen far away from home to minimise the shame."

"Naturally," agreed Blanche, "though bigamy is a far greater shame. When do we leave?"

Once again Hugh steeled himself to look into those dark, venomous eyes. He wondered what sort of witness this embittered nun would make, but surely her evidence would be sufficient in itself no matter how it was delivered? But deep down in his soul he felt disturbed. He had thought the opportunity for revenge would have appealed to Blanche, but instead of gratitude he sensed only mockery.

"We will depart as soon as you are ready," he answered, but even now he was beginning to wonder if a simple written statement duly witnessed by Chadwick would not be better after all. He decided that an urgent message should still be sent to Fastolf requesting the affidavit confirming the one-time existence of Robert Calveley's marriage record. It was best to be doubly sure.

* * *

III

In the twilight gloom, Henk de Groot stood as near to Fastolf's tent as he dared. He had shadowed the English commander ever since the Burgundian forces joined the Duke of Bedford's army on the Le Mans road. Military life was not to de Groot's taste, but as a Fleming he was a subject of the Duke of Burgundy and entitled to enlist under the Burgundian banner. Anyway, he consoled himself, it would not be for long but just until he had carried out Geoffrey's orders. After that he had promised himself a little treat. All those months of watching Richard's family had created a hunger in his loins which only Mary Calveley could quench. After Fastolf was dealt with, de Groot had determined to return to Rouen and have his will of her before beginning the search for the Franciscan who his master was so eager to have murdered.

But first he would be obliged to undergo the hazard of a pitched battle. The Franco-Scottish army was known to be marching north towards

Normandy in great strength; the rumour was nearly twenty thousand of them. Fastolf was constantly attended by captains and squires, which prevented de Groot from getting near him, so the Fleming had reluctantly concluded that his evil strike would have to wait until the clash with the enemy, for it was well known that many old scores were settled in the confusion of battle. Fastolf, like all the English commanders, led from the front. He would be in the thick of the fighting where a swift and deadly dagger thrust from behind ought to go unnoticed. After that, de Groot could easily drift away and depart from the scene before the battle was over.

The Fleming's silent scheming was interrupted by a French voice calling out for Sir John Fastolf. De Groot quickly intercepted the Frenchman and said in his heavily accented French, "I know the location of Sir John's tent. I will take you to him, but I hope you are not going to disturb him unless your business is urgent. He is a very busy man."

The Frenchman, a young page in service to one of Mary's friends, said, "I bring a personal message from Rouen of utmost importance."

"Then give it to me and I will take it to him."

"It must be delivered by word of mouth."

"What is it about?"

"A private matter."

De Groot at once sensed danger. Had his wicked mission been discovered? Could this be a warning to Fastolf about the threat from within his own ranks? He could not afford the risk. His voice became silky. "Very well, follow me and I shall take you to Sir John."

He led the page away from Fastolf's tent and into a thicket which separated the English from the Burgundian division. The page hesitated. "Where are we going? I was told Sir John's tent is close by."

"And so it is; well fairly close. The track we are following is a short cut."

The page died without a sound. De Groot wiped his dagger and quickly hid the body in the undergrowth. The message, whatever it might have been, was never delivered.

But Sir John was proving even more difficult to dispatch than de Groot anticipated, for next morning the Duke of Bedford made a decision which was criticised by some of his own commanders. In the face of the superior Franco-Scottish army, which was now closing rapidly on his little force, Bedford sent the Burgundian division away on the road to Picardy. The duke had never hidden his distrust of his allies and decided he would rather face the enemy with a smaller, but homogenous English army. Naturally, the frustrated de Groot deserted the Duke of Burgundy's force before the day was out. He would have to think of something else.

CHAPTER TEN

Loredan sat low in the water as her bow wave cut through the calm, blue sea. The weight of de Beaujeu's treasure far exceeded that of the fourteen Templars who had been interred within the walls of Pilgrim's Castle. Richard leaned against the stern companion rail watching the castle's grey walls getting smaller in the evening sun as the ship sped westwards to the steady beat of the bosun's drum. It seemed an age since that last desperate stand in the donjon but it was in fact only a single day. The fortuitous intervention of Captain Dandolo and his crew had saved their skins. One hundred and fifty burly Venetian sailors arriving under cover of darkness had surprised the Turks and turned the tide. The assault collapsed. This time Akurgal knew he had lost and resigned himself to waiting for the Governor of Jerusalem's men before engaging in further fighting with the Christian devils.

The suspension of the siege provided just enough time to load de Beaujeu's treasure on to *Loredan* whose hold was packed to the brim with heavy boxes and caskets. The Templars lay on the bow deck sleeping the sleep of the exhausted, but although he too was tired, Richard was still too exhilarated to sleep.

Captain Dandolo came to join him carrying two large goblets of Tuscan wine. He handed one to the Englishman. "Richard, have you the energy left to tell me what happened while we were away? All your comrades sleep now. Tell me nothing yet."

"Of course Captain. It's a story that will be told and retold in years to come. I have no doubt of that."

By the time Richard finished, the sun had dipped below the horizon and the clear, western sky was a pastiche of purple, pink and gold. Apart from the all too brief moments alone with Ruth, he had told Dandolo everything, for the ship's crew already knew the nature of their cargo.

"And what about you Captain?" asked Richard. "How did you manage to refit your ship and return in only three weeks? An hour or two longer and we would have been crow's meat."

Dandolo drained his goblet and smiled. "I, how you say, use stick and carrot; plenty stick, not much carrot. Those Cypriot dockers only work hard if they want to, and our Jewish owner give me no peace because he is frightened for his beautiful daughter. I too plenty worried so we work day and night until *Loredan* as good as new."

Richard felt a breath of warm evening wind brush his cheek. "I am sure the Grand Master will generously reward the efforts of you and your crew. He is a changed man. The discovery of the Templar legacy seems to have melted the ice in his veins."

The wind began to freshen and Dandolo looked up at a group of woolly clouds scudding across the sky. "We shall hoist sail now and the rowers can rest. Is a beautiful evening, no?"

"It is indeed," agreed Richard. "Tell me Captain, will *Loredan* be slowed down by the weight of the Templar treasure aboard?"

"Under sail alone, yes, but when we row she will be even faster. Extra weight means she is lower in water which makes rowing more efficient. Each time oars enter water, oar blades are fully submerged so all power from oarsmen is transferred direct back to ship. In normal Mediterranean swell, a few blades are only partially submerged at each sweep, so some rowers' effort is wasted. If we have to fight, *Loredan* will be better than ever."

"I see. Are you expecting a battle Captain?"

"I no think so. Anyway, we avoid battle until our mission is complete and treasure safely unloaded in Venice."

"Good, I've seen quite enough fighting just lately. I'm feeling tired now so I think I shall retire."

"Not just yet I think. Someone wish to speak with you." Chaim had just emerged from the quarter deck cabins and was walking unsteadily towards them. He wished Dandolo a friendly good evening as the captain went forward to order the hoisting of the sail, and came to stand beside Richard. This was the moment the Englishman had been hoping to avoid because he knew he would be questioned about Ruth.

"Hello my dear." The greeting was friendly enough, but what had Ruth told her father? She was no liar but the truth, if it came out, would end his friendship with Chaim.

Richard said, "Good evening Chaim. I was just about to retire."

"Of course my dear, you must be exhausted, but perhaps we could have a quick word before you do."

"Very well then," agreed Richard reluctantly.

"Good, good. First I want you to know that I attach no blame to you for Ruth's irresponsible behaviour."

What does he mean by that, wondered Richard. Clearly Chaim was expecting a response.

"She acquitted herself remarkably well," he replied, deliberately trying to divert the conversation. "She is a fine shot with a crossbow."

"Yes, yes, but I am referring to her disobedience to her father. I know you sent her back to the ship and that she secretly returned to the castle without your knowledge. She has told me everything." Please God not everything, thought Richard. "But," continued Chaim, "there is a matter upon which you could put my mind at rest if you would."

"Of course, if I can."

"I know my daughter well; we are very close. The loss of my beloved wife was a tragedy for us both, but it brought us even closer together than before, which is why I understand Ruth and she understands me. Since she left Pilgrim's Castle I have noticed a change in her."

"What sort of change?" asked Richard nervously.

"It is difficult to be exact, but I feel she is more distant from me. The tight bond between us seems to have been broken. It's not that she has said anything in particular to make me think this way, far from it, but I sense it through instinct rather than logic. It's as if my daughter has suddenly changed from a girl into a woman."

"Chaim, Ruth has been a woman for some time now. Only a father would not see that."

"Yes, I know. I suppose I should not expect you to understand. Your daughter is still a child."

Richard was now sure of the direction in which the conversation was heading and once again tried to divert it. "There is something Ruth may not have told you Chaim. She took an active and valuable part in the fighting. She saw things a woman should never see, guts spilling out from stomachs, brains splattered across battlements, blood flowing in rivers, yet she bravely stood her ground and stared into the jaws of death like the rest of us. We all believed we were done for just before *Loredan* arrived. Most important of all, she went against her womanly instincts by killing the enemy. Can you not see that the terrible experience she has just gone through would change anyone? She may be undergoing delayed shock which is something inexperienced warriors often succumb to after their first engagement. Have no fear, it will pass. Just give her a little time and be proud of her as we all are."

Chaim did not answer for a while. He thought about Richard's response and, though it brought him some comfort, it still did not answer the question that was burning up inside him. "Richard," he said quietly, "what you say makes sound sense of course, and it was selfish of me not to appreciate the effect the fighting would have on my daughter, but I must know. Is Ruth still entire?"

"Entire?"

"Has she been touched by a man?" The question was out at last. Richard wondered how he should respond. Should he be shocked, angry, or even indifferent? What had Ruth said, if anything? The only thing he had no doubt about was the truth; it must remain concealed.

"Have you asked her?" he asked.

"No, how can I? Surely Richard you would know if anything has happened?"

"Not necessarily. Of course I watched over her all the time I was with her but that was only when the fighting began. I hardly saw her before then. I think you should have faith in her. She is honourable as well as beautiful and has gained the admiration of us all. The fact that you will not ask her suggests to me that you are ashamed of your suspicions."

Chaim nodded sadly, "I am, I am. I know it is unworthy but if she has been touched, no-one will marry her."

Richard laughed humourlessly, "Anyone would marry Ruth."

"I meant no Jewish man would, at least no-one worthy of her."

Richard decided the conversation had gone on long enough. "Listen Chaim, if you have real reason to worry then speak to Ruth, if not then keep your suspicions to yourself. I will not act as a mediator between father and daughter. I am tired and need sleep now so I'll bid you goodnight."

Chaim watched him as he walked towards the foredeck and whispered bitterly to himself, "It was you Richard. I know it had to be you!"

* * *

II

On the twenty ninth day of March, *Loredan* rowed into the fortress harbour of Nauplion once more. It had been a cold winter in Greece and a mantle of snow covered the crags upon which the great fortress sat glowering over the Gulf of Argos like a gigantic, dark vulture. A chilly offshore breeze whipped the grey sea up into choppy waves which had forced Dandolo to reef the ship's sails and rely upon his oarsmen all morning. Now, as they passed through the short strait between the island of Bourzi and the mainland, which marked the entrance to the sheltered anchorage, the oarsmen knew their efforts would shortly come to an end for a while, and the pleasures of the port would be theirs.

The return journey from Pilgrim's Castle had passed uneventfully thanks to unseasonably good weather. The spirit of good cheer remained with the Grand Master; he had permitted his six Cypriot Templars, including Mamoun, to disembark at Nicosia and spend time with their families with instructions to rejoin the Order in France at Michaelmass. He had even provided them with a generous grant in Venetian ducats from de Beaujeu's treasury. Now there remained only sixteen Templars aboard *Loredan,* including Titus Scrope and the half blinded de Graveson.

As well as numerous small craft sheltering from the blustery wind, there was another, sleek Venetian war galley anchored offshore. It was similar in appearance to *Loredan* except that it did not boast the sumptuous stern quarters that Chaim had financed, nor did it possess cannon fore and aft.

"I wonder what *Sanudo* is doing here," said Dandolo who suddenly appeared at Richard's side. "She is one of the doge's own ships which he uses for personal rather than state business."

Richard pointed to a broad beamed barge which had just cast off from the shore and was rowing towards them. "I expect we shall soon know Captain."

Despite all his efforts, Richard had been unable to speak to Ruth alone during the voyage. Chaim closely chaperoned her whenever she left her quarters to take the air, never leaving her side until she returned to her cabin. Richard now sensed a change in Chaim's attitude towards him and guessed his erstwhile friend strongly suspected the truth. Whenever Richard tried to engage them in conversation, Chaim was polite but cool and gave Ruth no chance to speak freely. Apart from secret looks and smiles, the lovers remained frustratingly separated. The journey back to Venice was now three quarters done but Richard was determined to find an opportunity to be alone with Ruth before the end; perhaps a little time ashore in Nauplion might provide his chance.

The white robed figure in the rear of the barge waved an acknowledgement to Dandolo as a hemp ladder was thrown down to enable the Dominican to climb aboard. Despite his unsuitable clothing, Father Cavalli made light work of the ascent and presented himself to the captain. They spoke quickly in Italian so Richard was unable to follow the conversation but, from the number of times 'benissimo' was uttered by the priest, he knew they must be discussing the wealth that lay in *Loredan's* hold. But then the atmosphere suddenly changed. Dandolo began to shake his head, vehemently objecting to what was being said. Eventually, after much gesticulation and raised voices, the captain stormed into his cabin abandoning Cavalli in mid-sentence. The Dominican seemed untroubled by the outburst and glanced round the deck, but the crew studiously avoided his reptilian eyes. At last he saw Richard, smiled coldly, then climbed back down to the barge.

The silence Cavalli left behind him endured until the barge was almost half way back to dry land and even then, the normally garrulous mariners spoke only in hushed voices. Richard walked aft to see the captain in his quarters.

On his way he was joined by the Grand Master. "That Dominican must have brought ill tidings. I have never seen our captain so agitated."

"He has the same effect as a stoat in a rabbit warren," agreed Richard. "Everyone freezes until he slithers away."

They found Dandolo angrily pacing up and down in his little cabin.

"Can we be of assistance Captain?" asked the Grand Master.

"Is nothing can be done! Sit down, I explain." Richard and the Grand Master sat on some oak chests and, after a last angry glare through the cabin window at Cavalli's barge, the captain sat down too. "You know already that the Dominican is Doge Foscari's creature," he began. "Well that mean he has doge's authority when he travel as his emissary. Of course Cavalli plenty pleased when I tell him our mission is successful, but then he order me and all crew to stay aboard the ship to prevent news of the treasure spreading. This I no like but I understand, but then he say we must wait in Nauplion two days for some Dalmatian hostages to be brought here. We must then transport hostages to Venice where they will be kept for assurance of good behaviour of their people, who are all pirates."

"Two days!" exclaimed the Grand Master. "But what about the other ship? Can that not do the job instead?"

"Is exactly what I say to Cavalli," exclaimed Dandolo. "*Sanudo's* crew can go ashore so waiting two days no big problem for them. My crew stay here in sight of Nauplion after nearly a month at sea. Is unfair and bad for morale. I tell Cavalli I shall visit *Sanudo* and ask Captain Morsini, who I know well, if he will transport hostages. Morsini is good captain. His family and mine are allies through marriage. But then Cavalli say Morsini no longer captain of *Sanudo,* he replaced by Captain Spatafora." Dandolo spat on the floor with contempt. "Spatafora is bastard son of Sicilian upstart. His family little better than pirates. They support Foscari." He spat again. "I plenty worry about this. If Morsini removed from *Sanudo* by Foscari, then it cannot be long before Dandolo removed from *Loredan.*"

"Captain," said the Grand Master with a generous smile that still surprised Richard each time he saw it, "you have done so much for us, there is something that the Order of Knights Templar can do for you. When we return to Venice I will ensure that the ownership of *Loredan* is transferred to you or, failing that, I will purchase an equivalent ship for you. It is the least we can do to show our gratitude."

Dandolo was taken aback. He stood up, his warm, brown eyes moistening and looked once more out of the cabin window. "Is too much," he said quietly. "Every captain dream of owning a ship one day, but most never do. You offer too much. I no deserve such gift."

The Grand Master smiled again, "I am sure Captain Richard would agree it's the very least you deserve. You will become a true merchant captain deciding what commissions you take and how much to charge. You shall come and go wherever and whenever you please, and at least you will be far beyond Foscari's malice."

Those last few words were soon to be proven dramatically wrong.

* * *

III

In the end *Loredan* was forced to linger in Nauplion for five days during which time *Sanudo* and Captain Spatafora set sail on their own mission. When the Dalmatian hostages at last arrived, both Richard and Dandolo felt an immediate sense of unease. They were certainly fine looking people, tall, lean and aquiline but they were all young men. Usually hostages consisted of entire family units so that life in the host country could continue as near normal as possible.

There were twelve hostages in all, every one of them a natural warrior, so Dandolo personally checked the chains that linked them together, much to the annoyance of Cavalli's agent, an Argive Greek who had been sent to accompany them. The Greek was the opposite of his charges. Short, fat and profusely hairy, he reminded Richard of an African ape he had once seen in a travelling fair in Norwich. He wore a dirty, brigandine jacket which had probably not been removed all winter, and a broad, black belt from which the keys to the chains that bound the hostages hung. The Greek oozed menace and Richard determined never to show him his back.

At first the homeward journey began well. *Loredan* soon rounded the mainland of Greece, and after only ten days left Corfu in her wake, but when she entered the Adriatic Sea, keeping well clear of the Dalmatian coast, the Fates deserted her. The change of fortune began innocuously enough on the morning of the fourteenth day of April when the lookout hailed the deck from his lofty perch. Everyone strained their eyes northwards and soon a small, grey speck became visible on the horizon in front of them.

"What do you think?" said Henry who stood beside Richard close to the bow companion rail.

"Too early to say, but friend or foe it is only one ship, so I doubt *Loredan* has anything to worry about."

But it was not as simple as Richard thought because the ship, which seemed to be sailing on the same course as *Loredan,* increased its speed so that the gap between the ships failed to diminish. This aroused Dandolo's curiosity. He ordered the oars to be run out and rowed at three quarter speed for an hour. At first the gap narrowed a little, but then the other ship responded and the distance separating them remained constant once more.

Henry scratched his head. "That ship must be quick if it can keep pace with ours so easily. It seems to be shadowing us."

That feeling of unease, which Richard felt when he first saw the Dalmatian hostages, returned. Although the Adriatic Sea was said to be Venice's back yard, it was nonetheless infested with pirates who would spring out from any one of thousands of small islands which provided sheltered anchorages close to the Dalmatian coast, and attack helpless merchant ships.

"Henry, I shall go aft to the helm and speak to the captain," said Richard. "I am beginning to think the pirates might be returning to take back their hostages."

Richard's idea was quickly dismissed by the experienced Dandolo who explained, "Is no pirate Richard. The only ship that can match *Loredan* for speed is a large war galley. There is no pirate vessel like that. I believe that ship must be *Sanudo,* but I no understand why Spatafora play this stupid game. Cavalli and Foscari are behind it I think."

"Perhaps Spatafora just wants to race us?" suggested Richard, but Dandolo's only reply was a non-committal shrug. Seconds later the lookout hailed the deck again and pointed to the northeast.

Dandolo smiled grimly, "More sail approaching from direction of pirate lairs. Maybe now we find out why Spatafora play game of, how you say, mouse and cat with us."

Five ships appeared on *Loredan's* starboard bow closing fast under full sail. They were a motley collection, all lateen rigged with dirty, patched sails and no flags of identification, but they held their line abreast formation with remarkable discipline. Richard guessed, even before Dandolo ordered the crew to battle stations, that he was looking at Dalmatian pirates. He said, "Captain, I shall go forward to join the Templars. Five to one are formidable odds."

Dandolo looked up at the pennant fluttering from the main mast, which indicated a gentle but steady breeze from the starboard quarter. Then he looked at Richard with the light of battle in his eyes. "Not when you consider the quality of ships. And Spatafora, he see what is happening. The odds are five pirate tubs against two Venetian war galleys. Is nothing to fear. Even five to one is not bad odds. Is not like land battle. *Loredan* can keep pirates at distance using superior speed, bombard them with cannon and, if things look bad, can always turn and run. I shall hold off and sweep round front of enemy. Then I shall use cannon while we wait for *Sanudo,* but we must keep out of crossbow range. When Spatafora join us we give Dalmatian barbarians a lesson in the Venetian seamanship."

When Richard returned to the foredeck the Templars were putting on their chainmail hauberks ready for battle. As he lifted his own to slip it over his head, he felt the weight; at least fifty pounds, and looked at the blue green sea all around him. If something were to go wrong it might not be possible to shed the hauberk quickly and no man, however strong, could float with it on. He decided to trust to sword and shield alone and, when he rejoined Henry, he noticed that his sergeant had come to the same conclusion.

"I see you are playing safe too Captain," said Henry as he sharpened the edge of his blade on a whetstone.

"Aye Henry, I don't fancy being dragged to the bottom of the Adriatic by a hauberk, but Captain Dandolo seems confident enough. He reckons he can win the fight using cannon alone."

The pirates were closing rapidly from the northeast borne forward by the stiff easterly breeze. All had run out their oars to add to their speed and Richard estimated that if *Loredan* kept to her present course, she would meet the most westerly of the five ships in less than half an hour. But the wind was perfectly placed for *Loredan,* and Dandolo had plenty more speed to draw on if he wished because he was still only using sail power. As the ships drew closer, Richard was thankful the captain had decided to avoid close quarter work until *Sanudo* arrived because the pirates had crammed their vessels full of men. Although much smaller than *Loredan,* each pirate ship's complement seemed to contain at least as many men as Dandolo's crew. The middle ship of the five was larger than the rest, and to judge from the signals coming from it, was the pirate commander's vessel. It had the sleek lines of a small war galley, a daughter of *Loredan*; its capture must have cost the pirates dear.

The angle of the converging courses brought the westernmost ship into cannon range first. The Templars stood well back as the Venetian artillery men prepared the squat, evil looking black tube to fire a stone ball about two feet in diameter. If it found its target, the impact would be unimaginable. After interminable squinting along sights and lever adjusting, the bombardier ordered a slow match to be applied to the black powder in the touch hole. Everyone put their hands to their ears but the roar was still deafening. The whole ship shuddered under the recoil, but a few seconds later a sigh of disappointment went up as a huge spout of water appeared about fifty paces behind the pirate vessel.

By the time the cannon was ready to fire again, the gap between the ships had narrowed to about four hundred yards. Blood curdling yells and threats could easily be heard drifting on the wind towards Dandolo's ship. Richard picked up his crossbow to prepare for action but after the next discharge of the cannon he put it down again. This time there was no waterspout. Everyone stared at the pirate ship looking for evidence of the strike. It was not long in coming. First the rhythm of the oars on the starboard side collapsed into a tangle of confused, crabbing splashes and the ship began to slew beam on to *Loredan*. The single mast teetered for a moment as the rigging briefly held it in place, but the weight was too much; it came crashing down to the deck in a tangle of splitting wood and spars, crushing the oarsmen on the larboard quarter. The pirate ship began to drift helplessly, and as *Loredan* passed by, the cannon was discharged for a third time. The massive stone ball smashed a hole in the hull just above the water line and soon the ship developed a terminal list.

Dandolo chose this moment to order the oars to be run out and altered course half a point due west. The change of direction combined with the exhilarating surge of speed generated by the oarsmen took *Loredan* beyond the intercepting course with the pirates. Now her enemies were left trailing in her wake as she sped in the direction of the Italian mainland. In a few minutes she would be able to resume her northwesterly bearing with nothing between her and *Sanudo*. It had all been as easy as Dandolo predicted but strangely, Spatafora's ship did not seem much nearer than before. The Sicilian upstart was certainly taking his time coming to *Loredan's* aid.

Richard looked back over the starboard quarter at the sinking pirate ship wondering if any of the others would alter course to help it. They had responded to Dandolo's change of course and were pursuing in line astern, but even though they were rapidly falling back with every sweep of *Loredan's* mighty oars, none stopped to assist their stricken comrades.

The waste of life, even low pirate life, disturbed Richard. "I don't understand it Henry," he said. "It's obvious we've escaped their clutches yet the pirates are continuing a blatantly pointless pursuit."

"Perhaps they know something we don't Captain." The sergeant's words had barely been uttered when there was a commotion at the stern of the ship. Suddenly the trap door to the hold flew open and the Dalmatian hostages swarmed out from *Loredan's* murky depths. Before anyone could stop them, they had captured Dandolo and murdered two of his crew who tried to block their way. The ship lurched to starboard as the helm was thrown over by the hostage leader, a tall, fearsome man with long, black hair and wrestler's muscles. The billowing sail lost the wind and began to flap as *Loredan* slowly, fatally drifted off course.

Dandolo's first officer quickly took over command, ordering the sail to be reefed and the oars shipped so that he could gather enough men for a counterattack. He prepared a fighting party of twenty five of his best swordsmen to regain the helm, but he was unable to give the order to attack. The Dalmatians, who had gathered in a knot around the stern companionway, brought Dandolo forward held firmly between two of them. Their leader pointed a dagger to his throat and shouted threateningly in his strange tongue. It was clear that the hostages had gained the upper hand; Dandolo's life was the price for control of the ship. Seeing this, the first officer halted his counterattack and *Loredan* lay dead in the water while her crew remained frustrated and helpless. Dandolo called out to his crew in Italian, which was later translated for Richard. In essence, and with the expletives removed, he shouted, 'Do not give up the ship! I do not matter! For God's sake do not give up the ship!' A powerful Dalmatian fist struck him in the face knocking him senseless for a few seconds. Meanwhile the other pirate ships were getting closer.

Richard walked unhurriedly across the foredeck to where the Templars were standing and had a quiet word with the Grand Master. Then he returned to Henry and asked, "Can you shoot that big bastard without endangering our captain?"

"The one holding the dagger?"

"Yes."

"It will need to be a head shot but it should be possible at this range."

"Then do it Henry; it's our only hope."

The distance was not great but it was a difficult shot because of the rudderless, pitching deck. Henry slid behind a water barrel out of sight of the Dalmatians and prepared his crossbow. Once the iron quarrel was installed, he slowly got up to a crouching position and rested his elbows on the lid of the barrel to steady his aim. The pirate leader saw him a split second too late. He opened his mouth to bellow another threat but no sound came forth. Henry's iron bolt entered the eye socket and emerged from the back of the head spreading blood and brains over the other pirates like confetti. Recovering from the Dalmatian fist, Dandolo saw his chance and wriggled free from his shocked captors before they had time to realise what was happening. As he ran towards his first officer, cries of "Deus Vult!" came from the foredeck where the Templars began their charge to retake the helm from the Dalmatians.

"Captain, look who's with the hostages!" shouted Henry pointing to a squat, dark figure. "It's that bastard Greek!"

"It doesn't surprise me at all," answered Richard. "He was in league with them all the time. It must have been he who gave them the weapons they're wielding now. The question is who else is involved in the conspiracy?"

Henry placed another quarrel in his crossbow and smiled grimly, "Well I've got a little present for our Greek friend." The aim was true and the Greek fell to the deck clutching his ample stomach. After that the fighting became too confused to permit further shooting.

The Dalmatians, armed only with small swords and axes, fought like lions contesting every inch of deck, but gradually they were forced back by superior numbers and weaponry. Richard saw no need to involve Henry and himself in the brutal, gutter fighting taking place in the cramped space at the far end of the ship where he observed Titus Scrope doing evil work with a boarding hook. The grey haired Templar was in his element in this sort of conflict, having developed acute survival instincts in the back streets around Ipswich port at a very tender age.

But the hostages had achieved their aim, even at the cost of their own lives, because as the last of them was dispatched, the four remaining pirate ships closed in on the helpless *Loredan* like a pack of hounds round a wounded boar. The leading vessel had managed to interpose itself between *Loredan* and the sluggardly *Sanudo* while two others approached from either beam. The commander's ship stood off to watch its cubs finish off the Venetians.

Captain Dandolo had no intention of waiting resignedly for the end. Like all true leaders, adversity brought out the best in him. Holding a bloody scarf to his injured nose, he gave out a torrent of commands to his men. First, the oarsmen were ordered back to their stations, and the two cannon were reloaded. The larboard oars backed water until *Loredan's* bow pointed homewards once more. There was no mistaking the next order, "Avante!" The crew cheered, the ship lurched forward to the beat of the bosun's drum and surged towards the pirate vessel blocking her way to freedom. The bow cannon roared defiance but the stone ball overshot, harmlessly drenching the crowded pirate deck in salt water. As the gap between the two ships narrowed to about fifty yards, Dandolo ordered his bosun to increase the pace to ramming speed. At the same time he tweaked the helm so that *Loredan's* bow pointed directly at the middle of the pirate vessel. The enemy captain realised his danger too late and did not even attempt to avoid the inevitable collision. A space miraculously appeared at the point of the anticipated impact. All those not holding an oar on board Dandolo's ship gripped the nearest fixed object and braced themselves.

The collision was bone jarring. The crack of splitting timbers and shrieks of crushed men rent the air. *Loredan's* oarsmen were pitched from their benches. Their oars, which seconds before had been beating with disciplined rhythm, were now a tangled mass but the hull was still sound and both masts remained upright. Dandolo's ship was still seaworthy. The pirate ship fared worse. The larboard beam was stove in and Richard could see water flooding into the hold. Scores of bobbing heads dotted the sea where men had been thrown from the stricken vessel, but now desperation lent an edge to those still on board, for they knew they must capture *Loredan* or sink with their ship.

"Henry, make sure none of those pirates gets near our Jewish passengers," said Richard. "They must be protected at all costs."

"I'm not sure they need protecting Captain. Look!" Henry pointed to the stern where Ruth had already emerged from her cabin clad in the light mail shirt and white sailor trousers she had worn at Pilgrim's Castle. A crossbow was slung over her shoulder and a pouch full of quarrels hung from her belt. Close behind her was an extraordinary sight; Chaim ben Issachar ready for war. He had found a Templar helmet which was far too big for him; the rim came down to the bridge of his nose. He carried a boarding spike to serve as a weapon and a long sword which dragged along the deck as he ran towards Richard.

The Englishman said, "Chaim, what do you think you're doing?"

"Protecting my investment my dear. Anyway, I could not stop Ruth and I could hardly skulk in my cabin while she fights. Where do you want us?"

Richard had to think quickly because the shocked pirates had recovered from the ramming and were gathering to board *Loredan*. He pointed to the main masthead. "Ruth, can you climb the ratlines and carry your crossbow at the same time?"

"Of course I can."

"Then settle yourself in the crow's nest and shoot any target that presents itself."

She climbed athletically onto the first rung of the ratline and looked back at him. "Be careful my darling."

"I will," answered Richard, "God go with you." Chaim's reaction to the familiarity was unclear beneath his saucepan-like helmet, but that was of no concern now as the leading pirates leaped aboard *Loredan's* foredeck.

The Templar Legacy

"Chaim, stay close to Sergeant Hawkswood and me," said Richard, ducking the heavy boarding spike as it wobbled in his direction, "and be careful where you stick that thing!"

* * *

IV

Even with the addition of the ferocious ben Issachar, *Loredan's* plight was hopeless. Swarms of pirates were able to board her because both ships were locked together, and although the attack was checked on the foredeck by a small force of Templars and Venetian mariners, the second pirate ship was fast approaching the larboard quarter, grappling hooks at the ready. Dandolo ordered all oars to be shipped and the larboard oarsmen to repel boarders. They ran up on deck armed with a startling array of broadswords, axes and handspikes. Venice's policy of using freemen instead of slaves to row her galleys was about to justify itself; *Loredan's* close quarter fighting strength was effectively tripled.

Richard stationed himself, Henry and the gallant ben Issachar on the larboard deck to face the new attack, but just as the grappling hooks were lodging themselves into the ship's beam, an explosion drew everyone's attention to the starboard quarter. The Venetians had managed to fire the stern cannon at the third pirate vessel, which was also fast closing on them, but there was no time to assess the effect because the larboard attack was beginning. Here the pirates launched themselves in a tide of snarling, screaming hate. Some fell between ships to be crushed by the two hulls, others were impaled on the defenders' boarding spikes, but most were able to climb over the companion rail and gain a foothold on the deck where the fighting became cramped, confused and very deadly. Richard quickly discovered why the crew's preferred weapons were axes and short hacking swords; there was no room to swing a cat, never mind his forty inch sword blade. This sort of fighting required little skill and a great deal of luck because, due to the press it was impossible to wield a sword or raise a shield for much of the time. He was reduced to using his shield rim and sword pommel. He had intended to cover Chaim but it was all he could do to stay on his feet; the brave Jew would have to fend for himself.

Richard had still not dealt a fatal blow when the deck suddenly pitched and he found his arms pinned to his sides by two equally squeezed Venetians. A tall Dalmatian loomed up in front of him. Richard could see his white teeth through his filthy, black beard as the pirate smiled at his helpless victim. The Englishman had fought in many battles but he never expected to meet his end like this. He struggled to free his arms but it was no good. The Dalmatian slowly raised his axe and took deliberate aim at Richard's head. In that brief moment time stood still. Richard knew there was no more he could do. A great sadness came upon him as he thought of Mary and Joan vainly waiting for him to come home to Rouen. He hoped Henry would take revenge upon this unworthy pirate for ending his life so ingloriously. He offered his soul to God but last of all, as he closed his eyes and waited for the killer blow, he thought of Ann and hoped he would be with her soon.

The axe never struck home. Richard felt something brush past his right ear followed by a gurgling noise. He opened his eyes. The pirate dropped his weapon and gripped his throat where the white feathers of a crossbow quarrel were protruding through his beard. Richard craned his neck around and looked at the masthead where Ruth was already reloading her weapon. She saw him and gave a quick wave before shooting off her next bolt. He had protected her at Pilgrim's Castle; now she had done the same for him aboard *Loredan*.

The deck pitched again and Richard's arms were freed. He stepped back from the fighting and gave himself a few seconds to recover from his close brush with death. At the same time he looked round and saw the battle had reached a critical point. Although the pirates from the first ship were being held on the foredeck, those from the second were still pushing forward along the larboard beam. If the two groups managed to link up the end would quickly follow. Using desperate hand signals and what little Italian he had managed to pick up, he gathered about ten of the starboard crew who were waiting to fend off the third pirate ship, now almost upon them. Collecting Henry and Chaim on the way, he led them to the space on the larboard beam which still separated the two areas of fighting and, using the Jew as translator, explained to the Venetians what must be done. No sooner had he finished speaking than a groan of dismay came from the Templars holding the foredeck.

"What is it?" asked Chaim.

Richard scanned the foredeck. "I'm not sure; I think the Grand Master may have fallen." Then turning to Henry he said, "Take command here Sergeant, I will not be long." He ran towards two Templars who were dragging a third away from the conflict and saw his fears confirmed. Blood oozed from the Grand Master's chest where a boarding spike had pierced his chainmail armour.

"Sit him up against the main mast," ordered Richard. "He must not lie down or he'll choke on his own blood." The pink froth which bubbled from the Grand Master's mouth told Richard his lung had been punctured; the wound was mortal. The Templars gently laid down their leader with his back propped up against the mast and looked to Richard for orders. "There is no more you can do here. You have done well. Return to your posts. I will attend to the Grand Master."

The fighting had not yet spread to the main mast so Richard was able to put down his sword and shield and spare a few moments for the dying Templar. The old, grey eyes opened and slowly focused on Richard. The voice came in laboured gasps. "Richard, I am glad you are here. How goes the fight?"

"Well," lied Richard. "*Sanudo* is almost here. You will still lead your men back to France in glory."

The Grand Master shook his head, "We both know my wound is fatal, but no matter. I have done my duty to my Order and my God. Now listen to me, there is but little time left." The voice was already fading and Richard had to lean forward to hear the hoarse whisper. "I want it known that my wish is for Mamoun to succeed me. He shall lead the great crusade to recover the Holy Places. With our money you English will be victorious in France and then both great nations shall unite to follow the Templar banner back to Outremer."

"It will be a wonderful venture," agreed Richard sadly, knowing it would never happen. The days of crusades were long gone.

The Grand Master was sinking fast, his voice was barely audible. "Richard, one last favour."

"Of course," he answered, putting his ear close to the bloody mouth.

"I would like you and your brave sergeant to accompany Mamoun on the crusade. With you two at his side I am sure he will succeed."

"We will go with him Grand Master. Having started the great work, it would be good to see it through." The Grand Master nodded but words were beyond him now. The grey eyes closed for the last time. He gasped for air and gripped Richard's hand then, with a long, slow outward breath, his soul left his body. Richard looked down at the man who had dominated his life for the last few months. Charles d'Evreux had borne all the characteristic arrogance and fervour of the grand masters of old yet, after a difficult start, the two men had ended up as friends and d'Evreux's unhappy and inadequate life was eventually crowned with glory. He had died contented.

Richard stood up but while he was gathering his sword and shield the deck lurched to larboard. Chilling death screams and the ominous sound of splintering wood came from *Loredan's* stern. He looked back to see the fate of Dandolo's proud ship finally sealed. The stern cannon had destroyed the steering gear of the third pirate ship. Instead of swinging hard to starboard to enable his crew to board *Loredan*, the pirate captain had lost control and rammed her amidships. The impact was too much for the main mast. Large cracks opened in it near the base and quickly spread upwards.

Richard saw Ruth perched precariously in the crow's nest and yelled, "Get down here! Now!" She reacted immediately and scampered down the ratlines just before the mast toppled over, snapping the rigging and crushing friend and foe alike as it smashed into the foredeck. The devastation caused a brief pause in the fighting which gave Richard time for another quick assessment of the battle. He could see Chaim but there was no sign of Henry.

Richard called out, "Chaim, where's Henry?"

"Not sure my dear; I think he might have gone for some water. He said he would only be a few seconds."

"I hope so. A few seconds are all we've got!"

By now the pirates from the first and second ships had managed to join forces. The first ship, the one *Loredan* had rammed, had been cut free by the Venetians and had already sunk, but it was the third which dealt the final death blow; its bow was firmly wedged into *Loredan's* starboard beam and had smashed deep into the hold. Water was pouring in through broken timbers and it was then Richard saw one of those momentary, bizarre scenes which can sometimes happen in the midst of battle and etches itself deep into the memory. Some of the treasure caskets must have been split open by the collision because suddenly, a bright yellow stream of gold ducats began to spill out of the hold into the water. It seemed as if, having given her all, Dandolo's brave ship was gushing her golden lifeblood into the all-embracing, implacable sea. She was slowly sinking but *Sanudo* was still half a mile away.

As suddenly as it stopped, the fighting started again. While Richard watched the crew of the third pirate ship preparing to board, he spoke to Ruth. "Stay close to me. We'll make our final stand with Henry and your father." But before Richard could rejoin the melee, he was hailed from the stern of the ship. It was Dandolo who was frantically pointing to the second pirate ship which still lay alongside *Loredan's* larboard beam.

"Richard! Follow me and bring the Templars. We gonna take that ship!" Then the captain abandoned his position by the helm, calling as many of his crew as could hear above the din of battle, to follow him. Most of the pirates from the second ship were already aboard *Loredan,* so the few left on their own ship were quickly overwhelmed by the unexpected counterattack. At the same time the crew on the third pirate ship boarded

Loredan unopposed. Dandolo's ship was now in enemy hands except for a small section on the larboard beam where the Templars and the last of the Venetians were covering the retreat of their comrades.

But although the grappling hooks were still in position, boarding the pirate vessel was perilous because its deck was now higher than the listing, Venetian galley. Ruth leaped across the gap without difficulty, but Chaim lost his footing and would have fallen had it not been for the strength of two tough oarsmen, who hauled him on deck by his shoulders in an undignified but grateful heap. Last to board were the twelve surviving Templars, who had manfully covered Dandolo's counterattack against huge odds. Richard and Henry remained with them but the final seconds, when they would have to turn their backs on the enemy to board their new ship, were always going to be difficult.

Richard bellowed, "Templars retire!" They were fighting in a half circle formation with their backs to *Loredan's* larboard companion rail. Those at the edge of the half circle quickly boarded the new ship as the formation pulled back on itself until only Richard, Henry and three Templars were left on *Loredan*.

Richard gained a brief respite by dispatching the Dalmatian in front of him with a sword thrust through the throat. Then he shouted "Run!" This was the moment he had been dreading, but now the two Englishmen's decision not to wear chainmail bore fruit. They turned, scrambled over the companion rail and leaped the void between the ships. Richard felt a second rush of air pass his cheek as he grabbed one of the trailing ropes; it was another bolt from Ruth's crossbow covering him again. *Loredan's* deck was now at least five feet below the deck of the captured pirate ship, so the exhausted fugitives had to claw their way up ropes to safety. For the armoured Templars this was almost impossible; only one of the three was saved thanks again to the arm strength of the Venetian oarsmen. The other two slipped down between the hulls to a watery grave.

Some of the pirates were beginning to understand the severity of their plight. They were stranded aboard a sinking ship with no hope of escape because the foundering *Loredan* was dragging the third pirate ship down with her. Some tried to recapture Dandolo's new vessel but were easily driven off because of the different heights of the decks and the widening gap between the ships, which were beginning to drift apart now that the Venetians had cut the grappling ropes. Soon there was enough space to run out the oars, so Dandolo ordered his men to pull fifty yards away from his once proud galley. He watched *Loredan's* final moments, tears streaming from his eyes.

There was no danger of pursuit from the pirate commander's vessel, which had stood off from the battle, because *Sanudo* had belatedly arrived. The pirates turned tail and headed northeast as fast as they could go. The screams of anger and hate from the two sinking ships turned to wails of despair as they slid below the waves.

Dandolo, damp eyed and heavy hearted stood beside Richard and said quietly, "I shall see Spatafora in Hell for this."

"He certainly took his time," agreed Richard, "but at least you still have a ship. Indeed, surely you can claim this as your own personal prize; you did not own *Loredan*."

Dandolo shrugged, "Is true but I loved *Loredan*. Spatafora shall pay."

CHAPTER ELEVEN

Sanudo pursued and soon caught the last pirate vessel. The commander, hoping for mercy, surrendered without a fight but his hopes were unfounded; no-one had sympathy for pirates. He was hanged in front of his crew who were then thrown unceremoniously into the sea by Spatafora's men. The sun was well into the western sky before *Sanudo* and her prize returned to the scene of battle where Dandolo was making his new ship habitable.

Conditions on board Dandolo's ship were crowded, but they might have been worse had not half his men fallen in the fight. There was a single deck with sixteen oars on each side and a small, stern cabin big enough for just one person which was cleaned out and allocated to Ruth. The mast was a little forward of midships and there was enough fresh water on board to last until they reached Venice. Dandolo, who was beginning to realise he would end the campaign wealthier than when he started, gave the crew a short rest then ordered them to start the task of cleaning up the endemic squalor the pirates were content to live in. Even before *Sanudo* returned he had organised the crew into starboard and larboard watches, replaced his fallen officers with promotions and, following a short ceremony, rechristened his new ship *Maria* after his mother. By the time he saw *Sanudo's* signal calling him on board, the captain of the *Maria* was beginning to regain some of the old spirit that had deserted him when he witnessed the sinking of *Loredan*.

The same could not be said for Richard. A large, red evening sun cast a warm glow across the calm sea as he leaned against the mast watching Dandolo returning in *Sanudo's* skiff from his conference with Spatafora.

It may have been a reaction to the fighting or the disappointment caused by the loss of the Templar treasure, but Richard felt a glowering darkness come over him which subdued his spirit in a way he had not experienced since the murder of Ann and his sons. How was he going to break the bad news to Fastolf and, worse still, the Duke of Bedford? They had entrusted him with a vital and noble task but he had failed miserably.

"Is everything all right Captain Richard?" Henry's friendly Wiltshire burr cut across his gloomy thoughts like a bright ray of sunshine. "Are you feeling seasick again?"

The English sergeant crossed the deck and stood in front of Richard looking hard into his captain's green eyes. "You look like you've just seen a ghost!"

"I suppose it's a kind of sickness Henry, but not seasickness this time."

"Can I help?"

Richard smiled. The intervention of his cheerful sergeant had already lifted his spirit a little. "I was thinking about the failure of our mission and how I will explain it to the Duke of Bedford."

"No man could have done more than you Captain, I'll swear to that. Without you we wouldn't have found the Templar treasure in the first place."

"I think that's what troubles me most Henry. Looking back, it would have been better if we had never found it. We secured it, or rather half of it, but then we lost it which makes failure even worse. We came so close to tasting success only to have it taken away at the last moment."

Henry remained silent for a moment then suddenly a new idea entered his resourceful mind. "There's still the other half of the treasure hidden on Mount Carmel. We could return next year with a properly equipped expeditionary force and retrieve it."

"I may suggest that to Lord Bedford but I think it very likely we were observed by eyes unseen to us. I wouldn't like to recommend an expedition to Outremer only to find the cupboard bare."

Henry grinned, "And maybe next year would be a bit too soon. We stirred up a real hornets' nest did we not?"

"That we did," agreed Richard, "and talking to you has helped lift may dark mood somewhat. I see Captain Dandolo is back so we shall soon hear why Spatafora left it so late to help *Loredan*."

The stony faced Dandolo climbed on deck and beckoned Richard to follow him to the stern, where he cleared the area around the helm so they could speak privately. Although the captain could stand near the edge of the ship comfortably enough, Richard hung onto one of the ratlines because there was no companion rail on *Maria* to prevent ill-balanced mariners from toppling into the sea.

For a short while Dandolo looked back at *Sanudo* with hatred in his eyes, and when he spoke to Richard it was with uncharacteristic detachment, as if he dare not give vent to his true feelings. "Understand all now. Is treachery, treachery on a grand scale. Spatafora no say much but I read in between his words."

"Is that why he took so long to come to our aid?" asked Richard.

"Yes, but he miscalculate. He no expect *Loredan* to sink. He think if he wait long enough, the pirates will come close to capture my ship then *Sanudo* arrive and save us. He big hero and can claim *Loredan's* cargo by right of battle."

"So he would take possession of the Templar treasure."

"Yes."

"But how did he even know about it? At Nauplion none of the crew left our ship."

"But Cavalli did. He put so-called hostages aboard *Loredan* and then tell Spatafora about the treasure. I check hostage chains myself; they were secure. Only Cavalli's Greek henchman can unlock them. Cavalli must have got word to the Dalmatian pirates to attack us. This is why he make us wait in Nauplion. Then, when the pirates strike, the Greek releases the hostages on our ship. The plan almost worked."

"But Cavalli is a priest, a Domincan. What use is wealth to him?"

"None, but he ambitious for promotion like any other man. Perhaps he want to be bishop or pope even, I dunno, but his master is the doge and has big influence in Rome. Foscari also need much money for his wars in Italy and to, how you say, put plenty feather in nest. Spatafora is only small player in great game of treachery."

Richard was not surprised by Spatafora's involvement, but for a Venetian doge to be responsible for the deaths of one hundred and fifty of his loyal citizens was without precedent. "When we get back to Venice we shall expose his iniquity," said Richard. "All the traitors will face Venice's famous impartial justice."

Dandolo shook his head sadly. "Your faith is misplaced Richard. I will be blamed for everything. Spatafora will say he come to help as quick as he can, but escape of hostages my fault. A captain is responsible for everything that happen aboard his ship. It will be me, not Spatafora or the doge who will face trial."

"If you are found guilty what will the sentence be?"

Dandolo drew his finger across his throat, the universal gesture of death.

"But there are witnesses who will support you," said Richard. "As well as your own crew you have your passengers too. All will testify to *Sanudo's* slow approach which left *Loredan* fighting alone for the entire battle."

"Thank you Richard but is no use. The prosecutor will ask what naval qualification you have to make judgment about *Sanudo's* effort. Spatafora will claim he was rowing into wind, which he was, and testimony from my crew will be seen as slanted to me. It will come down to my word against Spatafora's. Jury sympathy will be with him because I am captain who lost a Venetian war galley. I doubt Foscari will even need to bribe jurors to find me guilty."

"Then surely you cannot go back to Venice like a lamb to the slaughter."

For the first time since the loss of his ship, the impish twinkle returned to Dandolo's brown eyes. "Can wager your last ducat on that, but is no simple. We are prisoners already. Spatafora has command now because he has senior ship. He order me to sail astern *Sanudo* but if I break formation he can turn and catch us easy because his ship much faster than *Maria*."

"Then what will you do?"

Dandolo laughed and pointed to his head. "Use brain! I have a week to think of something."

For the next few days, *Maria* dutifully kept her station behind *Sanudo* and in front of the other captured ship as the little convoy sailed up the Adriatic towards Venice before a steady southwesterly. During this time Chaim's attitude towards Richard reverted to the old, paternal friendliness he had shown before Ruth's unofficial sojourn to Pilgrim's Castle. It was as if his experience of fighting the pirates aboard *Loredan* had allowed him to see life's real values in a new light. He even seemed to accept the loss of his investment remarkably philosophically, so much so that Richard began to wonder if he had taken a blow to the head during the battle. But the new Chaim's tolerance did not extend to permitting Ruth and Richard to talk alone, so the two lovers were still limited to soulful eye contact and, when they were very lucky, a surreptitious hand squeeze.

Meanwhile, on Dandolo's orders, the ship's carpenter built a strange object out of the reserve oars and spars stowed in *Maria's* hold. It had three sides, a cross beam and was twice the height of an average man. It had a pointed top which was hollow in the centre and gave it the appearance of a capital 'A'. Venice was now only a few days away but Richard could not see how the carpenter's creation was going to save the captain from his fate. Dandolo showed no inclination to share his plan, if he had one, so Richard decided to force the issue because he could not stand back and see his friend sail calmly to his death.

It was late afternoon, Venice was now only two days' sail away, and Dandolo was happily chatting to his helmsman as if he did not have a care in the world when Richard approached him and said rather awkwardly, "Captain, I must speak with you."

Dandolo dismissed the helmsman and took the helm himself. "Well Richard, what is it?"

"Have you changed your mind? Are you going to face trial in Venice after all?"

"Answer is 'No' to both questions."

"But time is running out. When are you going to do something?"

The captain looked up at the clouds scudding across the blue sky and frowned, "Tonight I hope." He pointed to a heavy, grey bank of cloud in the east and said, "I think the wind shift at last. It starting to back to the southeast. If so we break ranks tonight and set course for Ancona. Ancona no friend of Venice; it lose much trade to us. We safe from Foscari's clutches there for the time being."

"Will not Spatafora be able to catch us before we reach Ancona?"

"Not if my plan work. Is why we wait for wind. We cannot row because of sound of oars and bosun's beat."

"Well that's good news," replied Richard, relieved that something was going to happen at last, "but why all the secrecy?"

"Is possible not all crew loyal to me. Cavalli may have put some of his creatures aboard before we set out from Venice. Maybe not, but I no provide opportunity to sabotage my plan."

"Is there anything I can do to help, Captain?"

"Not this time Richard; this seaman work. You and Sergeant Henry have done enough already. Now you rest until we reach Ancona."

Dandolo's forecast was correct. By nightfall the wind shifted to the southeast bringing with it the cloudbank which conveniently obscured the moon. The three ships maintained contact by using pilot lights of tallow protected by glass, which were set up in the bows and stern of each ship to prevent anyone getting lost. At ten o'clock, Dandolo ordered *Maria's* stern light to be carefully moved, slotted through the top of the carpenter's framework, and then secured to the small beam which was wedged through the middle of it. The framework was lowered into the water alongside *Maria's* starboard beam and, at the exact same moment, the pilot light in the ship's bows was extinguished.

To the watch aboard *Sanudo's* prize, which was the rear ship of the convoy, nothing seemed amiss as *Maria* turned a point to the west leaving the carpenter's beacon floating in the water behind them. The beacon light gradually became smaller as Spatafora's two ships pulled away, but it was more than an hour before anyone realised something was wrong. By the time *Sanudo* had turned and retraced her course to investigate, three hours had passed. Spatafora had no choice but to wait until daybreak before deciding on what direction the pursuit should take, but by then *Maria* was hull down in the west and half way to Ancona.

* * *

II

"What will you do now Captain?" asked Richard as he packed his travelling bag before disembarking from *Maria*.

Dandolo, leaning on the mast of his new ship, looked across Ancona's deserted dockyard, where the early morning sun cast long shadows across the empty berths, and said, "For now I make Ancona my home and use *Maria* for merchant trade to earn enough money until I can take revenge on Foscari."

"That might take some time my dear," replied a Jewish voice from behind them. Chaim had just returned from a quick look round the old town and was not impressed. "This place is dying. Trade, its lifeblood, has been enticed away by Venice. I should know because I was part of that process. You can see that Ancona was once rich and powerful from the large dockyards and impressive buildings, but now the port is almost abandoned, there are more empty shops than occupied ones in the town centre, and the fine buildings are unpainted and decaying. This is not a good place to begin a mercantile business."

"Then what would you do?" asked Dandolo.

"Come into partnership with Ruth and me. I have long wished for a maritime arm in the business which would cut out the huge margins taken off our profits by greedy Venetian merchant captains. The prices they charge Jews are inflated and always agreed amongst themselves in advance of any contract. With you and your ship as a full partner, we could outwit their price fixing."

Dandolo looked uncertain. Richard urged him to agree. "Accept Captain. It is an excellent proposal."

Chaim saw the captain's hesitation. "Is it because I am Jewish?"

Dandolo reddened with embarrassment at Chaim's intuition. The Dandolo family was one of the oldest and most noble in Venice. One of them, Doge Enrico Dandolo, old and blind though he was, had the influence to divert the Fourth Crusade from Jerusalem, its proper target, to Constantinople. The great Byzantine city was sacked and never fully recovered, but Venice became a world power as a result. For a Venetian aristocrat to go into business with a Jew was unthinkable, but the universal Christian bigotry against Jews was not shared by Paolo Dandolo. In the battle with the pirates Chaim and Ruth had done more than enough to earn his respect.

"You do me great honour Chaim ben Issachar," he answered.

"Then you accept?"

"Is no that simple. I shall be wanted for trial when Spatafora report back to Venice."

"That is not a problem my dear. The ben Issachar Dandolo partnership would set up its mercantile office at Ravenna, which is near enough to communicate with Venice but far enough to be beyond Foscari's reach and, as you already know, it has its own port which could be the home berth for *Maria*. While you would operate from there, you would of course need to be discreet when visiting Venice on business, at least while Foscari is doge."

"Chaim, I think you underestimate Foscari's reach, and if I join you he will say you his enemy too."

"I am prepared to take the risk if you are."

Dandolo held out his hand and beamed, "Then I accept with all my heart."

The two men shook hands and Chaim said, "Ruth and I will return overland to Venice to prepare the papers, then we shall come back to Ravenna to set up your branch of the business. It should not take long. I must also get permission from my partner, Ruth, to make this offer to you, but I am sure she will approve it."

Richard could not have known he was witnessing the beginning of a successful, long term partnership, but he knew in his bones it would work well for all three of them. But there was an inconsistency in Chaim's proposal which he needed to resolve. "Just a moment Chaim. Back in Venice when we were discussing the value of your investment in the Grand Master's venture, you said you were putting all the money in your business into buying *Loredan*. So when *Loredan* sank you lost five thousand ducats as well as your business, but now you're talking as if nothing has happened."

"Er, well, it appears worse than it is," stammered Chaim tapping the side of his nose, "but in Venice we were negotiating. Do you really think I would have risked my business on such a madcap adventure as we've just been on?"

"But you've just lost five thousand ducats!"

"Not really."

"Now I too am confused," said Dandolo. "*Loredan* was worth at least five thousand ducats."

The old Jew's eyes twinkled, "Not to me my dear. I will start my explanation by mentioning the city all Venetians hate; Genoa. Some years ago, Venice's bitter rivals found a way to mitigate the shipping losses they were suffering at our hands; it is called insurance. It was used by the ancient Romans when piracy infested the seas in their empire and was re-invented by the Genoese. I am proud to say that the Jewish community in Genoa played a large part in it. The concept came to Venice about twenty years ago."

"How does it work?" asked Richard.

"It is most easily explained if I use *Loredan* as an example. I didn't want to risk all my money on such a mad adventure but the potential reward was so great, I thought it was worth some risk at least. Ruth came up with the idea of speaking to a company of insurers, who operate in Venice, to offload our risk. They charge what is called a premium whereby for a sum of money, which they keep, they pay all the costs of a ship if it is lost at sea. Usually the insured ship returns to port unscathed, and after this happens a few times the insurers build up enough money to pay for the occasional loss of a ship and keep a tidy sum for themselves. I am considering going into the insurance business myself if I can find suitable partners."

"So you will get your five thousand ducats back?" asked Richard.

"Yes, less the premium I had to pay."

"How much was that?"

"The insurers wanted a thousand ducats, but when Ruth told them we would be retaining Captain Dandolo and his crew, they halved that figure."

"So you've only lost five hundred ducats."

"Three hundred and fifty. Ruth cut the figure further. She can be very persuasive when she wants to be."

Dandolo shook his head in wonder. "Chaim, is amazing story. I have much to learn about trade and commerce."

"You will soon learn my dear and you already know everything about sailing a ship which we don't. The ben Issachars can learn from the Dandolos too."

It took more than thirty years, but in the end the Fates turned their backs on Francesco Foscari. He fell from power and underwent the disgrace of becoming the only doge in Venice's proud history to be forced to abdicate. The flourishing ben Issachar Dandolo partnership played a small but significant part in his downfall, but Chaim did not live to see it and Paolo Dandolo never returned to Venice.

* * *

III

But there was another matter which Chaim wished to conclude before they went their separate ways. "Captain -"

"You must now call me Paolo," interrupted Dandolo.

"Thank you Paolo. May I have a few words with Richard alone?"

Paolo nodded and took one of Richard's large hands between both of his own. "Farewell brave Englishman. You will always be welcome at my home, wherever that may be."

"Thank you Paolo, and if you ever have reason to travel north, my houses in Rouen and Suffolk will always be open to you." The bold Venetian captain smiled and departed for the town centre where he hoped to find a ship's chandler.

"A fine young man," sighed Chaim. "What a pity he's not Jewish."

"Jew, Christian, they are just labels. The value of a man should be judged by what he does whatever his label."

"My, my, you are too young to be a cynic Richard."

"War makes you grow up quickly. Ask Ruth."

Chaim shifted uncomfortably. "I should not have questioned you about Ruth the way I did after we left Outremer, nor did I ever properly thank you for watching over her while she was there."

"There is no need," replied Richard guardedly.

"It is a good thing we are about to separate. I know Ruth feels great affection for you, but you must understand there can never be anything of substance between you."

"I am also fond of her as we all are."

"Not 'as we all are' I think, but no matter. It is high time she was married and there will be plenty of suitors in Venice."

Richard looked Chaim directly in the eyes for the first time in many weeks. "She will not marry just for business reasons."

"Of course not, but there are many fine Jewish men of good family she can choose from."

"Why are you telling me this Chaim?"

"Because I want you to tell her. She will accept it from you."

Richard hesitated. "I, I'm not sure about that."

"I am not a fool. I see the way you look at each other. I know it will be hard, but if you have any regard for me at all you will do this thing for me." Richard did not know it, but the kind old Jew was offering him an honourable way out because he had accidently discovered in conversation with Henry that Richard was already married. Henry had no reason to hide this information but the fact that Richard had not mentioned it spoke volumes. If Richard could break the tie now, before Ruth discovered the truth, it would be less painful for both of them in the long run. Chaim was certain they were lovers; he had tried to hate Richard for it but could not. He silently prayed that Richard would be strong enough.

For a tense few seconds the Englishman looked out to sea and remained silent. Then taking a deep breath he said, "Very well, I will do as you ask but I must be alone with Ruth when I do it."

Chaim was so relieved he would have agreed to almost anything. "All right, alone but where I can see you both."

"Agreed."

It was early next morning when Ruth met Richard in the dockyard adjacent to *Maria*. An onshore breeze had developed, which would have chilled anyone else to the marrow, but neither of them noticed it. Chaim stood beside *Maria's* helm watching them like a hawk, but no indiscretion could take place because nearby the Templars were preparing their mounts for the long overland journey back to France. The command of the Templars had devolved upon de Graveson, who had recovered from the wound he received at Pilgrim's Castle, but was now permanently blind in one eye. He had purchased a score of small, bony horses which even a Welsh freebooter might have thought twice about stealing but, with careful handling and plenty of fodder, they were expected to manage the trip home.

Ruth spoke first. "The only reason my father permitted this meeting is for you to say goodbye. Is that not so?" Richard nodded. "But," she added, "what if I were to go with you?"

Richard's eyes widened; he had not expected this. "My love, I am going to fight a war. How can you come to that?"

"Have I not proved myself as good as any man in battle?"

"More than proved it but I will not have you face death any more. If something were to happen to you I could never forgive myself, nor would your father, and rightly so. We were very lucky at Pilgrim's Castle, very lucky indeed. Also the army is no place for a woman, no matter how brave. Camp life is hardly decorous. You cannot come with me."

"Then if you have decided we should separate will you return or is this the end for us?" Her eyes were beginning to dampen as she spoke but she was determined to hold back the tears.

"We are of different faiths," he answered. "What future is there for us?"

She took his hand, uncaring of her father's eagle eyes. "But we love each other too much to let that come between us; we worship the same God in our different ways. Do you love me enough to abandon your faith to be with me?"

"I would need to have been born a Jew. I cannot become one just because I want to."

"Then I shall become a Christian. Will that satisfy you?"

"That would destroy your father."

"What then! Is there really no way ahead for us?"

Richard was in turmoil. He loved Ruth deeply and knew full well that had it not been for Mary and Joan, he would never have contemplated leaving her. All the grand talk of wars and different faiths sounded hollow in his own ears because it was only an artifice to extricate himself. If he had been free, he would have become a Muslim or a pagan, never mind a Jew, to be with her. He looked back at *Maria* and saw the lone figure watching them, no doubt going through a turmoil of her own. He put his arm round Ruth's shoulders and sighed,

"Listen my darling. No happiness can be built on other people's unhappiness. Perhaps in a hundred or a thousand years things that matter to us now like faith, war and family responsibilities may no longer matter so much. Who can tell? But we are creatures of our time. If we cut ourselves off from all we know our happiness will be short lived. You have my love, you always will. I wish there was more I could give you."

She rested her head on his chest, finally comprehending she was going to lose him. Now the tears began to flow. "So it is ended then."

He too was close to tears. "I will write to you from Rouen and, if you wish to write to me, any letter sent to English Army Headquarters in Rouen will find me. Perhaps one day, when you are settled with a family of your own, we might meet again."

"How can you say that!" she sobbed. "I shall only ever want you. I cannot bear the thought of you being in another woman's arms."

She wept quietly for a while, and as they stood silently together her large tears gradually penetrated his linen surcoat. He looked out across the calm waters of the Adriatic which mirrored the blue, spring sky but the beauty of nature no longer pleased him. The contempt he felt for himself cast a darkness over his spirit which would stay with him for years. Even now he was being dishonest with her. Ruth had done nothing to deserve the misery she was undergoing, a misery that could not have happened if he had been honest from the beginning.

Suddenly the shuddering in Ruth's shoulders stopped; she looked up at him through swollen, reddened eyes. Without a second thought they kissed each other long and passionately for the last time, uncaring of who was watching. Then, at last, she gently stepped back from his embrace and said huskily, "Go now while I still have the strength to watch you leave. If you linger I shall not be able to bear it." He turned and walked quickly back to the ship.

Richard boarded *Maria* to collect his travelling bag and spoke to Chaim in a dull monotone. "It is done."

The old Jew replied sadly, "It is for the best. May God watch over you Richard Calveley."

The Templar Legacy

Richard and Henry rode at the rear of the column of Templars that filed out of Ancona dockyard. Just before they were obscured from sight by a line of warehouses, Richard looked back. Ruth was still standing alone exactly where he had left her. He raised his arm in final farewell but she did not respond; she could not accept that she would never see him again. And there was something else. She had missed her monthly cycle. The next was almost due; then she would be certain. This had happened before when she was under stress, and there could be no greater stress than believing she had been within seconds of a terrible death at Pilgrim's Castle, but this time it was not the same. She could not explain it even to herself. Somehow her body felt different, changed in some way. But there was no-one she could talk to. She was an only child, her companions were all men and her mother had died before these matters could be discussed. Traditionally such things were only spoken of outside the family after betrothal. She never felt more alone than now. Should she have told Richard? Perhaps, but if she was wrong it would appear she had tricked him into staying. Yet deep down, she was sure his child was within her. She decided she would write to him after the baby was born; then he could make his own decision in the cold light of day without a sobbing woman to influence him.

She looked at her father who was still standing alone on *Maria's* deck. She must soon face him with her news, but nothing worse could happen now. She did not want to hurt him but she would keep Richard's child whatever the cost. There would be no sending it away or hiding the fact. Somehow she knew it would be a boy; had she not already had a premonition at Pilgrim's Castle? The child would be a constant reminder of him and nothing would ever separate them, nothing!

* * *

IV

Richard hardly spoke for a month during which time the travellers had crossed Italy and entered French territory. Henry knew his captain well enough to understand he was best left alone at times like this, but it was only when he saw him saying farewell to Ruth at the dockside that he realised their friendship was deeper than it should have been.

The journey was agonisingly slow, barely ten miles a day. The half starved horses could only travel at a snail's pace until they built up their strength with fodder purchased along the way. The fact that the Templars refused to travel on a Sunday only made matters worse; they spent the entire day fasting and praying. Nor did they have much money because most of their possessions were at the bottom of the Adriatic along with de Beaujeu's legacy, so Richard was obliged to help out with some of the gold ducats he had pocketed from the donjon at Pilgrim's Castle. Progress improved a little as the horses gradually became stronger, but Richard and Henry were obliged to remain with the Templars because there was no possibility of two Englishmen successfully crossing France in time of war. At least being part of a group composed predominantly of Frenchmen gave them a much better chance.

The Templar numbers gradually decreased as individual knights peeled off from the column to head homewards and, by the time they approached the Loire valley, spring had turned into high summer. They reached Orleans on the morning of the eleventh day of August. By now, only de Graveson and four other knights were left to accompany Richard and Henry; one of these was Titus Scrope. De Graveson, whose home was in the south of France, was travelling north to Evreux to report the news of the Grand Master's death to his family, so the Englishmen would still have cover at least until they reached English controlled France.

It was in Orleans that the travellers heard of the huge army that had recently passed through on its way to Normandy. The more restrained accounts spoke of an array of sixteen thousand men, nearly half of whom were tough Scots under the command of an experienced warrior, the Earl of Douglas. In addition there was a strong body of Genoese crossbowmen, who were the only archers able to match the range of the English longbow, though not its rate of fire. Finally, and most intriguingly, there were also two thousand mounted Milanese mercenaries who, along with their horses, wore the latest design of Italian armour which was said to be proof against the longbow. The whole army was commanded by the Duc d'Aumale, who would doubtless leave most of the tactical decisions to Douglas.

On the day after their arrival in Orleans, Richard and Henry sat outside a hostelry enjoying the late evening sun and discussing the news of d'Aumale's army. The comfort of good food and good wine did nothing to dissipate the Englishmen's desire to reach the Duke of Bedford's army before the battle began.

Richard finished his goblet of wine and placed it firmly on the roughly hewn oak table in front of them. "I think we'll have to leave our escort tomorrow Henry, and trust to luck we reach Duke John in time."

"But that means crossing a part of France outside English control. Is it worth the risk?"

"I don't know. We've heard the French are heading for Verneuil, which is near Evreux, but by the time the Templars get there the battle will be over."

"And the opportunity for ransom will be lost," agreed Henry sagely.

"The trouble is, the French are between us and Duke John so we'll have to use small tracks to skirt round them, but we'll probably get lost because neither of us has been to that part of France before."

"But I have," said an English voice behind them.

"How much have you heard Scrope?" demanded Richard.

"Enough to know you need me."

"Have you forgotten my oath? I have sworn to kill you."

"You may do as you wish; I do not fear death."

"Why do you not follow de Graveson? You are a Templar are you not?"

"The Templar cause is finished. The dream is over; it lies at the bottom of the sea. There is nowhere for me to go."

"What is that to me?"

Titus shuffled uncomfortably and stared at his feet. "I wondered if you could find it in your heart to take me into your service Captain."

Richard felt as if he had just been struck. "After what you did to my family! I shall go through with my oath even if it means meeting you again in Hell, but if you manage to set foot in England first, I shall see you hang."

"I have not been convicted of anything though I have never denied my evil past to you. I had hoped you would have observed the change in me. I do not ask for forgiveness, that would be too bold, but I could serve you for no reward to continue compensating you in a small way for the wrongs I have done you. I can turn my hand to most things despite my advancing years and I can still fight as you have seen. I also beg to remind you that it was I who saved you from the falling spar during the storm on the outward journey to Outremer."

"I have not forgotten," answered Richard, though in truth he had. He glanced at Henry who replied with an indifferent shrug. Then he looked at the darkening sky which reflected his sombre mood. "I need time to consider, but provided you get the approval of the Sieur de Graveson, you may join us for the time being, at least until we reach Verneuil."

Early next morning, under the shadow of the great cathedral in Orleans, the three Englishmen took their leave of de Graveson and the Templars, knowing they were unlikely to meet again.

"I am sorry our venture was not crowned with success," said Richard to de Graveson, "but we came close did we not?"

"Indeed we did, but God's will was done and the Templars will find other ways to serve him. God speed you on your journey Richard but, as a Frenchman, I can hardly wish you success. However I shall pray that you and your companions come through unscathed."

"We can ask no more. God go with you too."

The Englishmen hurried north towards Chartres which they reached on the sixteenth day of August. There they turned off the main road to Rouen and headed northwest to Verneuil which was now only thirty miles away. Fortunately the dry summer weather had hardened the narrow, mud surfaced road sufficiently to prevent it being churned up by thousands of hooves and feet, but even so, the evidence of a large army on the march was everywhere to be seen. Deserted, unharvested fields, plundered villages, occasional unburied corpses and the unmistakable smell of sweat and ordure, which lingered for days after the rearguard passed by, left Richard in no doubt that a mighty force heading towards English territory was not far in front of them. It looked as though a great battle was about to be fought with all the opportunities that would bring for ransom and plunder; Richard and Henry were desperate not to miss it.

But on the evening of the seventeenth of August, when they were still six miles from Verneuil, the Englishmen discovered they were too late; the battle had already been fought. They were approaching the village of Brezolles when two French knights appeared round a bend in the road spurring on their lathered horses as if all the devils in Hell were just behind them. It was clear that neither rider had any intention of drawing rein, let alone stopping to answer Richard who was bursting with questions, so the travellers stood aside to let them pass. A few moments later another group of horsemen, about twenty strong, appeared galloping in the same direction and as they flashed past, Richard noticed that at least half of them bore serious wounds. Soon the trickle of men became a flood as the first foot soldiers staggered past, eyes wide with terror at what they had just seen.

The Englishmen were forced to suspend their march and observe the wreck of the French army from the edge of a copse of beech trees which capped a small knoll about a hundred paces from the road. "We might as well camp here for the night," said Richard. "We are no longer in haste and we'll only get swept up in the chaos if we try to struggle against that sad tide of humanity."

"Indeed," agreed Titus, "and from the panic in the eyes of those men I do not doubt we would be parted from our horses before long."

"Well it looks like our chances of plunder are gone for this year," mused Henry sadly. "I don't suppose we could waylay a count or maybe a rich knight at least?"

Richard smiled, "A good thought Henry, but our first duty now is to report back to Sir John Fastolf and Lord Bedford with the sad news of our venture. I am sure both will be with the army, so at first light we'll resume our journey."

The Wiltshire sergeant looked across the field of golden wheat which separated them from the road. "A fleeing army is a terrible thing. Blind panic turns disciplined men into animals. I pray I never have to see an English army reduced to this."

Richard replied, "We've been fighting the French for nigh on eighty years. It has not happened yet so I see no reason why it should ever happen."

"We are fighting in God's cause as well as our own," warned Titus, "but if he ever turns his back on us things will be different." Richard ignored the comment as the ramblings of an old man, but within a few years he would have good cause to remember it.

The flood of terrified men continued throughout the night, but by daybreak the numbers had declined to a trickle so the three Englishmen deemed it safe to resume their journey towards Verneuil. Some of the sights that met them on the road moved even their war hardened hearts. The stragglers they passed were mostly severely wounded helping each other as best they could, but few were likely to survive the day. Clusters of black flies covered their congealed wounds which had hardened under the hot August sun, and fresh corpses littered the edge of the road where exhaustion finally overcame the weakest. Occasionally the travellers came across foxes and feral dogs already beginning to scavenge around the bodies, but the most heart breaking scenes came from the pathetic wretches, who had so recently been proud warriors, calling out desperately for water. The Englishmen quickly drained their flasks as they answered the calls, but after that they had no choice but to ignore the pleadings of the rest. All the ditches and streams had long since dried out during the hot summer; there was no water to be found in the open, rolling countryside and the travellers did not have time to conduct a wide ranging search for it.

The most sickening aspect was the sight of the local peasants plundering their own countrymen. Some of the victims, who were too slow to die, were helped on their way to the next world by the very people they had just been fighting for. There was nothing the Englishmen could do; even if they chased the scavengers away they knew as soon as they were out of sight, the grisly work would resume. They passed through Verneuil, where the frightened townsfolk had bolted their doors to both French and English alike, and followed the wreckage of the French army towards a village called Damville, five miles away, where the battle had actually been fought.

As they trudged towards Damville Titus, who had been particularly quiet, asked, "Captain, you have fought the Scots before have you not?"

"Twice. First when I was very young at Homildon Hill, and then again last year at Cravant."

"Do you see any of them amongst the dead?"

"Not a single one."

"Might they have escaped?"

"I doubt it. They never run and usually fight to the death, especially when they face us. They never know when they're beaten."

"What do they look like?"

"They are not a wealthy people so their armour is of a poor standard compared to the French, except for their leaders who can afford the best. They are generally short in stature but have the confident swagger about them of natural warriors. Some wear kilts, which are the butt of many English jokes, but any Englishman who has fought them would admit he would prefer to face a French army than a Scottish one."

"How is it that we can beat them then?"

"The English fight well too as you may yet see, but when it comes to the Scots, no quarter is given by either side."

The travellers reached the battlefield late in the afternoon. The English were camped in what had been the French position before the battle and, amongst the many banners fluttering in the cool breeze, the royal colours of English lions couchant quartered with the lilies of France Moderne, which marked the tent of John, Duke of Bedford, could easily be seen. Richard and his companions walked their horses slowly towards Bedford's tent unchallenged because all in the army knew there was nothing to fear from the enemy now. They passed the burial pits which were already almost full to the brim with bodies; burying the dead was always a priority especially in summer months, and arrived in front of Duke John's headquarters where a young equerry asked them what they wanted.

"Wait here," said the equerry after Richard identified himself, and disappeared inside the tent; most in the army had heard of the Calveley name. He returned a few seconds later. "You are Sir John Fastolf's man?"

"Yes."

"My Lord Bedford will see you immediately. I will arrange refreshment for your two companions while they wait here for you."

This was the meeting Richard did not relish for he was going to have to report complete failure for the first time in his military career. He entered the tent where he found Bedford pacing up and down dictating letters to a clerk. The duke had aged in the year since Richard last saw him. His hair was now more grey than brown and his face was lined with the cares of governing two kingdoms, but the broad smile with which he greeted Richard seemed to shed years from the gaunt features. Richard regretted more than ever that he was the bearer of ill tidings.

Duke John dismissed the clerk and said warmly, "Captain Calveley, how pleased I am that you have come through your venture unscathed. Pray be seated and let me pour you some of the excellent wine we captured yesterday." At least I shall be able to tell Mary I was waited upon by the

Regent of England and France before he threw me out, thought Richard glumly as he took the silver goblet handed to him by the duke.

Bedford sat down opposite him and crossed his long legs. "Now tell me your news, every little detail."

"That might take some time My Lord."

"No matter. Time is something I can spare for a change. Yesterday has altered everything."

It took Richard two hours to complete his report, but when he had finished the duke remained silent for a moment or two as if weighing up the penalty he should mete out for Richard's failure. His first comment was inconsequential. "You look like a Turk yourself Captain. I never saw an Englishman with such a brown face."

"The effect of the Mediterranean sun My Lord."

Bedford smiled, "Do not look so worried Captain, your efforts do you credit. You were sent on a mission more in hope than expectation. In truth I am surprised you came so close to success. If the opportunity ever arises, could you find de Beaujeu's cave again? You say you only took half of the treasure."

"I am sure I could."

"What a pity that Doge Foscari proved to be so untrustworthy. I shall bear that in mind should I have any dealings with him."

A wave of relief swept over Richard. Duke John was known to be a man of justice but Richard was still surprised at the lenient treatment he was receiving. "But what about the money we need? Was not our hold on France weakening because of the expense of the war?"

Bedford beamed, "It was, but yesterday changed all that. I never thought France would take us on again in open battle. We were wasting our money and energy on interminable sieges, the exchequer was being bled dry then suddenly, like manna from Heaven, the French changed their strategy and put all their might into another pitched battle. I think we have the Scots to thank for that. I am sure it was the Earl of Douglas who persuaded them to confront us in the open again."

"My Lord, where are the Scots now?"

"Still here but all dead except a few. More than seven thousand were killed yesterday and those who are prisoners are all badly wounded. What a battle! The French lost two thousand before breaking and leaving the Scots to fight on alone. But those Milanese horsemen gave us something to think about; I am sending their armour back to the Greenwich armoury to see if we can produce something as good. It is proof against our arrows except at very close range. They managed to ride down some of our archers; I have not seen that happen before. But I believe we killed more of the enemy yesterday than at Agincourt, and those who were at both battles say that yesterday was harder fighting than Agincourt."

"I was at Agincourt My Lord, so I can vouch for the ferocity of that encounter. What of our own losses?"

"Surprisingly few, about six hundred, and no-one of consequence. French morale is shattered again and their Scottish allies are broken. One more push and France will fall into our hands like a ripe apple. Only divine intervention can stop us now."

That last sentence came back to haunt Bedford in the years to come.

"What about plunder My Lord?" asked Richard.

"Should generate enough money to see us through what's left of the war, but rather too many French nobles were killed in the heat of battle I'm sad to say, otherwise the ransom money would have been even greater."

The mention of ransom brought Fastolf to the forefront of Richard's mind. "My Lord, I must report to my liege but I did not see his banner when I arrived. Can you tell me where I can find him?"

Duke John shook his head sadly, "I regret that Sir John Fastolf is displeased with me. He captured the Duc d'Alencon during the battle, but when I claimed my commander's right to a share of the ransom, he took umbrage. You know what he's like where money is concerned." The two men's eyes met and neither could help but smile at the thought of the crusty Norfolk knight whose reputation for making a profit out of war was unequalled in the entire army.

"I do indeed My Lord," answered Richard.

"He took a flesh wound, nothing serious," continued the duke, "but it gave me the excuse to send him back to Falaise to recuperate. I don't want one of my best commanders scowling at me every time we meet. He left this morning. It may take a little time, but he'll get over it."

"The wound or the ransom?"

Bedford laughed, "Both I hope."

"Then with your permission My Lord, my two companions and I will leave tomorrow and report to Sir John at Falaise and," added Richard with a gracious bow of the head, "my sincere congratulations upon your great victory."

Richard, Henry and Titus resumed their journey next morning. They did not leave early and allowed their mounts to canter at a gentle pace because the victory at Verneuil had all but ended the campaign of 1424. They had just passed through Damville when they saw a dust cloud created by a single rider approaching from the north at great speed. As the rider drew nearer, there seemed to Richard's eyes something oddly familiar about the ungainly figure in the saddle, but it was only when the newcomer drew rein a few yards from them that recognition finally dawned.

"God's holy balls!" gasped Richard. "What are you doing here!"

―――――――✦✦✦✦✦✦―――――――

CHAPTER TWELVE

News of Father Hugh's return to Calveley Hall spread like wildfire and a hostile crowd gathered in Beccles market square to meet him as he rode into the town on the morning of the second day of August. He was surprised by the number, more than a hundred, of those who believed they had been wronged in some way by his ministrations as a fallen priest, but he was obliged to face them because they had assembled outside the entrance to the moot hall where Geoffrey Calveley's petition was to be heard. At least Hugh was not alone, for burly Tom Riches rode beside him and behind them a large farm labourer drove the open wagon which carried Sister Blanche. The presence of a nun inhibited some of the worst excesses of the crowd which restricted itself to angry jeering and catcalling.

Hugh and Tom dismounted outside the moot hall leaving the horses and wagon under the supervision of the farm labourer, and walked up the steps with Sister Blanche who was turning out to be far less frail than she looked. Life outside the convent seemed to suit her.

At the top of the steps a large figure emerged from the hall and blocked Hugh's way. It was big Will Mullen who said, "A word if you please." Fear chilled Hugh's heart as he looked into the eyes of the huge blacksmith, the man in whose wife he had implanted his clerical seed. Just at that moment the sun disappeared behind a small, fluffy cloud as if even the heavens had chosen to abandon Hugh to his fate.

But Tom still was there and interposed himself between them. "And what be bothering you Will Mullen?" he said truculently. "We have an appointment to keep with the magistrate so if you're thinking of causing us trouble you'll answer to the sheriff's men and then to me."

"It's nought like that Tom," answered Will, "I just want a minute of Father Hugh's time then I'll be on my way."

His tone of voice was placatory and there was no anger in his eyes so Hugh agreed. "It's all right Tom, it's the least he's entitled to."

The crowd bayed with delight because it seemed as if the blacksmith was about to wreak his revenge. "First thing Father," began Will, "you should know that Annie has just given me a fine son, a son a man can be proud of. I've not laid a finger on her in anger since she told me she was carrying and now she's happier than she ever has been."

"I'm truly pleased to hear that Will."

"Course, I've heard all the talk and don't doubt some of it is true, but Annie reckons the baby is mine. Even if it isn't it's changed our lives and I wouldn't alter anything now, so you see we've got ourselves sorted and the boy can grow up calling me Father."

"Our Lord has blessed the three of you," said Hugh trying not to sound too pious.

"But," continued Will as his eyebrows knitted and a hint of the old aggression showed itself, "we need to be left alone. We don't want no third party meddling with us if you take my drift, and Annie certainly don't want to see you again, so now you're back I want to hear you say you'll keep away from us."

Hugh knew no good could come from trying to see Annie again, and Will was probably speaking the truth when he said she didn't want to see him, but he still loved her. This time he must keep his word come what may. "Will, I will do as you ask and keep away. I shall probably return to the priory at Dunwich, if they'll have me, and live out the rest of my life there. I am also very sorry for any harm I may have done you."

Will nodded his approval, "Well if that's the way of it, I'll bid you good day and wish you luck against that bastard Geoffrey Calveley. No-one likes him."

Hugh watched Will's large figure disappear into the crowd and wondered. Most people would say how lucky he had been to escape the blacksmith's wrath, but Hugh had just agreed to abandon Annie for ever. Deep down he had harboured secret hopes that she and her baby might be re-united with him when Will threw her out, but the blacksmith had not behaved as expected. Now that Hugh had returned to Suffolk and faced up to his past, he felt he had at last achieved the moral fibre to abandon the priesthood and live with Annie, something he could and should have done when he had the chance. But then he had weakly thrown the opportunity away and now his new found inner strength had arrived too late. He would have to live the rest of his life under the shadow of what might have been.

Life was full of surprises. Hugh recalled the sage words of Father Anselm when he visited the old priest in the depths of despair during the winter. Anselm had said, 'It is unwise to be too sure about human reactions before they occur. Will Mullen may not behave as you predict.' How true that was! Parenthood and a certain amount of self deception had brought out a previously unseen side of the blacksmith. At least Annie would be secure with Will to look after her.

"Come along Father," said Tom. "You can't stay here daydreaming all day. Geoffrey has already arrived."

* * *

II

The quiet moot hall provided a church-like sanctuary for Hugh away from the baying crowd outside. The high, vaulted ceiling and rows of public benches, which always filled up for the more juicy court cases, added to the ecclesiastical, almost reverential atmosphere. This was not inappropriate because in England, unlike all other countries on the continent of Europe, respect for the law was ingrained in everyone from an early age and was second in importance only to the Church in people's minds. Because of this, and despite the sneering of many in the crowd, Hugh had donned his grey Franciscan raiment again which he hoped might add to his 'gravitas' for the hearing.

Two men stood beside the bench nearest the magistrate's desk deep in conference. One was Geoffrey, the other was a well dressed, balding man of about forty. When they saw Hugh and his companions, they immediately ended their conversation and approached them. The balding man held out his hand to Hugh. "Good morning. My name is William Paston. I represent Geoffrey Calveley."

"I have heard of you Master Paston," replied Hugh. "You have chambers in London and Norwich. Your reputation is unequalled. I am Father Hugh of the Franciscan Order."

Paston gave a slight bow, acknowledging the compliment, then frowned. "You do not appear to have counsel with you Father Hugh."

"I am representing Richard Calveley. We believe our case is strong enough to forgo the expense of professional counsel."

"I should warn you against such confidence," said Paston with genuine concern. "In my experience few cases are as clear cut as you suggest when put to the test. We can adjourn if you wish to reconsider."

"That will not be necessary."

"Very well then, if you are sure."

Paston returned to the front bench but Geoffrey lingered a little, and when his counsel was out of earshot whispered, "Heard from your prize witness have you?"

"Sir John Fastolf?"

"Who else?"

"Of course," lied Hugh. "I have his affidavit with me."

The evil, triumphant look that swept across Geoffrey's face froze Hugh's blood, and although it only lasted a second, it was enough to warn the Franciscan of the fate that might have already befallen Sir John.

"Then you are to be congratulated," rasped Geoffrey, "for you must have received the first letter ever sent from the next world." Looking at Sister Blanche, who had already taken her place on the front bench with Tom, he added, "I trust your case does not rely entirely upon evidence from Heaven and Hell. The magistrate won't be impressed." He sniggered at his own joke and, as he turned to rejoin Paston, he left Hugh with a chilling, parting shot. "I shouldn't worry about Fastolf's well-being; you'll be joining him shortly."

Whatever the result of the hearing, Hugh now realised that his first duty was to find Fastolf and warn him of the danger he was in. He was angry with himself for not second-guessing what Geoffrey would do; the frustrated squire would stop at nothing to regain Calveley Hall. In Geoffrey's eyes, all that stood between him and the hall was Fastolf, the only independent, credible witness left. It was all so obvious now. Hugh sat down beside Sister Blanche and offered a silent prayer that his stupidity would not result in the murder of one of the bravest knights in the English army.

As the church of Saint Michael tolled eleven o'clock, the door to the magistrate's office opened. The recorder emerged first followed by a short, plainly clad man of advancing years. His slim frame and grey hair were familiar to Hugh because this was Sir John Satterley, a firm but fair minded magistrate who could not be influenced by the wealth or birth of those that came before him. He sat down at his desk and nodded to the recorder to commence proceedings which involved announcing the names of the main participants and a brief summary of the points of dispute.

When he finished Sir John said, "Gentlemen, this is a tribunal not a court of law, so you may therefore choose whether or not you give your evidence as witnesses under oath. If you take the oath your evidence will be given greater weight but you lay yourself open to the criminal charge of perjury if you are found to have lied. The choice is yours."

Both sides agreed to give evidence under oath, after which Sir John addressed William Paston. "Good day to you Master Paston. As counsel for the plaintiff, I ask you to present your case first."

Paston stood up. "Thank you Sir John. The defendant has no professional representation so I will keep my client's submission in plain English."

"I am sure we are all glad to hear it," replied Satterley.

Paston's case was much as Hugh had expected, claiming Robert Calveley's marriage to Maud, Geoffrey's mother, was not bigamous and that Richard's claim to Calveley Hall was based on spurious evidence invented to bastardise Geoffrey so that Richard could inherit. There was no physical evidence for the first 'invented' marriage, which therefore relied for its veracity upon the credibility of the so-called witnesses to the marriage entry in the parish register in Calais. Of these, Sir John Fastolf had not seen fit to present himself to the tribunal or even send an affidavit, while Richard Calveley was an interested party. Sir Thomas Erpingham was in his dotage which meant the entire case now rested on Father Hugh the Franciscan.

"So we must turn to the credibility of Father Hugh," continued Paston, after a slight pause suggesting that what he was about to say would pain him also. What followed was the worst humiliation Hugh ever suffered, worse even than that dreadful moment last Christmas when he had abandoned Annie Mullen. It was not so much what was said, though that was bad enough, but the clinical, dispassionate way that Paston delivered a character assassination of sustained venom. Every word burned itself into Hugh's memory.

The lawyer concluded with a theatrical sigh, "So it seems my client is separated from his rightful inheritance by the word of a known liar, deceiver, fornicator and adulterer who is even prepared to use his status as a Franciscan friar to send souls into the next world unshriven for the sake of his uncontrollable lust. Surely this is without precedent. By contrast my client is a man of impeccable character, a magistrate himself whose prime purpose in life is to uphold the rule of law and whose word no man has cause to disbelieve. Consequently we look to the law, as dispensed by you Sir John, to put right the injustice that has taken place over the last eight years."

Satterley looked up from his notes and said, "Thank you Master Paston for a most eloquent rendering of your case as usual." Then turning his attention to Geoffrey, he asked, "And do you Master Calveley support all your counsel has said with the strength of your oath?"

"I do Sir John," replied Geoffrey smoothly.

"Very well, I have just one question before I hear from the defence. For how long to your knowledge has Father Hugh been behaving in the way described by your counsel?"

"At least a year I believe," said Geoffrey.

Satterley looked at the white faced Hugh, "Do you confirm that?"

The Franciscan's mouth was dry. He spoke in little more than a whisper. "About eighteen months Sir John."

"Speak up man!"

"About eighteen months."

Satterley rubbed his chin thoughtfully. "I see, but from the records in front of me, the hearing which transferred the ownership of Calveley Hall from Geoffrey to Richard Calveley took place eight and a half years ago. There is no mention at that time of you being the monster just described, nor am I convinced that Sir John Fastolf, who I know well, would simply ignore a matter of such importance to one of his captains as suggested by Master Paston. However, this is a civil case not a criminal one, which therefore will be decided on the balance of probability rather than beyond reasonable doubt. Perhaps the defence can throw some light on the matter?"

Hugh stood up to present his case but he felt weak at the knees and had to steady himself before speaking. Few men could have remained unaffected by Paston's skilful character demolition, and Hugh was more sensitive than most. But he was also beginning to realise he might not need to use Sister Blanche for evidence because Satterley seemed favourably disposed towards him, perhaps seeing him in legal terms as a David against Paston's Goliath. That brought some relief because there was something about Blanche which had troubled Hugh since their first meeting at the Calais convent. From that moment his disquiet had increased, though he could not understand why, except he felt she was playing a game of her own that he knew nothing about. He determined not to use her unless absolutely necessary. The translator he had booked for the hearing had not turned up, so at least he would be saved the effort of translating Blanche's French into English for the benefit of the recorder; Satterley of course understood French as did every properly educated man in England.

Hugh cleared his throat and began the case for the defence. "Sir John, everything Master Paston has said about me is true except he forgot to add 'coward' to my list of vices. However, as you have already noted, I was in a state of grace at the time this case was previously heard so I beg you not to allow my failings since then to reflect upon my master, Richard Calveley, a bold and honourable captain who has spilled much blood, including his own, for his king and England. I would first like to outline the circumstances in which three good English warriors and I saw the marriage entry in the Church of Our Lady of Calais shortly after the Battle of Agincourt. Unfortunately, the page upon which the entry was recorded has since been removed."

"But," interjected Satterley, "it would be possible to remove any page from a marriage register and claim it recorded whatever suited your purpose, would it not?"

"That is of course true Sir John," acknowledged Hugh, who then proceeded to recount the events of those heady days in the aftermath of the great battle.

Even before Hugh had finished, Satterley had already decided on the proper course of action and interrupted the Franciscan. "Father Hugh, I must stop you there." Then addressing both sides he said, "It is clear to me that this dispute should not be decided without word from Sir John Fastolf, who has nothing to gain whichever side wins. It may be that he is unaware of this hearing due to one of the unpredictable turns of fate that occur in wartime. I therefore propose to adjourn until -"

"Stop!" All eyes turned to Sister Blanche who had spoken for the first time. She stood up, walked slowly to Satterley's desk and said in English with little trace of a French accent, "You must hear what I have to say."

Tom leaned over to Hugh and whispered, "I didn't know she speaks English."

"Nor did I until now." Thanks to Satterley's fairness during the hearing so far, Hugh had started to relax but suddenly his heart began to pound again. The situation was now out of his control and he regretted, more than ever, uprooting Sister Blanche from her sanctuary.

Satterley remained calm and spoke gently to the old nun. "Do you have material evidence that your representative has not yet given?"

"I do."

"Then you may proceed."

"Thank you sir." The nun turned and faced the public benches. "Although I am known as Sister Blanche of the convent of Our Lady of Calais, my real name is Blanche Calveley. I am Robert Calveley's first and only true wife."

"Impossible!" shouted Geoffrey as he leaped to his feet. "Impossible! Where's the proof? This old woman could be anybody!"

"Sit down Master Calveley," snapped Satterley. "I will thank you to show the self control befitting your rank." Then the magistrate's eyes turned on Hugh; his brow creased into a deep frown. "And as for you

Father Hugh, I think this tribunal deserves an explanation. If you have been playing games with me you will regret it. Why did you not call this witness at the beginning?"

"I did not think it necessary Sir John."

Satterley was unimpressed. "Do you take me for a fool? This is a properly constituted hearing, not a stage for a Chester play. I shall speak to you later. Sister Blanche, please continue."

The uproar subsided and everyone listened intently as Blanche told the story of her sad and brief marriage to Robert Calveley. Geoffrey held his head in his hands as he listened to his carefully prepared case disintegrate before him, while Paston sat quietly giving no hint of his own feelings.

At last Blanche brought the account up to date and Satterley said, "Thank you Sister Blanche for your evidence. You may return to your seat."

The nun's dark, spider eyes flickered towards Hugh before resting upon Geoffrey. Then a spiteful little smile spread across her lips. "I have not quite finished Sir John."

"Then make it quick if you please," said Satterley patiently.

"The words I have spoken are God's own truth, but there is another truth which I thought would die with me until that Franciscan came to the convent." Then she addressed Geoffrey. "You bear two round birthmarks, one above the other, upon your lower back. Is that not so?"

Geoffrey took his head out of his hands and spluttered, "How….how can you….nobody knows that! Who told you?"

"But is it true?" asked Blanche quietly.

"Yes, but not even my wife has seen them."

"But you agree your mother would have?"

"Of course, but what has she to do with this!" demanded Geoffrey.

Hugh was the first in the moot hall to understand where the exchange was leading. He cursed himself for a fool as the enormity of his error dawned upon him. Blanche's crackly but firm voice continued relentlessly. "Geoffrey, through your mother you are the rightful owner of Calveley Hall but you are not Maud's son."

Geoffrey, confused and sweating profusely, mumbled, "Then who …." His voice faded away.

"Yes my son, you are looking at her. You were never a bastard. When your father deserted me I was already carrying you in my womb. I bore you; you are the fruit of Robert's only true marriage. I returned to my parental home for your birth but when your father heard of your existence, he returned and my father sold you to him like a chattel in a market. You were called Guy then, but there was nothing I could do to prevent my father's greed separating us. After that and disillusioned with life, I entered the convent where I expected to end my days until Father Hugh's fortuitous intervention."

Tom whispered, "No wonder the old hag insisted on coming with us."

Hugh shook his head sadly, "Everything I do seems ill fated. We would have won this hearing had I not unwittingly brought the cause of our downfall with us. I should have followed my instinct. I always sensed there was something wrong about Blanche. She even reminded me of someone when I first saw her; now I know who it is!"

Geoffrey was unable to speak but Paston, professional as ever, stood up and said, "I think Sir John, that Sister Blanche's evidence proves beyond all doubt where the rightful ownership of Calveley Hall lies."

In response, Satterley addressed Hugh. "It appears the evidence from your witness was not quite what you intended. Do you have anything to add before I pronounce judgement?"

"No Sir John."

"But I have!" interjected Paston as he ushered Blanche across to Geoffrey's side of the bench.

Satterley frowned, "Well Master Paston?"

"Sir John, I wish to submit a claim for compensation on behalf of my client for the loss of estate revenues during the eight and a half years of wrongful occupation by his cousin."

Satterley glared at the lawyer. "Master Paston, you go too far. I reject your claim out of hand. Your client's cousin made his claim eight years ago in good faith and based on all the information available at the time. It was therefore a reasonable thing to do. I doubt as much can be said for your client now. The basis of his contention that no first marriage took place is manifestly false, which begs the question of what happened to the marriage record in the Calais Church, does it not? Someone, as Father Hugh says, must have removed it; a criminal act in itself. Master Paston, as I speak I am considering whether or not your client should face a charge of conspiring to pervert the course of justice, and I marvel at you being associated with such a thing. I advise you to accept your success, undeserving though it is, while my patience lasts."

Paston did not need telling twice and Satterley duly pronounced judgement in Geoffrey's favour. The magistrate and his recorder then retired to their chamber leaving the two opposing factions alone with each other.

Hugh spoke first. "So Master Calveley, you need not have loosed your assassins on Sir John Fastolf after all."

Geoffrey, recovering rapidly from the surprises of a few minutes before, gloated. "You cannot prove anything. I wonder what sort of reception you'll get from Richard when he receives this news."

Paston neatly folded his papers and at last let the scorn he felt for his client show. "I have heard quite enough. I shall render my account shortly Master Calveley. After that is paid, do not trouble to contact me again." He nodded briefly to Hugh and walked out of the moot hall. The Franciscan looked at Geoffrey and Blanche seated side by side quietly laughing at him.

They are indeed of the same kin, he thought, which explains much. "Come on Tom," he said, "there is nothing more for us here."

When Tom and Hugh emerged from the moot hall, the crowd had dispersed. They paused at the top of the steps and Tom sighed, "Well, what now Father Hugh?"

At least on that matter Hugh's mind was clear. "Tom, you must return to Calveley Hall at once and ensure that whatever belongs to Richard is packed up and sent to his house in Rouen. I shall return to France immediately to warn Sir John Fastolf of the danger threatening him if it's not already too late."

* * *

III

And so, after a frantic ride through northern France, Hugh came across Richard, Henry and Titus just after they had left the English camp at Verneuil. Richard's initial surprise and pleasure at seeing his old friend in such an unlikely place quickly turned to consternation when he saw the worry on Hugh's face.

"Is Sir John Fastolf with the army?" panted the Franciscan, omitting all the usual opening pleasantries one might have expected.

Richard answered, "No, he left for his house near Falaise yesterday morning. That is where we are going now."

"Thank God, we might not be too late!"

"Too late for what Hugh? Calm down and explain what's happening."

At that moment Hugh recognised Titus. "What I have to say is not for his ears. I thought he was dead."

"So did we all but I too have much to tell. Let us dismount and talk."

"No time! No time! We must hurry. We can talk as we travel."

"Very well then," agreed Richard. "I will tell Scrope to ride a little way behind us."

Hugh's sorry tale about his affair with Annie Mullen did not surprise Richard because he had always known the Franciscan was unsuited to the priesthood. Indeed he felt some sympathy as he cast his mind back to his treasured moments with Ruth, but as Hugh began to recount the fate of Calveley Hall, all Richard's feelings of understanding were replaced first by incredulity, then horror as he learned how his treasured estate in England had reverted to his cousin. The driving force in Richard's life of exile had always been the hope that one day he would be able to return to his Suffolk home with Mary and Joan. Now it was gone! He was a tree without roots; a nomad. True, he had a dwelling in Rouen but that was only ever intended to be a temporary arrangement to last just until the Lollard persecutions in England were ended. To make matters worse, his closest friend had been the instrument of Geoffrey's triumph. He felt like throttling Hugh but even at this moment of anger, Richard knew his friend had done his best.

Hugh waited nervously for his master's response, but for a while Richard dared not reply for fear of what he might say. The rhythmic pounding of cantering hooves on the sun baked, dusty road and the occasional rustle of a midsummer breeze in the branches along the tree lined highway were the only sounds that broke the heavy silence. Eventually Henry, who had heard every word of Hugh's sad tale, spoke first. "Captain Richard, do you recall that moment during the fight with the pirates aboard *Loredan* when you were looking for me, and Chaim said I was getting some water?"

Richard had to think for a moment before he was able to drag his mind back to that mad, terrifying sea battle. "Yes Henry, what of it?"

"Well Chaim was mistaken. In fact I had gone down to the hold to rescue some of those Venetian ducats which were about to go to the bottom of the sea along with the ship."

"Well done Henry, you always were the best plunderer I know."

"No Captain, that's not the point. There were about fifty gold coins. What I am trying to say is that you are welcome to have them all. I know it is only a fraction of the value of your estate but it will offset your loss a little bit."

Such a generous offer from his loyal sergeant helped Richard realise that his world had not ended. There was more to life than material wealth. "Sergeant Hawkswood," he said, "you honour me with your friendship which I value far more than Calveley Hall. Please keep your ducats, you have earned them."

"Thank you Captain," replied a relieved Henry.

"And," continued Richard, "it is only fair, under the circumstances, that you should know I removed a similar amount from de Beaujeu's legacy when we were still at Pilgrim's Castle!"

"Holy Moses!" laughed Henry, "I'm not the only plunderer here then."

"Indeed not, but you have helped me see things in their true perspective." Then turning to Hugh, Richard said, "So Geoffrey was never a bastard after all. He was the rightful owner of Calveley Hall all the time. Well I suppose all is now as it should be."

"And you have had the estate revenues for eight years," replied Hugh helpfully.

"True, though it's galling my cousin has beaten me even if the hall is rightfully his, but I still thank you my constant and faithful friend for your support. I know you have faced many difficulties even though they were largely of your own making, but when it would have been easier to abandon me, you remained loyal. It took great courage for you to return to Suffolk and face your angry flock."

"Thank you Richard," said Hugh. "You will never know how much better that makes me feel."

"But, my fiery Franciscan, you have still not explained why we are in such a hurry to reach Falaise."

The Templar Legacy

"Just before the tribunal, your cousin made it plain to me that Sir John would never be able to testify. Not yet knowing his true parentage, Geoffrey had made arrangements for the only witness who could destroy his case to be eliminated, we must assume by assassination."

"That would be his style," agreed Richard. He glanced back at the old Templar riding twenty paces behind them. "He must have secured a replacement for Scrope."

"So," continued Hugh, "after the tribunal I hurried to Rouen to find out from Mary where Sir John was. She said he would either be at home, or more likely with the army. I therefore headed south following the army while Mary set out for Falaise just in case the imminent battle with the French had already been fought and Sir John had returned home."

"She didn't go alone?"

"No, she took a servant with her."

"I doubt that will be enough if the assassin is already at Falaise waiting for Sir John. When did she leave?"

"Yesterday morning, the same time as me."

"That means she'll reach Falaise before us. Spur on your horse my friend, we can't get there a moment too soon."

The four Englishmen arrived late the following day. Their long shadows preceded them in the warm light of the setting sun as they trotted their mounts down the gravelled track which branched off the main Falaise road a mile east of the town. Saddlesore and tired, they drew rein outside the substantial, two storeyed manor house which was one of the many properties given to Fastolf by King Henry V in appreciation of his services to the crown.

Dismounting stiffly, Richard said to Henry and Titus, "Best to be cautious so draw your swords."

Henry squinted at the dark windows, "Looks deserted Captain."

"Aye, but I've been here a few times before. Even when Sir John was absent, there was always a servant to greet me and look after my horse. Stay close."

They tied up their horses and warily approached the heavy, iron framed front door. The front of the house was in shadow, which cast an ominous darkness as if warning the travellers to beware.

Richard raised his sword pommel to knock at the door but then paused and gently pushed it open. "Strange," he whispered, "the house seems empty but it's not locked up."

"What's that odd smell?" asked Henry.

"Cloves," replied Titus, "an expensive eastern spice which relieves toothache. Does Sir John have trouble with his teeth?"

Richard answered, "Not that I know of." The pores in his skin opened as he carefully entered the dark interior. His sense of imminent danger was overwhelming.

Henk de Groot had seen them coming. He had had an eventful day. At noon he presented himself at Fastolf's house having followed the English knight the sixty miles from Verneuil at a discreet distance. By claiming he brought news of Richard Calveley he was given a hospitable reception, so putting the drug into Fastolf's wine had been easy. With the veteran warrior sleeping the sleep of the dead, de Groot quickly disposed of the manservant who was the only other person in the house. The body lay hidden in the bushes which flanked the rear courtyard. During the afternoon de Groot set about preparing Fastolf's demise which must appear to be an accident. It was well known that as a student of modern war, Sir John liked to experiment with various types of gunpowder, for he believed England lagged far behind France in the development of artillery. With injudicious disregard for his volatile hobby, he kept numerous large kegs of gunpowder stored in his cellar, quite sufficient to blow up the entire household many times over, thus presenting de Groot with the opportunity to create the perfect accident.

The Fleming's preparations were nearing completion when he was disturbed by a noise outside. His irritation turned to eager anticipation when he saw Mary dismounting in front of the house accompanied by just a single servant. She would also become a victim of the accidental explosion, but not before he had vented the lust that had been building up inside him during those months he was observing her in Rouen. A single shot from his crossbow dispatched the servant but she fought hard until a backhand blow from de Groot's mighty fist knocked her senseless. When she recovered, her hands had been bound by a rope attached to a ceiling beam in the main hall. She had not yet been violated, but the hungry leers from the revolting, goblin-like creature going about its work in the lengthening evening shadows warned her she soon would be.

De Groot was placing the last keg of gunpowder in an upstairs room, where Fastolf still lay drugged, when he heard horses approaching. He ran downstairs and roughly gagged Mary with a piece of cloth ripped from one of the curtains. Then he went to his horse, which was tethered at the back of the house, returned with a pouch full of crossbow quarrels, and waited.

"Not a step further you English or she dies!" The sight confronting Richard was much as he feared. At the far end of the main hall Mary stood bound and helpless. De Groot sat near her lounging in a chair with his feet casually resting upon the long dining table and a loaded crossbow pointing at her heart. The Englishmen edged towards him but de Groot shouted, "One more step and I shoot!"

Richard pleaded with his companions, "Stand still for God's sake!"

"Dat is good English. Now we talk. First drop your swords." The Fleming grinned baring his crooked, yellow teeth, now that he controlled the confrontation.

Henry gasped, "God's teeth, what an ugly bastard!"

De Groot ignored the insult, "Listen to me very good English. Now I walk out of here wid dis woman. You will not stop me. I let her go if you do not follow. If you do she die." Geoffrey's orders meant nothing to de Groot now. All that mattered was survival.

Richard spoke calmly but with steel in his voice. "If you harm my wife I shall kill you."

De Groot jumped angrily to his feet. "You tink you can frighten me English! You tink you can frighten Henk de Groot do you! Do you!" Still holding the crossbow firmly with one hand, he gripped the neck of Mary's bodice with the other, and in a single powerful movement ripped it off stripping her naked to the waist. Richard froze, terrified that de Groot's loss of self control might end with a crossbow bolt deep in Mary's heart. The gag stopped her speaking but she looked at Richard, imploring him with her eyes to check his temper. He long, fair hair lay tousled around her shoulders, her breasts heaved with fear as the Fleming stood behind her and began to taunt Richard.

"You brave English. You tink you better dan anyone." Keeping a firm grip on the crossbow he stepped behind Mary and began roughly fondling her breasts with his free hand. "I teach you to respect Henk de Groot proper."

He roughly massaged her nipples as he spoke in his vile, guttural English, but from behind Richard a voice shouted, "Bastard!" Titus Scrope pushed past Richard and strode purposefully towards the Fleming; he had never stopped loving Mary. Whether it was surprise at one of the other Englishmen attacking him or simply the murderous look on Titus' face will never be known, but de Groot hesitated, changed his target and fired at the old Templar. The bolt entered Titus' body just below the heart and buried itself deep in his chest. Even before Titus fell, de Groot dropped the crossbow and was feeling for the hilt of his dagger, but he was not quick enough. Richard had already rushed the few paces separating them, and head butted the Fleming in the face with all the power he could muster. De Groot howled in pain but did not fall. His powerful arms snaked round Richard's waist and began to crush his spine. But the Englishman's right arm was still free. He drew it back and finger punched his enemy in both eyes. This was true gutter fighting; de Groot was forced to release Richard and, as he put his hands up to his blinded eyes, Richard drew his own dagger. All this happened in a few seconds. Henry ran to his captain's aid but was not quick enough to stop Richard plunging his dagger into de Groot's black heart. The ugly goblin bellowed like a wounded boar but Richard's strike was mortal and, with a long exhalation of foul, stinking breath, Henk de Groot sank to his knees, rolled over and died.

"That was a mistake Captain," said Henry.

Richard frowned as he cut Mary's bonds and covered her nakedness with his cloak. "Why so Henry?"

"We could have used this creature to testify to your cousin's murderous nature in open court. You might still have been able to watch him hang and have Calveley Hall transferred back to you."

"Damn me to Hell. I didn't think of that."

"Quite understandable under the circumstances," replied the Wiltshire sergeant soothingly. "I doubt not I would have done exactly the same."

From behind them Hugh said urgently, "Come quickly, Titus still lives!"

* * *

IV

Titus Scrope, Knight Templar and erstwhile murderer, liar and thief, lay on his back beside the oak dining table. Blood oozed from his mouth staining his short, grey beard dull red. A rattling sound deep in his chest warned that death was only a minute or two away. Unaffected by the blood, Mary cupped the old head in her lap to ease his breathing a little, but Richard could tell from the dilated eyes that Titus' sight was almost gone. The Templar's hand searched for Richard's and gripped it with unexpected strength.

"Mary, is she all right?" he whispered hoarsely.

"I am thanks to you Titus," she answered as she stroked the long, wire-like hair which lay in grey strands across her skirt.

"Thank God!" gasped Titus. "I have done something to atone." He turned his face towards Richard. "Captain Richard, can you forgive me now?" Richard did not answer immediately. He was indeed grateful for Titus' selfless bravery, but when he thought back to that terrible day ten years ago, the day Titus destroyed his family, he knew forgiveness was beyond him.

"Titus," he said, "I heartily thank you for what you have just done."

The old Templar was sinking fast. Speaking was now only possible with a huge effort. "But do you forgive?"

Richard remained silent so Mary intervened. "This man has just saved my life. I am your wife. Can you not do as he asks?"

A surge of anger pulsed through him. How dare she ask that! She could never understand. To forgive would be tantamount to betraying the memory of Ann, the woman who bore his children and stood beside him when he was little more than a penniless farm labourer, the woman who worked and gleaned in the fields with him when times were hard, even though she came from gentle stock and, above all, the woman he still adored. Ruth would have understood; she was so like Ann.

He looked at Titus and said softly, "I believe God will forgive you but I cannot." The old Templar nodded as if he understood but speech was beyond him now. Richard turned to Hugh, "Shrive this man now, before he dies."

"But I...," then seeing the look on Richard's face Hugh came forward, knelt beside Titus and gave him the last rites. Richard looked up and his eyes met Mary's. A yawning gap had just opened between them. This was the moment she finally realised she would always have to give best to Ann in Richard's heart, yet how was she supposed to compete with a memory?

Richard knew he had hurt her deeply. Titus was still holding his left hand in a vice-like grip, so he held out his right to comfort her but she drew away from him, something she had never done before.

"He has gone," said Hugh as he closed the lids of Titus' blind staring eyes, "but where to God only knows."

Richard unpicked Titus' fingers from his hand and whispered, "God can forgive when Man cannot. I do not doubt that Titus Scrope will enter the Kingdom of Heaven, though only by the skin of his yellow teeth. We will bury him here. Falaise is as good a place as any for a man with no home."

Next morning the travellers went their separate ways. Apart from a thunderous headache, Sir John Fastolf was fully recovered from the drug though somewhat ashamed at the ease with which de Groot had overcome him. Mary and Hugh took the road to Rouen from where Hugh would continue onwards to England and Dunwich Priory. Richard and Henry headed back to the army to assist with mopping up operations after the Verneuil campaign, while Sir John remained at home to recruit a new manservant and recuperate from his war wound.

Richard's parting from Mary had been cold. She felt a bitterness he was unable to sweeten without the use of artifice. The bond between them had been loosened, perhaps irreparably so. As he cantered, deep in thought, along the road back to Verneuil with Henry, Richard felt his life was in turmoil, a turmoil likely to get worse before it got better. He knew he could not abandon Mary for that would mean abandoning Joan too, but he had yet to discover that Ruth would bear his child. He had unwittingly left more than just fond memories in Italy.

But there was still a war to be won. After Verneuil the rampant English carried all before them and during the next two years swept the French back to the line of the Loire. Orleans, where the English determined the final breakthrough should take place, was soon under siege. If this city fell, victory would be within sight at last. Only a miracle could stop them.

But in the small village of Domremy, in far off Lorraine, a twelve year old peasant girl was already hearing heavenly voices. Her name was Jeanne, but to the English she eventually became better known as Joan...........

THE END

ACKNOWLEDGEMENTS

I must thank my two excellent proof readers and editorial advisers, Lawrence Tallon and Nick Meo for their invaluable contribution in turning an error strewn manuscript into the finished article. Once again I am indebted to Neil Amos for his creation of legible maps and Rachel Wright for her I.T. support. Thanks also to my wife Jennifer who has gone to the trouble of constructing a well fitted out tree house in the garden so she can regain possession of her orangery when I am writing.

Finally, I thank the friendly Authorhouse team who have produced another well presented book. Richard Calveley will return again for a third adventure quite soon.

Also by Peter Tallon

The Lion and the Lily (2016), published by Authorhouse

Part 1 of the Richard Calveley trilogy.